# THE
# NEWLYWEDS

BOOKS BY ARIANNE RICHMONDE

*The Wife's House*

# THE
# NEWLYWEDS

ARIANNE RICHMONDE

bookouture

Published by Bookouture in 2021

An imprint of Storyfire Ltd.
Carmelite House
50 Victoria Embankment
London EC4Y 0DZ
www.bookouture.com

ISBN: 978-1-83888-637-0
eBook ISBN: 978-1-83888-636-3

*For my mother, who taught me all about creation, taking things into my own hands, and being brave.*

# CHAPTER ONE

In the cold clarity of hindsight, I would not have married Ashton Buchanan.

I thought I had my life under control, that I was the architect of my future.

I was wrong.

On the day of our wedding, I questioned everything. But the wheels were in motion and it was too late to turn back. I could not let go of my dream. The painstaking plans that had kept me up at night and every waking hour for all this time were finally happening. My wish had come true.

Ashton and I were getting married.

It was a fantasy wedding beyond anything I could have hoped for. The sort of wedding you design in your head from the age of six, a make-believe princess's fairy tale. Grand and elegant: the big white dress, the something-borrowed-something-blue gifts, the ever after speeches.

Distant Island, where Ashton's family house had stood for nearly two hundred years, and where our wedding was set, could not have looked more beautiful. Glorious in its antebellum magnificence, the mansion, Distant Sands, presided over the coastal waterfront and its private dock, reflecting the pale blue, late April sky. As if it knew my secret, as if it held our history in the eyes of every windowpane, the limbs of every door. Watching us.

Watching *me* as I moved ahead with my mistake.

There was no stopping me now.

Huge white marquees on the lawn and tables dressed with the finest linen, and silverware—real, not plate—shimmered in the afternoon sun, while guests chatted and laughed, sipping champagne from crystal glasses, throwing back their heads in abandon, and toasting the happiest couple in the world. Waitstaff weaved between the throngs, carrying canapés and trays with drink refills, as children circled and skipped between grownups' knees and elbows, and dogs in bow ties barked happily on the gleaming green spread of lawn.

Everything was perfect.

Except… it wasn't.

I couldn't believe I had actually gone through with this, but I had, and you would never have known from the smile on my face what I felt deep down inside, because, despite my reservations… despite myself, I did feel like the luckiest girl in the universe.

"Honey, are you all right? Everything okay?" Ashton, his face brimming with consternation, swept a tendril of hair from my brow—careful not to dislodge my perfect hairdo, styled and fussed over all morning by South Carolina's top hairdresser. Ashton looked like the perfect Southern gentleman in his tailored tails, the rosebud buttonhole he sported, the shiny black shoes polished to within an inch of their lives. His sandy hair—that turned blondish in summer and back to brown in winter—flopped over his liquid brown, multi-century eyes. Observing Ashton did make you believe in reincarnation. As though he'd lived so many lives already. His wise, heavy brow that told you he had it covered, that he could fix any problem. The strength of his jawline spoke of quiet determination and justice, but even a hint of his boyish smile took all that away. The paradox of him confused me. Ashton was so much more than just my husband. He was—

"Vivien, honey, are you all right?"

Teary-eyed, I fixed him a smile and said, "Ashton, it couldn't be more beautiful, I only wish I could have shared all this with my parents."

"I know, sweetheart, but I swear I'll make up for what you've lost. I'll make you so happy, you'll see."

Ashton had extraordinary self-belief. Something I so admired about him. He was a fixer—not just because of his job as one of the best neurosurgeons in the South—but because of his unwavering confidence in himself. Why shouldn't he be confident? Full scholarship to the best medical school in the country, Johns Hopkins, top of his class. Board certified neurosurgeon before he'd reached thirty. Had written papers on this and that, published in science journals, lectured all over the world. Respect was a word that came to mind. And awe. People were in awe of him.

*I* was in awe of him. And that was the truth. But not the whole truth.

I mulled over what he'd said: "Make up for what you've lost."

I clung onto that belief.

The wedding spilled into the evening, until the inky gold of the sun dipped below the skyline, and guests ventured—some of them, the more adventurous ones—into waiting sailboats. They took off across the smooth water, the white sails looking like pretty handkerchiefs against the horizon, until the first stars twinkled in the Carolina sky. I didn't take a boat ride myself but chatted with the other guests, my smile a beacon, my wedding gown's beaded hem and train heavy around my ankles, swishing and swinging and making me feel that my life was indeed fit for a character in some classic romance novel, centuries ago. Then Ashton and I had our first dance, and when he fixed his gaze on me, I felt my heart leap inside my chest all over again, the way it did the very first time we met.

The way it still did when I wasn't thinking.

"Darling, oh my darling, you look *divine!*" My reverie was interrupted by Georgia-May, Ashton's mother, who had been released from her care home—supervised of course—for just a few hours, to partake in the nuptial celebrations. All elegance in her double strand of pearls and pink chiffon dress, she looked at me dreamily for a moment and then a furrow of confusion scrunched her brow, and she suddenly seemed to not remember who I was nor why she was even here at all. The poor lady had Alzheimer's. Something Ashton always hated to discuss.

I remembered in that brief moment—after my dance with Ashton and between Georgia-May's hazy confusion and several sips of champagne—confiding in a friend, one time, that I was unhappy about something (I couldn't remember what), and my friend had told me, "I'm so sorry your life hasn't turned out exactly as you wanted it to be." Her words had shocked me and angered me too. But it also gave me a kick up the butt. I decided in that second, *I am going to make my life turn out exactly as I want it to be. And no one's going to stop me.*

And here I was now, marrying Dr. Ashton Buchanan.

# CHAPTER TWO

Everything was perfect for us for the first five months. We honeymooned in St. Barts. Ashton could afford to holiday on exclusive islands like St. Barts. It wasn't that he was from old money, or even wealth; his father had been a shrimper. Ashton had inherited Distant Sands after his dad's death. His great-grandfather had owned great chunks of the island—had won the land and several houses in a bet, over a century ago—but Ashton's father had sold most of it off for practically nothing. Ashton had held onto Distant Sands, though, and its seven-acre lot. His was the only historic mansion that was still left standing. Romantic and beautiful as the house had always been, it was a dilapidated mess during Ashton's childhood: the roof half caved in, dry rot eating at the wooden wrap-around porches. Passing nearly two centuries, the mansion—a three-story Greek Revival—had served for myriad purposes, notably a hospital during the Civil War. Ashton had made this house what it became: an exquisite piece of history shrouded in splendor and beauty. I say "shrouded" because nobody could look at this antebellum landmark and not feel just a little bit intimidated. Distant Sands could be a museum. Ashton had restored it with love, putting all his heart into everything: the grand, sweeping, curved marble staircase with wrought-iron bannisters lording over the marble-floored entrance hall, lit up by an original Venetian crystal chandelier and where the baby grand piano lived.

Ashton had brought everything back to its former glory. The French windows, the library with mahogany woodwork with top to bottom judge's paneling. The heart pine and cherry wood inlay parquet floors, the windows—which didn't look remade at all, of course, but as if they had been there forever.

There were two parlors, one a drawing room with Chippendale settees, where men once drank cognac and smoked cigars, the other where the ladies would "retire" after a formal dinner or sip iced tea and catch up with gossip. The house still retained the air of bygone days, with its Queen Anne wingback chairs, needlepoint and tapestry footstools, and silver tea sets displayed on mahogany or cherry wood sideboards and eighteenth-century cabinets. It was almost as if you could hear their chatter in the walls, the hazy, heated summer days. Ladies with fans sipping long, cool glasses of iced lemonade. I couldn't help but feel this place would always haunt me—it wasn't me; I would never fit in, never feel at home here, no matter what I did. Distant Sands. Its name spoke volumes to me. *Distant.* So true.

Distant Sands maintained its classic, Deep-South antebellum design, with wide wood plantation shutters and upper and lower front porches. The back porch overlooked shaded green wooded land, and the front of the mansion faced the water and a live oak tree of such magnitude—at least eighty feet high—that people would come and visit it in awe. The tree was older than the house itself, and the most beautiful, majestic thing I had ever seen. Draped in swathes of gorgeous Spanish moss, it seemed like some elegant grand dame in her finest clothes, or a wild Medusa standing proud, guarding Distant Sands—her very own Greek Revival mansion—garlanded and festooned with streamers in her leafy hair.

The minute I arrived, Distant Island gave me a feeling that I was on a remote, going-back-in-time, Carolina sea island. I felt a little isolated.

The mansion is perched on just a little bit of a slope. The façade of the house faces a lagoon surrounded by a meandering web of creeks and inlets teeming with oystercatchers and winding salt rivers and coastal marshland buffering the land from the great Atlantic. Distant Island, on Lady's Island, neighbors hundreds of other sea islands, most of the inhabited ones connected by a bridge. Bays, rivers and sounds meander their way around them, like arteries flowing between the Intracoastal Waterway and the Atlantic Ocean.

When the tide is low the salty marsh exposes itself with all its secrets and God's little inhabitants amidst the wild sea grass shimmering in the breeze: the marsh birds, blue herons and egrets, crabs and crayfish, and silver oysters wedged in the sand.

And when the tide is high you can dangle your legs in the water, perched on the house's private deep-water dock that stretches wide across the marshy creek. You can watch pelicans dive-bombing for fish and sometimes spot bottlenose dolphins flitting across its smooth waters, pewter at dawn, and copper at sunset. Of course, there can be riptides that sneak into these waters and wild storms sometimes, even hurricanes, although, so far, I hadn't experienced any crazy weather. I have made Distant Island sound as if it's in the middle of nowhere, which isn't quite true, because it's only fifteen minutes from Beaufort, a beautiful little town set between Savannah and Charleston. Beaufort's downtown district was designated as historic by the National Trust for Historic Preservation.

Still, even with the town close by, I felt out on a limb.

I couldn't help sense that I was a visitor. A ship passing in the night. A shooting star exploding into dust. I knew from the outset I'd have to start counting my memories—the good ones—because they'd be fleeting. Call it premonition or sure-fire knowledge, it didn't matter. My days at Distant Sands were numbered.

I was still trying to acclimatize myself to married life with Ashton. A Yankee as I pretty much considered myself, the South

Carolinian ways were new to me: the food, the polite, unsaid rules, the unhurried gaiety and social norms that spoke a new language I hadn't yet mastered. I'd heard some of their jokes, told with a grin: "Yankees are like hemorrhoids. Pain in the butt when they come down and always a relief when they go back up."

I longed to fit in, to be accepted. I had yet to find out that cruelty would be wrapped in lace, and that if anyone said "*Bless your heart*," you knew that heart was damned.

I often wondered if confidence is something you're born with or something you acquire. I mean, *real* gut confidence, not the bravado kind or the fake veneer. I'd certainly had to acquire bucketloads of confidence since I'd been married to Ashton. The way you pick seashells from the shore, I had to collect confidence amidst the grains of sand, make myself sparkle, ease myself into feeling at home in a foreign world. Because the Lowcountry *was* foreign to me. Everyone was more than welcoming, but I wanted to be the perfect wife, to look as if Ashton and I matched, and that we had been made for each other, belonged together.

But being perfect doesn't come easy; you have to work at it, and work at it I did. The understated clothing, but always quality brands. Never flashy, never brash, but effortlessly well-turned out. My dark hair long enough to be sexy but always styled and cut so it was neat. Makeup applied with such precision that it looked as if I hardly wore any. A touch of mascara, maybe a dash of brown eyeliner to bring out the blue of my eyes, a dab of rouge or lip gloss. Natural was the byword, the key. Shoes: low heels or pristine sneakers. I favored pearl stud earrings. The only thing that drew attention was my solitaire diamond engagement ring that Ashton had had made especially for me. I tried so hard to be one of them.

I watched my diet, too. Salads and low carbs, no red meat, and rarely dessert. I drove an electric Volvo. Safe, expensive and top-of-the-range, but not ostentatious. I exuded *class*, or at least that's what I was aiming for. Ashton may have been a Southern boy at heart, a shrimper's son and a dab hand at the barbecue, but he was ambitious and a hard worker and had made himself a pillar of the community. It wasn't that he asked me to do these things or behave in any particular way, like going to the gym or practicing tennis till I could slam a backhand and challenge anyone to a decent game, but I knew it was part and parcel of my marriage, and I had to keep up. This marriage was everything to me. Without parents to call my own I clung to it like a lifeline, and I needed to make it work. And the truth was, Ashton was the only man I had ever loved. The only one I could ever imagine being with.

I didn't make friends easily but Lindy, the wife of the owner of the Sea Oats Country Club we frequented—where Ashton played golf—had taken me under her wing and we soon became fast friends. Not best friends, though. I needed to keep her curiosity at arm's length. Trust is not something gained overnight. There were secrets I would always leave unwrapped. Skeletons that could stay right there in their creaky old closets. But Lindy was kind, and kindness is a gift. I knew only too well about life's blows and switchback bends. Grateful was a word I cherished. I reminded myself every day how grateful I was for my marriage with Ashton and the chance to make things right again.

As well as keeping up with our social life at the country club, I worked long hours at a local foundation, Community Promise. We provided safe, temporary shelter and meals for those in need. Transportation to employment interviews, or medical appointments, or school. It gave women and youngsters a chance in life, to learn skillsets that would offer them jobs, or places at college. Our life skills program provided assistance in securing employment, access to medical care, school placement and, ultimately, help in locating affordable housing. We helped kids who had been abandoned by their parents, steered them away from temptations of drugs or crime. We also offered shelter from family abuse, or to runaway kids who had been molested. Troublemakers who were doing badly at school. Give a troublemaker responsibility and those troubles can melt away. So many kids are just not given a chance. It was a way of giving back, and my job meant the world to me. Our music classes in particular were transformative. With some youngsters it had been like watching the morning break, seeing the sun's orb rise from a dark horizon, and then shine slowly, brighter and brighter, lighting up the sky, making everything gleam in its wake. Some of these teenagers had made one hundred and eighty degree turns. Nothing gave me more pleasure than being part of their journey, a key element to their healing process. Ashton loved what I did because, being a doctor—a surgeon, no less—mending people (and cutting out the bad parts) was in his DNA.

I did everything I could to make Distant Island feel like my second skin. I wanted Ashton to be proud of me, I wanted—no, needed—his mother, Georgia-May, to love me as her own daughter, especially since my parents were no longer in my life. I began visiting her at her care home, Heritage Park Assisted Living, and I believed she now recognized me as her daughter-in-law and was really starting to warm up. Next were Ashton's friends in the community and his work colleagues. I left him to his own devices with his old fishing buddies and friends from childhood. What interested me more was the social scene at the country club and bonding with the other women.

A social climber, trying to hook my foot onto the middle rungs of the ladder and haul myself up to the top? You might assume that, if you didn't know me better. Let's just say I cared about being accepted by good society people. I cared about fitting in.

Our first dinner party I gave was a huge success. I spent weeks studying various different cookbooks, unsure of what to give them. The trick was to make it seem casual and second nature as if I were born into the laidback, unhurried, easy drawl of their world but was also effortlessly chic. I pretended that the dinner was no big deal. The guests were just Lindy and her husband Richard, and another younger couple, June and Michael. Michael was an intern at the hospital where Ashton worked in Charleston. A protégé, who had an uncanny resemblance to one of my favorite actors, Sidney Poitier. Neurosurgery is tough to master, obviously, and there aren't so many neurosurgeons in the States, not even throughout the world. You have to be meticulous. Have hands like Leonardo da Vinci and a brain like Einstein. Something I'd tell Ashton if he was stressed after a long day, if he needed to be bolstered.

"Leo and Al, remember?" I'd say. He'd always laugh.

For the entrée, I cooked a Basque *pipérade* of stewed green peppers, local clams and white fish, followed by a wine-braised chicken sprinkled with pearl onions and button mushrooms, and for dessert a cinnamon apple bostock splashed with French Calvados with frangipane cream and toasted almonds, sweet and crunchy. I'd baked bread, too, dripping with butter and garnished with herbs from the garden. I served it all with a crisp, cold Pinot Grigio, but had a good red on standby for those that might not like white. And a sweet French Sauternes for dessert. I was out to impress.

"So tell me how you two met?" Michael asked, dabbing his mouth with one of the linen napkins we had been given as a wedding gift. I had brought out all the best china and glasses and silverware too. I wanted his friends to approve of me.

"At the Citrus Club," Ashton and I said in unison and then laughed at how in sync we were.

June's eyes lit up. "The Citrus Club in Charleston?" We nodded. "And who spoke to whom first?"

I looked at Ashton, and he told them, "Me. Of course. I don't think Vivien would have even noticed me otherwise. What do you say, honey?"

"Oh, I don't know," I answered shyly, remembering how my heart had missed a beat when he entered the room.

"Vivien was waiting for a friend, who luckily never showed. She was sitting there, legs crossed, that gorgeous dark mane of hers hanging over one eye, sipping a cocktail so daintily—and I… well, I fell in love at first sight. And if anyone tells you love at first sight isn't possible… well, I tell you it certainly is."

"Nonsense," I protested. "You didn't fall in love with me at first sight."

"Oh no?" Ashton said. "I think I can be the judge of that."

"Get a room, you two," Lindy joked.

Michael took some bread and passed it along. "Sounds romantic."

Ashton smiled at me. "Oh, it was romantic, all right. I had to court her. But Vivien was hard to pin down. So busy with work. So elusive! Of course, I asked her on a date immediately—after we'd been chatting a couple hours. But she said she was busy, remember, honey? Took a while before I could get her to go for dinner with me. And after that first date, well, it took me forever to get her to have dinner with me again. And the third time. She was one cool customer. I had to work very hard to win her love."

"But it was worth it, right?" Lindy said. She swallowed a mouthful of chicken and licked her lips. "How do you do it, Vivien? I know you're busier than a moth in a mitten with your job. I mean, this food is out of this world. Weren't you working all day at Community Promise? How do you find the time?"

"Well, I don't have kids," I said, looking optimistically at Ashton.

"Oh, my word," Richard, Lindy's husband, agreed. "This really *is* exquisite. Where did you learn to cook like this?"

"Paris," Ashton replied. "Vivien *is* an astonishing cook. Even when she makes biscuits and gravy. I've really lucked out." He turned to look at me, his brown eyes glinting with pride.

I gave him a small smile. "The biscuits and gravy I *really* want the recipe for is your mom's, Ashton, honey. I hear Georgia-May has a secret biscuit recipe?" I had been hounding Ashton to let his mother come over and spend the day here, cooking, or doing something fun. The poor woman hadn't been let out of Heritage Park since the wedding. Ashton being an only child, we were the only family she had.

But Ashton swiftly steered me away. "I'm sorry, Michael, your glass is quite empty." He sprang up from his seat and gave everyone a refill. Ashton had such gentlemanly manners. As he was going around the table, in one hand a bottle of red and the other white, he said, "Vivien's far too humble. She did a cordon bleu cooking course in Paris, you know."

"How wonderful to do something like that in *Paris*," Lindy gushed.

I smiled, just a tad embarrassed. All eyes were on me. "Yes. I lived in Paris for a couple of years with my parents when I was nineteen, but I had to leave, sadly."

Richard, with his mouth full, said, "Why on earth did you leave Paris? Isn't that every person's dream to live there?"

"What took your parents to Paris in the first place?" June cut in.

"My dad's job," I said. "He worked in the fashion business, the rag trade. And my mom taught English as a foreign language to French students."

June raised a brow. "How glamorous," she drawled. "You must find it very backwater here in boring old South Carolina."

I caught Ashton's eye. "Not in the least. Distant Island's one of the most beautiful places I've ever lived, ever seen. And if I feel like a bit of shopping, or the theater or whatever, I go to Charleston. Or Savannah. And there's always New York, just a plane ride away. But seriously? My life here is so fulfilling, with Ashton and a large house to keep up and Community Promise, big cities don't really hold a place in my heart any longer."

"And why did you leave Paris?" Michael asked.

I hesitated then said, "My parents died." I spoke to the table, feeling too much in the spotlight. "In a car crash. I was staying with a friend at the time and Mom and Dad took a weekend trip to Normandy. My dad was fascinated with anything to do with the Second World War. It was on the autoroute, you know, the freeway?—except it isn't free in France, you have to pay a toll. People drive crazy fast in Europe, and my parents were wiped out in a horrific pileup. It wasn't their fault. A drunk driver in a truck, out of control."

I swallowed. Took a sip of water. Everyone was staring at me expectantly, so I went on with my story. "When the *pompiers* arrived—the fire fighters—my parents, and several other unlucky souls, had to be cut out of their cars. It was such a terrible scene of destruction. It was all over the news in Europe." I cleared my throat, took several gulps of wine and realized I'd given way too much detail and had made my guests uncomfortable. I felt as if I was failing and almost wished I hadn't spoken at all. I stole a glance at Ashton to gauge his reaction. I so wanted—and needed—to say the right thing. To not alienate his friends, his colleagues.

The room lost its warmth and people shuffled their shoes under the table, or fiddled with their napkins.

"I'm so sorry," Michael was the first to say. His dark eyes cast down, he stared at his plate and winced, mortified, it seemed, that he'd initiated this conversation.

"Thank you," I murmured, squirming in my chair.

Then everyone else mumbled their "So sorry for your loss" and, "I had no idea."

"*C'est la vie*, no? Or in English we translate that as, 'Life sucks,'" June offered, giving me a pitying smile. Her nonchalant attitude rubbed me up the wrong way. I wondered why silver-screen-handsome Michael was dating her—or were they married?

Ashton leaned over, held my hand and whispered in my ear. I looked at him with tears falling from my eyes prompted by what he'd just told me.

There was a strange silence. Nobody dared speak. But I could tell that everyone in that room wanted to know what my husband had said to me.

His words pulled me into a dark place.


Ashton and I made passionate love that night. I wanted to stay strong, stay focused on the positive. Marriages are whatever you let them be. My marriage was a turning point in my life and there was no way I was going to jeopardize everything I'd worked so hard to create. I needed Ashton. I *had* to make this marriage work.

Whatever the cost to my soul.

# CHAPTER THREE

Sundays with Ashton were my favorite. That domestic bliss when you're in the same room doing whatever you're doing and you don't have to say anything to each other. You just are. But when you've only been married six months—still just newlyweds—there is still so much discovering to do. *Who is this man I've married? What makes his mind tick?*

We had done things the old-fashioned way. No living together first. I suppose I didn't want to entertain any possibility of failure, and by living together first so much could go wrong. Of course, that's the whole point, isn't it? Checking to make sure you're right for one another for a couple of years before really committing? But we had gone in headfirst. I wasn't someone who'd had a string of beaux trailing behind me before I got married. I knew Ashton was the only one for me the second I met him.

Ashton looked up from his paper, glanced at me and smiled, then went back to reading. We were in one of the parlors, sipping iced tea… Georgia-May's secret recipe, with a dash of maple syrup and sprigs of fresh mint. It was too hot outside today, so the laziness of the sultry heat had chased us inside. The weather had been up and down. Just yesterday we'd had a rainstorm.

A pastel portrait of Georgia-May stared down at me with her pale blue eyes, as if to say, *Perhaps you made the tea too sweet, my dear? Too much syrup? I hope you're doing right by my son. Are you living up to my expectations? Oh, and by the way, don't let me down.*

Isn't that pretty much a given, that you'll let your mother-in-law down? I could feel it in my bones: dread, like a long frosty winter staring ahead of you, nipping at the windows of my soul, trying to weaken me, to make me slip up.

I was curious about their mother-son relationship, because Ashton never visited Georgia-May in her care home, and I wondered why. Whenever I asked, he used work as an excuse, or say something like, "Honey, I'd rather spend what little free time I have with you." There was some underlying history there between them, I knew.

Today I had Ashton all to myself, and felt covetous of my time with him. Sometimes he might be whipped away unexpectedly to the hospital. Neurosurgeons like Ashton did not grow on trees. I had learned, as the wife of a doctor, you not only have to share but take a back seat where patients are concerned. It's a lesson in humility. You can never believe you are number one because you'd be kidding yourself.

"Why are you smiling to yourself?" I asked, also smiling.

"Busted." Ashton looked up from the article he was reading. His brown eyes held a glint of mischief.

"What's so funny?"

"Are you ready? Something tells me you aren't." His smile lifted into a grin.

"Ready for what?"

"The test."

"What test?"

"The test of true courage."

"I'm a lot more courageous than you think," I told him. "I'm tougher than you, probably."

He roared with laughter.

"I am. I'm a strong woman. I'll surprise you one day, you watch. What are you reading about? Bungee jumping or something?"

"They've spotted her again. One thousand and ten razor-sharp pounds of her, roaming the shipping channel jetties near Charleston."

"Who?"

"Twenty miles offshore."

My heart missed a beat just thinking about it. "Not that shark again?"

"She's a true beauty. You see, when they satellite-tag white sharks we get such important tracking data. Discovering more about where they mate and give birth and their migration patterns is important. It's been discovered that great whites use the East Coast as a type of highway from Canada to the Gulf of Mexico. And this particular shark, Pearl White... well, we've learned so much about her lifestyle."

I chuckled. "Lifestyle? You make her sound like an Instagram star."

"She is. She's got a lot of followers."

I shivered. "Sharks scare me."

"Why?"

"Ever heard of the film *Jaws*?"

"Peter Benchley once said he wished he'd never written that book. He's done a lot for sharks and oceanic conservation since. You know getting in a car is a hell of a lot more dangerous than swimming in the ocean?" Ashton's face turned serious, suddenly aware of what he'd just said. He leaned over and stroked my hair. "Sorry, Vivien, I didn't mean to make you think about your parents again. That was a tactless remark."

I shook my head. "It's fine."

This shark hobby Ashton had I found disconcerting. There was nothing more powerful than a great white. Is that what he valued above all else? Power? The unknown? The fearful? He had made friends with a non-profit organization that tracked these apex predators and had even gone on a couple of expeditions. It was a charity he supported financially, too. He also went diving whenever he could, especially up the coast, to the Outer Banks in North Carolina, to a place where there were more than three thousand shipwrecks known as the "Graveyard of the Atlantic," where sand tiger sharks had made their home. For some reason, Ashton was absolutely fascinated with all types of sharks.

It gave me the chills.

"Come on, scoot over," he said.

I shifted closer to him, and he pulled me into an embrace. I let out a long sigh. It was a strange feeling I had with Ashton, the dichotomy of safety and vulnerability overwhelming me in one fell swoop. I wondered if I would ever be able to truly relax or be myself with my husband. He was so self-assured. So comfortable in his own skin.

Trying to sound upbeat, I said, "I heard on the news the other day that a woman from around here reported finding an ancient megalodon shark tooth that weighs a pound." I so wanted to take on Ashton's passions as my own, and someday I hoped to go diving with him. If I could dredge up the courage. "A pound! That's crazy. Near some muddy riverbanks near Charleston. A great big gray tooth was sticking out of the sand!"

He stroked my hand. "These parts were and still are their hunting ground. When you're ready we'll go diving and check out the sand tigers. They're cute, with a kind of snaggle-toothed grin. Graceful too and very docile. It's pretty risk-free. You'll be fine."

I furrowed my brows and grimaced. "*Pretty* risk-free?"

Ashton laughed again as if teasing me with all this was sport for him. "Another glass of tea?" He leaned over and grabbed the jug and filled up my glass. He was always making me drink more liquids to avoid dehydration. Before my marriage, I had never had anyone tell me what to eat or drink. It was always for my better good, Ashton's urging to drink more water, or eat the right foods, but still, I had been single for so long, I was unused to it. It did show he cared, though.

He stopped midway and held my gaze, long and hard. I couldn't work out if it was a sexy bedroom look, or if he was evaluating me, sizing me up. I looked away uneasily, and then the Georgia-May portrait caught my eye again. Or I caught hers, more like.

"When are we going to see your mom?" I asked, changing the subject.

"Whenever you like."

"Really?"

"Sure. She'd be thrilled if you paid her a visit."

"I thought we could go together."

"I'll check my schedule," he said. I knew that meant a "no."

We watched a couple of movies, cozied on the sofa, feet up, relaxed and easy. Later we made dinner together in the kitchen, and it all felt so natural and meant-to-be. I pushed away my fears and worries about where our marriage was heading and imbibed all the beauty and happiness of the day as if it were a magic elixir.

That's the problem with magic, though; it can turn. Because later, at night, while Ashton was sleeping, and the light of the moon crept through the open window, lighting up his face, I remembered again.

I was fooling myself.

All the beauty our marriage held… was only a half-truth.

# CHAPTER FOUR

For the next week I busied myself at Community Promise. A new girl had arrived—a sixteen-year-old—and I was doing everything to help her.

I made sure dinner was on the table at seven sharp or whenever Ashton got back from work at the hospital. Sometimes his shifts were erratic. He kept an apartment in Charleston, in case he had to work nights. Sometimes he stayed over.

The truth was I was beginning to feel the stress of trying to stay on top of it all. Keeping my body in shape, cooking fabulous meals, working so many hours at Community Promise. Although we had a cleaning lady and a gardener, I also liked to lend them a hand. The gardener, John, was a sweet, elderly man, who really should've been retired. He had suffered from Lyme disease and it had left him with a lot of pain in his joints, but he refused to stop working—he loved his job so much, so Ashton had kept him on. That's what John said, although I knew better. When people need to put food on the table, of course they love their job. I knew what it was like to live from paycheck to paycheck. The stress. The insecurity. Sometimes it made me feel guilty, living in luxury in a big house while others had so much less. I blessed my luck and good fortune every day. Who would have thought a regular woman like me would end up in a fancy house like Distant Sands?

I wished to put my stamp on Distant Sands, to make myself feel that the house belonged to me as much as I belonged to it. But sometimes I got the sensation it owned me. We had a beautiful rose garden, and I wanted to contribute, but between the gardening, the cooking, and work, I was bushed. It wasn't easy keeping up appearances.

After tennis, later that week, when Ashton was spending the night in Charleston, Lindy insisted I go over to her house for a girls' dinner. Just the two of us and an old friend of hers from school. But I didn't feel comfortable at the idea of getting to know yet another person, so I asked her if it could just be the two of us, without the friend. She agreed.

Lindy's house was lovely—not antebellum like ours, but a brick Colonial, full of beautiful but practical furniture, and homier than Distant Sands. It was overflowing with life. She had two black labs, and her children, Sally and Billy, were twelve and ten. Baseball bats, football paraphernalia, ballet shoes, tennis rackets, dog leashes—it all filled up the hallway and kitchen. It made my heart ache with longing. I wondered if Ashton had any intention at all for us to have a baby. So far, it seemed like that was the last thing he wanted. Both Lindy's kids had already had supper and were supposedly doing their homework, but I could hear them watching TV in the next room. *This is how Distant Sands should be*, I thought. Effervescent with children.

Lindy and I had the sunroom to ourselves. It was still light and we sipped her special-recipe margaritas as the sun turned golden, and we listened to birds chirping in the oak trees and the dogs chasing squirrels and the pow! pow! of a blockbuster in the next room. Or maybe it was a video game. Lindy had made some delicious cheese nachos and homemade salsa. I was starving; I'd hardly eaten all day and had played a grueling game of tennis at the country club. After the second margarita, I was a little tipsy, wondering if Lindy had done it on purpose: ply me with alcohol so my tongue got loose. If that was her intention, it had worked.

"Honey," she began, and then paused as she smoothed her wild red hair away from her face.

Lindy was pretty. Curvy and big-breasted, and she liked to show off those curves in tight, flowery, stretchy pantsuits. Pantsuits that might have come straight out of the 1970s. I often wondered if her clothing was retro but hadn't asked. She, I decided, was one of those born-confident people. She wore her extra weight with a sexy swagger and delicious self-assurance. She had big green eyes and her mascara and lipstick were always slightly smudged. I liked Lindy. She didn't care what people thought of her. She spoke her mind and called a spade a spade. She was fun. She also enjoyed her cocktails.

She took a deep breath then continued, "I've been worried about you all week, Vivien. That dinner party you gave was so wonderful, the food to die for, but I have to admit I saw the sadness in your eyes when you told us about your parents and..." She hesitated as if she couldn't find the right words.

I helped her out. "It's been a good long while since my parents died. Don't worry about me, Lindy, I'm, you know, over it."

She sighed and inspected her long nails. "You can *never* get over that kind of thing. You don't have siblings? Anyone to commiserate with?"

I took a gulp of my margarita then licked some salt from the rim. "No. Just me."

Lindy handed me the nachos and took some herself. "Tell me what happened after you left Paris?" she said, crunching.

"I went back to live in New York."

"That's where you were raised? In New York City?"

I nodded. "It was lonely. I was miserable for a long time. But I had a good job—worked at ... look, Lindy, I'm not as... I mean, I'm not from a wealthy family. There was no life insurance money after my parents died. I had to work. Had to struggle some."

"Of course you did, honey. I understand. I'm from a regular family, nothing special. In fact, when I met Richard, I was so poor I couldn't afford to pay attention." She laughed. "It's Richard who gave me this lifestyle. He's from 'old' money. Insurance is what built his great-grandparents' fortune. I'm just a regular girl trying to make good."

I smiled. "Looks like we're cut from the same cloth then. Except you and Richard seem so…" I felt tears building up. The need to tell Lindy everything was clamoring at me. I made to get up. "I should get going…"

She laid a hand on my arm. "You're not going anywhere, Vivien, you're three sheets to the wind, honey, you've drunk too—hey, what's that on your arm?" Lindy pushed up the sleeve of my sweater. "Is that a bruise? How did you get that nasty purple bruise?"

I shrugged, suddenly tongue-tied.

She looked into my eyes. "Please don't tell me you 'bumped into a door.' This is the third time I've seen you with bruises."

I said nothing.

"This is not a run-into-a-door bruise. This looks like a pinch. Like someone pinched you! There are *marks*."

"It's my skin. I bruise at the slightest thing. Honestly, it's nothing."

"Did someone do this to you?"

"No!" I said. "I'm really clumsy, always walking into things. My thighs, too. Always banging into corners of tables. I was born with two left feet!"

Lindy looked at me with suspicion.

"It's not… nobody touched me!" I protested, "Please don't think Ashton would ever lay a finger—"

"But it looks like someone *did* lay a finger on you! *Two* fingers, by the looks of it!" she shouted, then looking in the direction of where her kids were, simmered her voice. "You know you can trust me and share anything with me, right?"

"Sure," I said, wondering if I *could* trust Lindy.

"But, Vivien, this seems to be a recurring thing, these bruises."

I pressed my lips together. Lindy was trying to squeeze it out of me.

"Did this happen even before y'all got married?"

I gave her a neutral look but couldn't bring myself to say a word.

Lindy tightened her mouth into a narrow line and shook her head in what seemed like slow motion. Her eyes were wide with both shock and anger. "I'm amazed, frankly. I had Ashton pegged for the perfect Southern gentleman. Perfect manners. Kind, too. Okay, he has his past—he was a bit of a ladies' man in his day—but, boy, did I read him wrong. Turns out he's lower than a snake's belly in a wagon rut. What the heck? He's one of Richard's best friends! I'm dumbstruck." She glugged back her margarita in several furious gulps. I wasn't sure if she was angry with me for ruining her perfect vision of Ashton and spoiling her husband's relationship because they were best friends and now it might be awkward, or if she was angry with Ashton himself.

I sat there quietly, wondering what she'd say next. I wanted to defend Ashton, but the words felt blocked behind my mouth.

"What was it that Ashton said to you, honey, when he whispered in your ear at the dinner table the other night? It looked like you'd seen a ghost."

"Ashton's an amazing man. He's everything a girl could wish for… he had nothing to do with this! Please don't assume things!"

"Vivien, please. Please be honest with me, honey."

I fidgeted with my fingers, my heart beating erratically with a sort of fumbled panic. "There's this expression I've heard," I said. "And I wonder if it's typical. 'If you don't have anything nice to say, then keep your pretty little mouth shut.'"

"He said that?"

"No! Of course not! I just thought about it a second ago. Ashton's crazy about me, you know that!"

"Well, dang it, that's what I thought too! The way he looks at you with stars in his eyes. But it was your face, your face when he whispered those 'sweet nothings' in your ear and you misted up, I just knew something was wrong."

"You read that wrong, Lindy, he did say something sweet, I promise. Ashton's wonderful to me. So generous, amazing in bed, kind and caring." I swigged down the rest of my margarita. I could feel the liquor rush to my head. "I'm tipsy, I need to get home before I—"

"It's no wonder you're not as drunk as a fish, considering. The way you keep everything going so smoothly with all this *nastiness* going on behind closed doors. Spend the night here, don't go home. We'll watch a silly comedy and stuff our pie holes with chocolate chip ice cream and cookies. That sound good? Lord knows you could do with a few extra pounds on you." She embraced me with a cozy hug, and I couldn't help but burst out crying.

I wanted to run away from her that minute knowing that now she'd set eyes on this particularly pronounced bruise mark, she wouldn't let it rest. I said, between tears, "Lindy, Ashton and I are great together, I promise. Scout's honor. Our marriage is doing great."

"Hmm," she said. "I wasn't born yesterday."

# CHAPTER FIVE

Ashton arrived home late morning, exhausted. He'd been on the night shift at the hospital, had had to operate on a gun accident victim. A little boy had found his dad's revolver under the bed and had shot his older brother. The brother was still in the ICU, and Ashton didn't know if he would make it.

I brought Ashton breakfast in bed: fresh-squeezed orange juice, brewed coffee, and pancakes with fresh strawberries slathered in maple syrup from Vermont—his favorite. I was always amazed at the way he was able to operate and work for so many hours straight and then come home and leave his harrowing work behind. But he never lost his cool.

In his spare time, Ashton read a lot of spiritual books. Stuff about Buddhism and embracing your Higher Power. *I* was a whole lot simpler. I'd been raised a Catholic and still half believed all that mumbo-jumbo about Heaven and Hell. *Once a Catholic always a Catholic.* I couldn't shake it off. I tried to be more "spiritual" but it never quite jelled with me. Ashton never lost his temper outwardly. He was cool, calm, and collected. If he was ever angry it would be in a quiet, whispering way. He would rarely raise his voice or shout or scream or make a scene in public. Or dispute a check at a restaurant or argue with a contractor or tradesperson. He didn't need to. Ashton exuded authority. But when he looked at you with his deep brown eyes, it made you want to do anything for him.

I rolled Lindy's words over in my mind as I observed my husband with a smile spread across his handsome, tired face.

There were half-moons under his eyes. The sign of a benevolent doctor who put his patients before everything.

He sat up in the carved mahogany four-poster bed, bolstered himself up with some red, damask pillows behind his shoulders and let out a great yawn.

"You look exhausted," I said, placing the breakfast tray in front of him.

"I am, but these pancakes cannot wait! You spoil me, Vivien, and you always seem to know what I'm in the mood for. You're perfect in every way, you know that? Never change, honey."

I thought of how he'd whispered in my ear at our dinner party.

"I wish I could," I answered. "I wish I could believe you."

"You *must* believe me, honey." He put the tray aside and pulled me toward him. "You're beautiful. Come lie down, and let's spend the morning making love."

"For recreation? Or something more?"

He chuckled as if I were joking. "Honey, you know the deal. No kids, remember?"

I bit my tongue. Right now wasn't the moment for an argument. I hated that Ashton always used protection when we had sex. But it also gave me hope. He had said he didn't want kids, but if he really, *really* didn't want kids, he would've had some kind of medical intervention by now, surely? And he hadn't, so there was still that window open. I pictured what a son of ours would look like. I wondered if he'd inherit my looks or Ashton's. If our child would have brown eyes like him, or blue eyes like me. I assumed brown because brown is the dominant gene. I wondered if he'd be tall like Ashton.

"Come here," Ashton said, nudging me out of my reverie.

"Hold on, I'll just go freshen up." I headed to the bathroom, and even though I had already brushed my teeth, I brushed them again. Splashed cool water on my face and took several deep breaths, then faced myself in the mirror and took a long hard stare at the woman before me, feeling defeated, like I'd lost a part of myself—the good part—and for a moment, I wondered what my sense of purpose was in life.

When I came back into the bedroom, Ashton was fast asleep, the food only half eaten. I drew the silken damask curtains closed and left a note on top of the bedroom hearth. I decided to head out for work, even though it was Saturday and my day off. Ashton would be out for the count all day, probably, so there was no point waiting around for him to wake up. I needed to go to Community Promise and sort out Cady, the sixteen-year-old girl from a broken family.

I started the car and called Lindy.

"Lindy, thanks for last night. You cheered me up so much with that ice cream."

She laughed her special raucous Lindy-laugh. "Oh, honey, I was doing what any friend would do. Everything okay at home? I've been thinking round the clock about what you should do about Ashton."

"What do you *mean*?"

"Well, if anything like that happens again you call me straight away and I'll have words with him *myself*! There's nothing worse than a bully. Picking on someone who isn't your size, I can't abide that."

"Lindy, *please*. Everything's fine. Please don't jump to conclusions all because of that silly bruise." I changed the subject. "I feel badly I haven't gotten to know your kids that well yet. I hardly got a chance last night."

"Yeah, well, I didn't want to involve them yesterday because I wanted you all to myself! Come over next week. They say the weather's going to be gorgeous, so how about a barbecue? I do a great oyster roast too."

"That would be great. I can't wait to spend time with Sally and Billy. I love kids so much. I guess for now Community Promise will have to do."

"Aren't you planning on having your own kids soon?"

I hesitated, not knowing how much I should share. "I'd love to, but Ashton isn't on board yet. I guess he has all the time in the world. We women don't have that luxury. Ashton's thirty-nine—that's a newborn chick in male terms, right? I read that Richard Gere fathered a kid at seventy. For a woman, forty's over the hill, yet for a man... well, it's not fair, is it? I'm nearly thirty-five, I can't wait forever."

Lindy snorted. "Ashton doesn't want kids?"

"I need to convince him. He just doesn't seem to jell with children that much. That, or he doesn't want me spoiling my figure by getting pregnant and putting on weight." Then I added, "That was a joke, by the way. Of course, he wouldn't care if I put on weight. It's just he's very busy at the hospital. I think he's stalling because he wants to be a very hands-on dad, you know? And right now, he doesn't have the time."

Lindy sighed. "That's a shame. A real shame. But maybe, in the scheme of things, Vivien, it's a blessing in disguise?"

"What do you mean?"

"Maybe he doesn't even *deserve* your kids. If he doesn't show—I mean really prove—in every single way how much he loves you, then, honey, I think you better look elsewhere. I'm saying this to you as a friend. You're still young, don't waste yourself on the wrong man."

"Oh dear, Lindy, I think you have the wrong impression. Ashton and I—"

"You take care now, and I'm on standby if you need me, ya hear?"

I needed to cut this conversation short. "Listen, I better go because I'm late and I need to talk to this new girl, Cady, who's just arrived at the center. She's a sixteen-year-old runaway and she really needs my help."

"I don't know how you do it," she said. "You're busier than a one-legged cat in a sandbox! It's like you've got energy for twenty people, always putting others first."

I laughed. "Speak soon. I'm definitely up for the barbecue, and I know Ashton will be too."

"Well, don't blame me if I give him the evil eye."

"Please don't, Lindy! I swear to God, Ashton and I are doing great. *Please* don't stir things up. He hasn't done anything!"

"You're too sweet, you know that? Come next Saturday, six o'clock? Casual."

I put the car into drive and as I was pulling away something made me look back at the house. There was Ashton standing on the upper porch outside the bedroom looking longingly after me. He gave me a sad little wave as if to say, *You abandoned me?*

It genuinely seemed like he was a man who was crazy in love.

I felt my heart break, just a little.

# CHAPTER SIX

As well as a shelter, Community Promise was a day center for our "guests"—as we called them—to receive mail, do laundry, complete employment and housing searches in our computer center, and discuss plans with whichever case manager was on duty. Today, it was Susan's rota, a friendly, warm woman who had been working here for several years. I was sure she could use some help. It was all go-go-go, people hustling around the Xerox machine and busy staring at screens and talking on phones. In that moment we had about ten teenagers we were helping. I'd had personal success with several, namely an eighteen-year-old named Tom, who had been sexually assaulted, and a battered woman who had found refuge here from her husband. Both had started new jobs at a local boatyard.

There were all sorts of skills classes at Community Promise, too, with an array of tutors, a lot of them teaching them practical things like woodworking or cooking. It was rewarding to help our guests fill out forms or whatever they needed to move to the next level. We'd even had some success with kids ending up getting places at good colleges.

Cady was here, looking teenage-bored and surly, a typical sixteen-year-old pout plastered on her small, oval face that said, *The world owes me everything.* But there was something adorable about her too—when she smiled, that was. Her skinny frame was clad in equally skinny jeans, and a black baggy T-shirt that dwarfed her. The print was a turtle eating a plastic bag, and, LET'S FIND A SOLUTION TO OCEAN POLLUTION. Cady had dyed, tomato-red, spiky punk rock hair and a few piercings in each ear, with an assortment of different style earrings. Despite the pout, she was pretty, her skin pearly, and so translucent you couldn't tear your eyes away. And a deer-in-the-headlights gaze, all dark and soulful. She wore slashes of thick black eyeliner that swooped into wings either side of her eyes to give herself a feline look, which didn't quite work. But she was cute. She told me she had become estranged from her single mom who had moved states. We'd found her a place at Community Promise in one of the dorms until we sorted out a plan for her. Meanwhile, I had enrolled her in the local high school. I remembered what my life had been like after I no longer had parents to call my own.

I gave her a high five. "Hi, Cady, how's it going? How's school?"

She sneered. "I don't know… okay, I guess. Wish I had a mom who gave a shit about me."

I said carefully, "Well, I'm sure your mother wants the best for you. I'm sure she'd be delighted you're back at school."

"Oh yeah? I think she only cares about *herself*."

Susan caught our conversation and peered over her glasses. She bustled over to the worktable, where we were sitting. "You want to talk to one of our therapists, Cady?"

"Nuh-uh. It is what it is. I was just telling Mrs. Buchanan here that my mom doesn't give a *shit* about me." She chewed on a pen. "She found a guy and basically just dumped my ass."

"She was staying with a friend, a girl," I explained to Susan. "It was Cady's idea to spend the vacation in New York with her friend—her mom agreed—until she went to live with her mother in her new house and—"

"Yeah, but me and Amy fell out, so it was, like, complicated, even though Amy's mom was super cool. I think Amy got jealous. Then I had nowhere to go," Cady said.

"And your mom?" Susan asked.

"She like, bailed on me, basically." Cady bit her cuticles, her nubby fingers half in her mouth.

Susan asked gently, "Did you try living with your mom and her new partner?"

Cady looked at us tearfully. "I called my mom and she told me I couldn't live with her until things got settled. What the hell does that mean? '*Settled*.' She obviously doesn't want me around."

"Maybe things might change soon," I said to her. "Meanwhile, you're safe here at Community Promise."

A tear plopped onto the legal pad she was doodling flowers and guns on.

I explained Cady's situation to Susan. "It was a temporary solution, but then Cady heard about Community Promise from another friend of hers and got on a train and came here."

"But her mother's responsible for her until she reaches the age of eighteen!" Susan said. "In every way, especially financially."

Cady wiped her tears away with the back of her wrist. "I don't need my mom. I make my own money. I have a drop shipping business and make real good money selling stuff online."

Susan looked blank.

"You know, like an ecommerce store?" Cady explained. "Without the hassle of keeping goods in stock or owning the inventory?"

"Wow," said Susan, "that's very impressive. You're only sixteen?"

"Yeah. Seventeen in three days."

I said, "Well, that shows you have a lot of gumption and talent and you'll go places in the world. You should be proud of yourself that you got this business together. Like Susan says, impressive. Did anyone give you a hand?"

"In the beginning my mom helped me, but now it pretty much runs itself. Like I say, it's drop shipping so I don't have to do any packing myself, it's pretty cool."

"Can we speak to your mom?" asked Susan. "Maybe if she realizes you're here she'll be very worried and want you to come home. Maybe you can work something out with her and her new husband? Or is it boyfriend?"

"Same difference."

"Well, I can see that you're a very smart kid," I said. "Really smart. And I'm so sorry about your situation. We'll call your mother and work out a solution."

"I was raped," Cady suddenly said.

Her words hit me in the gut. "Are you *serious?*"

"Yeah, I'm serious. You think I'd make something like that up?"

I held her gently by the wrist. It was frail and thin. "What happened, Cady? That's so awful!"

Susan laid a plump arm around Cady's shoulder. "Oh, my word! I'm so, so sorry this happened to you, honey. You must be in a state of terrible shock. Would you like to see a doctor?"

After a long while, Cady shook her head. "What can any doctor do? This happened, like, a few months ago. They want a rape kit and all that crap. They wouldn't believe me anyways. It was like a date rape kind of thing, you know. I knew the guy. We went to a movie and then he... he took me in an alleyway. It was dark. He pushed himself on me and I told him no, but he forced himself. He was real tall and big and there was no way I could get him off me. Anyways, I just... kind of didn't react. Figured by being like a zombie he'd leave me alone, but he didn't. He finished what he came to do and strolled away. I don't think he even got that it was rape, that's how sick the whole deal was."

"Oh my God," I gasped. "Did you report this to the police?"

"Nope."

I took Cady's hand again and looked into her eyes.

She shook my hand away, fuming. "Dammit, you think I'm making this shit up?"

"No! I know there's nothing worse than a woman who isn't believed."

Susan said, "We need to report this. This guy cannot get away with this! You have his name and everything? Of course you do, you went to a movie with him. You have any phone calls or text messages we can show for proof?"

"Yeah, I can prove I went out with the guy, but I can't prove he raped me, can I? It happened so long ago now."

"When?" Susan and I said in unison.

"Like a few months ago. Look, the guy's a jerk, it happened, I'll just have to get over it, right?"

"We'll help you," I said. "I promise."

She looked at me with her teary doe eyes and managed a trembling smile.

My heart felt splintered in two.

Yet why did I get the feeling she was hiding something? Something dark.

I drove home so I could quickly change into something nicer. Ashton was still fast asleep and I didn't disturb him. Today was my day of giving back, paying it forward. Georgia-May was next on my list.

I passed by our mailbox at the end of the driveway. There were six letters and two small parcels. I sifted through them. Mostly bills. Then there was one that was stuck between two local flyers that looked like it had been sitting there for ages. Neither Ashton nor I had gotten around to throwing the flyers out. The envelope—a good quality one—had gotten damp at some point; the postmark was smeared and unreadable. I couldn't make out the date, nor the place. I opened it.

On expensive white paper, someone had written, in slanting capitals:

*LEAVE ASHTON WHILE THE GOING'S GOOD.*

# CHAPTER SEVEN

On the drive to Georgia-May's care facility I turned that freaky note over and over in my head. Who could have sent it? Lindy? What did people know? Was Lindy a gossip? A jealous ex-girlfriend? It had to be someone who knew my address. Easy enough to find out, I supposed. I slipped the paper back into the envelope and decided to keep it. Just in case things got worse and I needed to ask the police to scan it for fingerprints. Who, who, who?

*Who* had sent that ominous note? Was it a threat? A "friendly" warning?

It felt to me like a threat. But maybe I was being paranoid?

I arrived at the gates of Georgia-May's private care facility, where she lived full-time. There was quite a lot of security at the fenced-in property. I guessed they were worried about the residents wandering off, because a lot of them had dementia or Alzheimer's, Georgia-May being no exception.

Ashton had told me horror stories of how his mother would forget who she was and wander all over the place, venture into town, get on random buses. She had even hitchhiked. Another time she took the boat out, all on her own, thinking she'd seen a mermaid and she needed to rescue it. Ashton explained that she had been struck by the disease quite early in life and had been in the care facility for seven years already. It happened after her husband, Ashton's father, died in a boating accident. I had always gotten the impression that they were very much in love, and that

Buck's death had destroyed her and, literally, made her lose her mind. Georgia-May was now seventy. Poor thing, she seemed so vulnerable. I wanted to help in any way I could and be present in her life. As Georgia-May did not have a daughter of her own and I didn't have a mother, it made sense for us to become close. I could bring her peace and friendship. We could support one another, she and I, and form a sort of mother/daughter bond. At least, that's what I was aiming for. Maybe I felt I needed to make up for Ashton's disinterest in his mother? His distance? It was strange the way he just didn't appear to show an active concern with his mom's care. Or spend time with her.

I guess that's what wives so often do for their husbands: compensate, take on their family duties, fill in the gaps. Maybe I was reaching too high, but I could try.

It was such a shame for her to be living in seclusion when she was clearly a very sociable person, and I was tempted to persuade Ashton to let her live with us—at least in our self-contained guest house attached to the property—and hire a full-time nurse. But I also knew his mom was probably better off here, with her bridge games and activities, her regular, wholesome meals taken with friends. With my work at Community Promise and Ashton's at the hospital, there was no way we could give her the same care and attention.

At the gates, I gave the security officer my name, parked, then presented myself at the reception. They knew me well. Usually Georgia-May would come down with her nurse and we'd go for a walk around the grounds. There were sweeping lawns and rose bushes and azaleas and paths that meandered through the nine-acre lot. Huge oaks laden with Spanish moss and sugar maples and beds of black-eyed Susans and hibiscus and canna lilies were in bloom. There were plenty of benches to sit on, peppered along the paths. The place was beautiful and, appraising it all again, it made me feel so much better, because she was extremely well looked after, or so Ashton always assured me, and certainly the members of staff were smiley and friendly. They did seem genuine.

"Don't be surprised if Mrs. Buchanan doesn't recognize you," Ruby, the receptionist warned. She was an ample-bosomed, portly lady, with sparkly eyes that tilted up at the edges and freckles that dotted her earth-brown skin. She had worked as a nurse before but had switched her skills to receptionist when arthritis got the better of her.

I shrugged. "I know, Ruby. I know how it goes. But last time she knew exactly who I was and remembered our wedding and everything."

I couldn't deny feeling hurt on the occasions when Georgia-May forgot who I was. It was foolish. It wasn't personal, just the disease, but my pride made me want her to always know me, to need. Silly, but I couldn't help myself. Not having a mother in my life, I craved that connection.

"She's been a little testy the last few days," Ruby let me know. "She lost at poker."

"You let them play *poker* here?"

"Not with real money, of course. But, yes, ma'am, once a year we let 'em play poker. They love it. But it does tend to cause mayhem. Mrs. Buchanan isn't talking to Saul. Lord willing and the creek don't rise, she'll be right as rain again." Saul, a feisty and talkative widower, was Georgia-May's best friend. They were always "splitting up" then the greatest pals once more.

Georgia-May approached the reception with her nurse, Mariama—whom she adored—a hearty and jolly woman, who was very proud of her Creole heritage—from the sea island Gullah people—and sometimes brought homemade treats to work. I had tasted her shrimp 'n' grits and okra soup and had begged her for the recipe. But Mariama wouldn't share her family secret.

Georgia-May shrugged Mariama off her with a shoulder-shake and waved her tiny wrist at her. "I am absolutely *fine* and you can leave me now with this very nice young lady who has kindly come to visit. She looks quite *adorable*. Hello, my dear," she said to me. "I hear you've come to pay me a visit and I'm quite charmed, I'm sure."

Mariama tittered. "Mrs. Buchanan, you know exactly who this is. This is your daughter-in-law, the lovely Miss Vivien. She's married to Ashton. You remember, you went to the wedding and you told me what a fabulous time you had. You told me all about the wedding cake, that it had five tiers and was decorated with red roses and tasted like heaven. You told me about the sailboat rides and the beautiful outfit you wore. You remember? The pink chiffon? That was the same dress you told me that you wore when you were only twenty-five."

Georgia-May looked at her blankly.

"Don't you remember? You told me all about that dress, that you bought it in California. And, ma'am, was I impressed that you were able to wear that same gown. Lord knows, I myself am four sizes bigger than I used to be but you, you fit right into something you wore when you were twenty-five!"

Georgia-May's smile reached her eyes, twinkling with memory. "I remember going shopping in Atlanta and buying a beautiful pink chiffon dress. I also bought a yellow one. My husband spilled bourbon all over it, and I could never get the smell out. Not even with dry cleaning. It was quite ruined. I should've picked a husband who was less of a klutz!"

Mariama looked uneasy. "Are you ready for your walk with Miss Vivien?"

Georgia-May took two steps forward and offered me her arm. "Vivien! You look absolutely divine. I'm so delighted Ashton married you. What a lucky man he is. Forgive me, my dear, for not recognizing you sooner. I've been a little confused lately."

"No problem. Shall we go for our walk? It's such a beautiful day. I thought we could wander down to the pond and look at the goldfish."

"That would be lovely. You may leave us now, Mariama." Georgia-May held up her head haughtily and motioned for her nurse to leave us.

Georgia-May had no trouble walking; physically she was in great shape. It was just this "forgetfulness" she had trouble with.

"Isn't it the most stunning September day?" I said brightly. "I love it here, those huge trees and so much chattering birdsong. It's such a lovely place to live, don't you think?" I wanted to make her feel positive about her life, that she wasn't cooped up in some sort of institution, that she was here by choice.

"I guess I have to take the rough with the smooth, but then I *do* feel like I'm in jail some days. Ashton hasn't visited in forever. He doesn't want anything to do with me."

"That's not true, Georgia-May, he talks about you all the time," I lied. "He misses you terribly."

"That's a fib and you know it."

"I promise. Ashton misses you. Misses his dad too."

She turned silent, and I could sense an invisible barrier draw up between us. It wasn't true what I'd said. I just wanted to make her feel good. Also, I was hoping she'd share a little about Ashton's past. Ashton never mentioned his father. Only that he had died at sea during a storm and Ashton was with him on that fateful day. Every time I fished for details, Ashton changed the subject, or became taciturn—a trick he used often. And then I always felt tactless pushing or prying for more information. Last time I'd asked him, he'd said, "I'll tell you all about it some other time, I promise."

But he still never had.

Ashton hardly ever spoke about his childhood. Just occasional anecdotes about going fishing with his dad or about high school or college—how he excelled at football and always managed top grades, despite being a pretty wild partygoer. Once, he did share something deeper about himself—after he'd had a few too many beers. That his cheerleading girlfriend, Belle, the love of his life, had married his best friend, Bradley. He and Bradley had never quite made up.

No, Ashton had not shared too much of his past or his family dynamics with me.

In contrast, *I* had a thousand stories about my mom and dad. How in love they were, how they talked together in French when I was a little girl, so I couldn't understand. How spoiled I was. How Mom had had several miscarriages before me, so by the time I came along, I was the most treasured thing in their world. I told him that my life had basically ended when they died, and how I had to do everything to stay strong. I often chatted to Ashton about my life growing up in New York. Picnics in Central Park, visits to the New York Public Library, where I first learned about my passion for books. And Ashton had continued with this picnic tradition. Our marriage, I told him, had pulled me out of my grief. He was everything to me. He was my world, my kingpin, my one hope for repairing everything I had lost.

Georgia-May and I ambled through the grounds with linked arms. A squirrel dashed across the path then scrambled up an oak tree. Tweets of birdsong filtered through the branches, the sunlight catching its leaves with lashes of pale gold. Our gazes simultaneously followed the creature as it zipped along to join its friend.

That weird note popped into my head. I pushed it away. My mind wandered back to Ashton, wondering if he was anything like his father. Every scrap of information I gleaned would help me know my husband better. Marriages are like gardens; you have to tend them constantly. Just when the roses bloom little weeds peek through the earth, and if you don't pluck them out when they're tender, they grow thick and stubborn.

"What was Ashton's father like?" I asked Georgia-May as we ambled along together, slow as snails.

She stopped walking. "Buck Buchanan had powers of persuasion. And charm. Jackson Holt had asked for my hand in marriage, you know, but I foolishly turned him down. Chose Buck instead. Jackson became an attorney. Very wealthy, but I lived a life of relative poverty with Buck. I was a real beauty, you know, I could have chosen any number of beaux." She looked up at the tree as if in another world.

"I bet you were. You're *still* a beauty, Georgia-May." I hid my surprise at what she had alluded to… that she had made a mistake marrying Buck.

She was really stunning for her age. She had a heart-shaped face and a cute, pointy little chin and big, big, blue eyes. Silvery blonde hair and high cheekbones, and what really made her lovely was her beautiful nose. I noticed noses. Noses can make or break a person's face, and Georgia-May's nose was fine and elegant, ever so slightly retroussé. It fit her countenance perfectly. She was petite, slim, and probably quite athletic in her day. She still had very fine ankles and wrists and an elegant long neck. She always wore double pearls, even when paired with sneakers and a jogging suit. Today she was all in white.

She began to shake with excitement, and yanked my arm closer. "You hear that? That musical series of rapid warbling notes? See if you can spot those frisky, elusive birds. It's the painted bunting that sings like that. The one with the bright reddish-orange breastplate and purple-blue head? Look! You saw it? He just flew out of that oak! Such a beautiful bird. That's the male. The female is yellowish in color."

"I'm sorry. I missed it," I said, disappointed. "Darn, how did I miss that?" I let a good amount of silence lapse then pressed her again. "Tell me more about Buck. Ashton says he was the best shrimper in South Carolina."

Georgia-May started walking again and replied dreamily, "You know, Ashton is such a good boy, a sweet-natured child. He likes to collect butterflies. He loves beautiful things, he has quite a collection. He even helps me bake cakes sometimes. Always full of concern always kind. He thinks about others less fortunate than himself. Says he wants to be a doctor when he grows up. Such an adorable child. He takes our eggs to old Mrs. Zachery, offers to wash her car for her. Never asks for a cent in return. He's a darling boy. And, oh, what a smart mind! He's not like his father at all." Her face suddenly darkened and a fire lit in her eyes. "Oh, no, siree. Nothing like than mean son-of-a-gun, Buck. Ashton's father is a *brute* sometimes."

I noticed how she was suddenly talking in the present tense. "Why?" I asked, all ears. "What did... what does Buck do?" I was tempted to ask her if Buck had been abusive, but of course I couldn't... that would have been too intrusive.

She smiled and looked all sweetness and light again, the flashing fury I'd just witnessed wiped clean from her face. "Buck? Why he was a real charmer, very handsome, the most charming man this side of Beaufort County. We were extremely happy. The envy of all. Such a happy marriage." Georgia-May stopped walking and glanced up to the trees again then back to me.

I was agog, her sudden change of humor, and her story changing on the flip of a dime.

"May I offer you a little snippet of advice, Vivien, my dear?"

"Of course." I tried to appear relaxed and unfazed, so I smiled at her.

"If you don't have anything nice to say then keep your pretty little mouth shut."

Was she referring to me, or herself? That expression was not new to me. "What are you saying?"

She beamed at me sweetly, a tiny splotch of fuchsia pink lipstick stuck on her front tooth. "I'm telling you that Buck and I had the perfect marriage, and if anyone—I mean *anyone*—tells you different, they are quite simply... lying."

# CHAPTER EIGHT

By the time I got home it was already six-thirty. I had meant to call Ashton but ended up not having time. I did send him a text to let him know I'd be late and that I hadn't organized anything for dinner. I hoped he wouldn't be too disappointed. I checked the mailbox again. No new note. I still had no clue, no inkling who had sent it.

Ashton was waiting for me, all bright and happy as if I'd been away for months.

He opened the kitchen screen door with a flourish and let me pass through. Ashton always opened doors for women, and if you were at a restaurant and got up to go to the bathroom, he would rise from his chair and give a nod, in a true gentlemanly fashion. He behaved this way with all women, not just me. Once, I witnessed him stop his car in the middle of a traffic-choked street, get out and help an old lady cross the road. The vehicles were honking their horns, but he didn't care one whit.

"Honey," he said. "How was your day?" He pulled me into a bear hug. His hug said it all. A release of tension from doing such a demanding, high-precision job. Operating on people's nervous systems, with vulnerable lives in his hands every day of the week must be beyond stressful, I thought. Just one slip of the scalpel or laser. It didn't bear thinking about.

He clasped me even closer and inhaled my hair. Then out came a long, appreciative sigh. We stayed like that, our hearts beating at different rhythms, but connected. These were the moments I treasured so much.

*If only it had been like this always.*

I finally broke the embrace. "I'm sorry it took me so long to get home, but I got involved at Community Promise and then I went to see your mom."

"I know, thanks for the text."

I waited for him to ask me how she was doing, but he said nothing.

"I wish you'd come too sometime," I said. "She'd adore to see you."

"I will. I will. Just so busy at the moment. She doing okay?" He said this without feeling, as if it was his duty to ask. He got some white wine out of the fridge and poured me a glass then fixed himself a Scotch on the rocks.

"She was in pretty good spirits," I let him know. "Talked about your father, actually." I hoped this would act as a springboard for Ashton to say more, but all he did was tell me a few stories about his dad and him going fishing.

After a while, I said, "It's such a shame your mom can't live with us in the guest house. Be independent yet close by."

Ashton didn't respond, just came out with, "I've made dinner, by the way." He held both of my hands and appraised me for a beat as if to show how much he approved of me. I had made an effort for Georgia-May and was wearing a floral print silk jumpsuit and makeup.

"Vivien, honey, how come you decided to work on your day off?"

"I figured you'd be sleeping most of the day. And there's this kid, this teenager, who really needs my help right now. You didn't have to make dinner, Ashton honey, there's a lot of stuff in the freezer we could've heated up."

He led me to the kitchen table, where he'd set it up beautifully, with candles, linen napkins, and an open bottle of red. He poured me a fresh glass and handed it to me, then one for himself. We made a toast to our happiness.

I took a long sip then set my wine down. "The table looks beautiful."

"I felt like cooking. It's simple, just salad and pasta, nothing fancy. Informal, just here in the kitchen."

I grinned. "Your lasagna with sun-dried tomatoes? My favorite?"

"Lasagna with the sun-dried tomatoes, your favorite." He kissed me on the forehead and held my face before laying his lips gently on mine. "I've missed you," he breathed into my mouth. "You escaped earlier. My fault, I guess, for falling asleep on you."

I abandoned myself to his kiss, my body blazing from the intimacy. He clenched me close again, this time with more urgency. It felt so good to be in his arms. I was safe in that moment. Treasured. All my troubles melted away as if there had only ever been perfection between us all along. As if hurt and betrayal and those degraded feelings I'd suffered had never played a part in our relationship.

"If you carry on doing that, there'll be no dinner, I'll carry you straight upstairs," he said, and laughed.

"Fine by me. But the only problem is I'm ravenous."

He pulled out a chair for me. "Sit down, relax. Thought I'd take you out on the boat tomorrow. It's Sunday, we need a break. We've both been working too hard. I'll show you some secret places that I used to go as a boy. Since I was knee-high to a grasshopper. Little islands that belong only to the birds, and inlets leading to places that nobody knows about. Would you like that?"

"I'd love that."

Through the summer, although we'd been out sailing, the ferocious heat of the sun was something I wasn't used to. The weather was humid, unrelenting and, in the evening, the air thick with mosquitoes, so we tended to go swimming during the day or have dinner in the screened-in porch, rather than venture out on long boat rides. I was excited at the prospect of finally discovering these places that Ashton had told me about. He had two boats. The sailboat and a smaller motorboat that could slip its way through lagoons, sounds and riverine estuaries, even salt marshes teeming with seagrass.

Ashton stood there, his six-foot three frame hovering halfway between the table and the kitchen. He rubbed his weary, shadowed eyes. Dressed in jeans and a black T-shirt, the ropes of his muscles strained as he stretched his arms and yawned.

"Excuse me, I probably should've slept longer than I did." He suppressed another yawn.

"Did the boy make it?"

Ashton didn't answer.

"Your patient?" I prompted.

A sad resignation flickered in Ashton's eyes, but then he said, more upbeat, "He's in the hands of my team. If anyone can keep Brady alive, my team of doctors and nurses can. I say 'my team' but, you know, we're all equal, we all have a stake in our patients' lives. We work as one unit." He shook his head resignedly. "I hate to say it, but Brady's chances are very slim. I'll spare you the details, sweetheart, they're not pretty."

"I'm so sorry. It's heartbreaking. His family must be out of their minds. They'll live with that guilt for the rest of their lives."

*The loaded gun in the house.*

I took a long sip of wine, tasted the fruity warmth on my tongue and prepared my next sentence in my head. I came out with it in a gush. "I don't like it, Ashton, that you keep that loaded shotgun in the house. It terrifies me. Considering—"

"Honey, if we had kids, there's no way I'd keep a loaded gun around. But I like to know it's there, just in case. My father taught me to have a gun handy in case of emergencies. One time, when I was too young to remember, some criminals broke into the house. I'll teach you to shoot, if you like. Maybe it'll make you feel a little bit more confident, make you understand it's not as scary as it seems."

"Maybe," I said, without enthusiasm. "Maybe, but some other time."

"Yeah, some other time."

Ashton strolled toward the other side of the kitchen, took the dish of pasta from the oven and brought it, piping hot, to the table. It smelled delicious and my stomach rumbled in appreciation. He then stood behind me, massaging my neck and shoulders. The wine, the effort he'd made with the cooking, his touch—desire for this man spread through my body. In a couple of hours, we'd be making love.

"Let's just have a great day out tomorrow and concentrate on each other," he said. "I've missed hanging out."

My knots melting, I let out a sigh. His full-on attention and kindness made me feel equal parts sad and equal parts in love.

# CHAPTER NINE

We were racing along choppy waters out to sea, the wind warm, the salty air a springboard for my soul.

Ashton was in his element, too. "For shallow waters and chop, this little boat has done me proud. It's the second Action Craft FlatsMaster I've owned. You have to watch out for sandbars along here. Navigating these waters is no easy feat."

"It's a fun boat," I shouted above the roar of the motor, glancing up at him. "I love boat trips."

Ashton had prepared our picnic himself, stowed away for later. He'd done it all while I was fast asleep in bed this morning. I looked at him now, the waves of his sandy hair bleached all summer by the sun, and his dark eyes crinkling with happiness. Yesterday's tired neurosurgeon was quite gone. His spirits lifted with every wave, with every bounce of the boat. He looked boyish and younger than his thirty-nine years.

I thought about what Lindy had told me about Ashton: that he was a ladies' man. He was a catch, I was well aware. I reminded myself how I had lucked out, how hard I worked—so careful to dress the way I knew he liked women to dress and behave. Feminine, but not too flouncy. Assertive but never aggressive.

Ashton slowed down the boat some, as he navigated through a narrow channel. "You know, Beaufort's history is as old as the hills. All kinds of nations and cultures have put their mark on this place. A lot of different European explorers—from the Spanish to the French, usurping Native American tribes' lands along the way, and then the English with Sir Francis Drake—staked their claim on these sea islands."

"Francis Drake was no more than an aristocratic pirate, really. Queen Elizabeth I's pirate, who was rewarded for looting and stealing," I said, feeling pleased with myself that I could offer some tidbits of knowledge.

Ashton laughed. "I like your take on it."

"They all acted like pirates," I said. "They all behaved badly."

"True. You know that the European settlers brought the first strain of malaria to the Lowcountry? Then a new strain came along with slavery."

I grimaced. "Ugh, I hate that evil part of American history. It's so shameful."

"No denying that. I'm proud that one of my ancestors—a doctor—was an abolitionist; he was part of an underground movement to help slaves gain their freedom. The Gullah are an important part of our culture. Probably the most important African-American community and linguistic heritage in the United States. You know some of the largest populations of Gullah are here in Beaufort? They were from the west coast of Africa. Brought over for their expertise in rice cultivation. Rice became one of the most successful industries in early America. Charleston, for a good hundred years, was the richest city in the country, thanks to the skill and ingenuity of the West African culture."

"I didn't know that about the rice," I said.

"And their incredible talent for music? Gullah music was the basis for gospel, jazz, and the blues and influenced all American music, really. And, of course, their sweet grass basket weaving is famous."

"Not to mention their cuisine," I added, thinking of Georgia-May's nurse's amazing dishes. I told Ashton about Mariama's fabulous recipes that I was trying to get my hands on, but the mention of his mother made him go quiet again. I wasn't going to let him get away with clamming up about his family and his past yet again. Not today. I broached the subject of his father. There was a backstory there, and I needed for him to share it with me, once and for all.

He groaned. "You really want to go there?" And then he sped the boat up so the noise made it hard for us to hear each other.

"You bet ya!"

Just then, as if by miraculous timing, a dolphin rose out of the pearly water and broke through the waves beside the boat and began to swim alongside us. Then there was another.

"Look! Dolphins!" I cried out.

Their speed was amazing as they steered with their tails like the sterns of boats. The sunlight caught their backs as they shimmered and arced through the waters. A third arrived.

"They're the bottlenose variety," Ashton shouted above the motor.

I leaned down as far as I could over the boat, mesmerized by the grace and rapidity of these incredible creatures. It was as if they had magical propellers as they streamlined through the water, their dorsal fins slicing along like sails. They steered with their noses, too, weaving and cutting through and under and over each other. How anything so fast could glide with such grace amazed me. Their skin was a little bit mottled, a beautiful silver gray—no, several shades of silver, platinum-gray—and their bellies pearly white. I caught their smiles as I looked from one to the other, and then down they went into the water and disappeared. My heart dropped with disappointment at such a fleeting visit from them.

But Ashton shouted, "They're over here, starboard!"

I scrambled to the other side of the boat, my eyes darting around the water, and I made out the moving shadows beneath. Then they came up again, one and then the other, and the third, smaller one. Their curving, powerful leaps almost took me by surprise. Water unspooled off their backs like ribbons as they dived back down, bottlenose-first.

So free! I shuddered to think of their cousins, captive and imprisoned at sea parks around the world, hiding their misery with default, permanent smiles. These dolphins were so liberated, so one with nature. Tears—wind tears or real tears I wasn't sure—were streaming down my face. The flutter in my heart told me they were tears of happiness, because I had never been up so close and personal to an exotic and majestic wild animal before. A free wild animal.

Then, as miraculously as they had appeared beside our boat, they vanished deep into the Carolina waters. I looked around, bereft.

They were gone.

My gaze finally tore itself reluctantly away from the water as Ashton slowed the boat down. The creek became smaller, dividing itself into thin arteries like veins on a leaf. Spartina flanked the marshy, narrow channels with abundant grass. After Ashton navigated a left, we arrived at a tiny island, where a thick grove of palmettos and a fountaining sound of cicadas welcomed our arrival. Sea oats flipped their tawny-green colors in the salty breeze, and the wind lifted a little, shimmying feathery ripples through the water. The boat puttered in the suddenly shallow creek, then he killed the motor and we drifted noiselessly.

A scatter of crabs and creatures in shells scampered on the muddy sand.

A gull cried in the distant, clear blue skies.

The cicadas kept up their shrill chirp.

Ashton lifted the motor out of the water, rolled up his pants and jumped from the boat, hauling it toward land. He locked the motor then offered me his hand as I stood balancing on the bow. I jumped out, my feet meeting an oozy squelch of muddy sand, which seeped thickly between my toes. *I wouldn't want to be marooned out here alone*, I thought.

Ashton said, "My dad and I used to camp here when I was a boy."

"I'm amazed you remembered how to get here. It's a maze of estuaries and possible dead ends."

"It was our secret," he said. "Not many folks know about this place."

"You were telling me about your dad before the dolphins so rudely interrupted us," I joked, the experience of seeing them one of the highlights of my life so far, and something I knew I'd never forget. I inhaled the air. Imbibed the scene around me. The brackish odor smelled as ancient as time, and in that moment, the dolphins, this boat trip, everything infused itself into my soul, latched onto my memory cells—or so I prayed—to be picked up and savored another time, another place, somewhere in the future. Whether Ashton chose to trust me or not and open up about his father wouldn't matter. This day would still be forever perfect, either way.

He attached the boat to a dead tree stump, tying an expert sailor's knot in the rope. I needed to learn how to tie knots like that. He looked around then back at me. Linking his long fingers behind his neck, he stared up into the blue as if he couldn't decide what to do next, or what to say. I waited patiently, fixated on those fingers that did the most complicated stomach-churning medical procedures.

*What kind of a person cuts into someone's brain and skull?*

Finally, Ashton lowered his gaze and spoke to me in his baritone woodwind voice. "My dad wasn't out shrimping that day," he began, "but had taken his other boat, a small motorboat, to drop off fuel for a friend in downtown Beaufort. Instead of getting around by car, Pa preferred to go by boat. I happened to be home for the weekend. I'd heard a storm was brewing, so I told him to go another day. But he wouldn't hear of it. Told me old Mr. Briggs had waited long enough and he'd be quick. So, I figured I'd accompany him. Didn't want him going alone. The storm came in earlier than we thought it would, whipped up out of nowhere like a bat outta hell. My dad had forgotten his cell phone, and mine wound up going overboard, so we couldn't call for help. The boat capsized. There was so much wind, boy, the two-hundred-something-mile-an-hour wind and hammering waves were mean, out of control. By that point we were in a narrow estuary quite a way from home. Guess Papa's feet got tangled in weed. Or he got knocked out by a piece of flying driftwood. He was a pretty strong swimmer. But I lost him. Swallowing water, trying to keep afloat, I couldn't see more than a foot in front of my face. Eventually I…" Ashton paused, took a breath and gathered his composure. I thought he'd cut his story to an end. He turned still and quiet. I watched his every gesture, wondering how he felt inside.

After a long while, he continued, "By the time I saw Pa, he was face down in the water floating out to sea. I dragged him to shore—I'd done some lifeguard training years before—gave him the kiss of life but… but it was too darn late."

"I'm so sorry," I said, almost wishing I hadn't forced Ashton to share this tragic incident with me. I'd been so pushy for information; I felt callous. "How awful. How traumatic for you." I stood in the sand awkwardly, the water lapping softly at my calves.

Ashton shrugged. "Worse for him."

"Yeah, but I feel for you, honey. There's nothing worse than losing a parent."

"Especially when you could have saved—"

"It's not your fault," I broke in. "You did everything you could. It was your dad's choice, he insisted on going out that day."

"I could've stopped him."

"We can't live our lives with woulda shoulda coulda mantras stuck in our heads." *Woulda shoulda coulda.* There were plenty of woulda shoulda couldas competing for space in my head, too. "Honey, I'm so, so sorry," I added.

He pressed his fist to his mouth. "Life's a bitch sometimes."

"And your mom? Is that when she deteriorated and needed to go to a care facility?"

"Exactly," he said, offering no more details.

"So you were all alone after that?"

"Yep, being an only child, I felt the brunt of it."

"I sure can identify with that. What was your dad like?"

An almost imperceptible flicker of Ashton's brow told me he did not like my question.

"He was a wonderful man. Let me show you around this miniscule Treasure Island."

We meandered around. There were some old, broken down, rotten planks with rusty nails peeking out from behind the grove of palmettos. The breeze idled through the leaves.

"Your camp?" I asked. I took out some sunscreen from my cloth bag, where I had some mosquito repellent, hat, water and my camera. I smeared some cream on my face.

"Yep, this was our hidey-hole. We'd fish. Catch crabs. Play cards. Then barbecue the fish we caught that day and cook it with grits. Seabass usually, or shrimp. Tell jokes. First time I ever drank Wild Turkey was right here. On my fifteenth birthday. My inauguration. Pa told me I was ready to be a man."

"Your mom didn't join you?"

"Hell, no. Mama had no place here. This was *boys'* alone time."

"Were they very happy, your parents? Did they have a good marriage?"

Ashton's gaze fixed on mine and he held it there for a beat, his face enkindled by the late morning sun, the light catching his hair. I caught a flash—just a fleeting flash—of what I could only describe as a covert look in his eye.

He said with a smile, "Let's have lunch. We got chilled champagne and all kinds of sandwiches. And pecan pie for dessert. Come on, I'm starving."

Again, I persevered, but dressed the question more prettily. "They were very in love then, huh? Your parents?"

Ashton strode off toward the boat, grabbed his baseball cap, and while he was busy bringing out the cooler, with his back to me, he mumbled, "Uh-huh."

"They were really happy?" I was determined to get a straight answer.

He turned, smiled, and said decisively, "The envy of every married couple this side of Beaufort County."

Those were his mother's words, weren't they?

Like mother like son. Both were lying. Not that I cared. Those lies didn't affect me, personally. But other lies might. Case in point, because later, after Ashton and I got back home—after this perfect day out on the water—and I'd fixed a simple salad for dinner, the phone rang. The caller a total surprise, a ghost popping up from the past. Ashton's ghost. Ashton's past. My nemesis. Which also made it my past.

And my future.

It was then my marriage deviated along a new road, setting a whole new set of wheels in motion.

# CHAPTER TEN

I sat opposite Dr. Becker the following morning, feeling sheepish and dishonest.

"Vivien, aren't you going to take off your sunglasses?" She spoke in her soft Savannah accent that was so appealing to me.

"It's okay, my allergies are pretty bad, so I'll just keep them on, if that's okay."

"All right, please yourself. But I find it very disconcerting not being able to look you in the eye. This is therapy and we need to be straight with each other. I need to see your thoughts and feelings or, quite frankly, we are both wasting our time."

I had been seeing Dr. Becker for three months, once a week. She was very no-nonsense. Not unfriendly, but a take-no-prisoners kind of person, and I often felt uncomfortable. It was as if she had X-ray eyes and could see right into my soul. I had thought about changing therapists but so far, I had stuck with her. Not being a Southerner myself I felt a little bit out of my depth living in South Carolina, and I needed someone to talk to. I had a suspicion that Lindy might have gossiped and that was why I had received that note in my mailbox. I wasn't sure if I should share that information with Dr. Becker or not.

Dr. Becker reminded me of Oprah Winfrey. I always ended up opening myself up to her. She was like Oprah on a serious day with her glasses on, the Oprah who discussed heavy topics, not the joking, fun Oprah. Dr. Becker was extremely professional. Sometimes too professional for my liking, and although she made me uneasy because she sucked information out of me with effortless ease, I had continued with my sessions, despite this.

Her office, in downtown Savannah, was simply furnished but chic. She had a large library of books, not just books on psychology and psychotherapy—Freud and Jung and all that stuff—but big fat biology and chemistry books, and there was even a smattering of literature there. A few bestsellers, Nordic noir books, and Stephen King, and some Jane Austen, too. Quite a mixture of taste, which flummoxed me. I couldn't pigeonhole her.

There was a large gray couch just off-center of the spacious room, but I never got to lie or even sit on the couch—God forbid! No, I was relegated to an upright chair placed strategically opposite Dr. Becker's large wooden desk, classic in design, where she sat, her posture always erect. My chair was so-so comfortable, but firm enough to remind me who was in charge: Dr. Becker. She had a swivel chair. Not me. I guess she didn't want me swiveling around, losing eye contact with her, which was exactly what I was aiming to do today by wearing dark glasses. Perhaps I shouldn't have come in the first place.

"Tell me about your week, Vivien. How's work been?"

"Busy. Teenagers take a lot of energy out of you, though."

"Last time you told me about that family, the mother and her three kids. How are they doing?"

"We found them an apartment and they're doing just great, thank you so much for asking. The latest person to arrive is a young teenager whom I'm trying to help. She's very independent, makes her own money drop shipping—only sixteen, pretty impressive—and I'd like to find her an apartment round here. But because she's a minor, I need to talk to her mother about it. If and when I can get in touch with her, that is. I just remember how I felt so out on a limb as a teenager with nobody to turn to."

"Go on," Dr. Becker prompted.

"Well, I've had problems. I had problems today at work. This morning Susan told me that we can't keep Cady at the shelter any longer without permission from a guardian. So that's why I'm trying to hunt down her mom, but she's a little bit elusive. I feel compelled to help Cady, you know? But it's hard juggling everything."

Dr. Becker nodded. "And how's everything going with Ashton? Last week I asked you about the bruises."

"Bruises?"

"Yes, Vivien. The bruises that I could tell were from someone pinching you. I asked you if it was Ashton, and you promised we'd discuss it today."

She let the words hang in the air. I said nothing. Just sat there waiting for her to keep talking. But, of course, therapists don't work that way, do they? They're smarter than that. They wait for you to throw the ball before they catch it. I blew my nose, pretending I had hay fever.

"We discussed how you were going to ask Ashton if he would like to come here for a couple's session to talk things through."

I sat there dumbly.

"Don't you remember?"

It was true. I had promised Dr. Becker that I would put the idea to him of us coming in to see Dr. Becker together. I hadn't done that. I had not discussed anything with Ashton at all. Why would I rock the boat? Except the boat was already rocked. That was why I was wearing sunglasses.

"Vivien? I would so appreciate it if you would take off your sunglasses." Dr. Becker said this gently. In fact, she always spoke in a kind, calming voice. Some of what she said, though, was less calming.

I swallowed. I took off my shades and set them on the desk in front of me. How I wished I were lying on her soft gray couch this minute. It was no coincidence that she had me sitting face to face, which always made it awkward for me to tell lies, because I guessed she could read the deceit in my eyes.

"I see," she said.

Silence. I didn't say anything back, but I knew what she was looking at.

My black eye.

Well, it wasn't black yet, but it would be in a few days. Right now, it was a sort of magenta-mauve.

She sucked in a breath. "Can you tell me what happened?"

"We had the most incredible day yesterday. Ashton took me out on his boat. Prepared an amazing picnic and showed me his childhood secret island where he used to go with his dad. We saw dolphins, we drank champagne. It was one of the most beautiful days of my life. I felt so in love with him. But... but when we got home everything changed. The phone rang. The landline. I picked up. It was a woman asking for Ashton. I asked who was calling, and at first, she didn't want to say. Then she reluctantly told me she was Belle. I knew Belle was the name of his childhood sweetheart. Who is married, by the way. Married to Ashton's ex-best friend, Bradley, who stole her away from Ashton centuries ago. Anyway, the tone of Belle's voice made me realize that something was not quite right. She didn't come to our wedding. Ashton is not speaking to Bradley. If Belle was just another friend of his then why would she not have chatted to me for a few minutes or asked me something nice or, you know, made an effort to be friendly? But no, she was all shifty and weird. Ashton came to the phone, and I handed him the receiver. If it had been a friend, he would've been friendly and chatty or maybe would've put me on the line to say hello. Don't you think?"

Dr. Becker nodded. "Go on."

"Well that's the kind of thing he usually does. He shares. Shares his friends with me. Wants me to get to know them." I could feel tears welling in my eyes. "Then he took the receiver and walked out of the room with the phone. I heard him breathe into the receiver quietly: 'I'd rather she didn't know about that.'"

"Did you ask him what the call was about?"

"Yes. He said she had some old photos of him. That she'd been clearing her attic and felt bad for throwing them away so wanted to ask him if he wanted the pictures."

"Maybe he was telling the truth," Dr. Becker said.

"I got the feeling he was lying."

Dr. Becker nodded again in her impartial way. "Did you see your doctor?"

The change of subject took me by surprise. "My doctor?"

"For your eye."

"Uh… no."

"Did you at least take photographs of your wound? A selfie, so the time and date show up on the picture as evidence?"

"*Evidence?*"

"I suggest you take some pictures of yourself and you go and see your physician. You never know, there might be some lasting damage."

"I guess," I said, feeling the weight of the truth.

I noticed she still hadn't asked me what had happened. That was her technique. She never pushed for answers but let me unravel my story in my own time. Dr. Becker looked me over with her gaze as if searching for more bruises.

I supposed I'd have to tell her the story sooner or later. I continued, "Belle lives in Charleston. As you know, that's where Ashton's hospital is, and he has an apartment there for times he has super late shifts. Now, of course, I'm thinking about all those times he stayed overnight, and I'm feeling suspicious. Anyway, that's why we fought last night. I asked him about this woman and I got angry with him. At first it was just a discussion, but then he got furious with me for being jealous and told me there was no way he could live with someone if he was under suspicion all the time, that I needed to trust him. Anyway, I did something really foolish. I threw a plate on the floor. One of our fancy wedding plates that cost a fortune."

Dr. Becker nodded. No judgment. No reaction.

I hesitated. But she held her gaze with mine. The ball was rolling now; I couldn't turn back. "He told me to pick up the pieces, in a really cold voice. He ordered me to get down on my hands and knees and crawl like the cat I was and pick up my mess. Said I was being catty and cats go around on all fours. It was the *coldness* in his voice that got to me. And by the way, he hates cats. He used his neurosurgeon's cold *chilly* voice that just terrified me. But instead of doing what he wanted, I started screaming and told him that no, I was not going to pick up my mess because it wasn't my mess, it was *his* mess. That *he* had started. He shoved me to the floor. I was on my hands and knees, the broken pieces of porcelain digging into my flesh, because I was just wearing shorts. Anyway, he pushed his knee into my face. Well, not pushed exactly but, like, sort of nudged my face with his knee. And that's, I guess, how I got my black eye."

Dr. Becker arched her brow. "*Nudged?*"

"It didn't feel so violent in the moment," I said. "I mean, it wasn't like a punch or anything."

Her other eyebrow shot up. "Are you excusing him?"

"No! But I can't say he *hit* me, exactly, 'cause he didn't. He didn't punch me or kick me either."

"Vivien, he *did*. It just so happened to be with his *knee*, which I admit, is a little bit unusual, but it is still a violent act. Do you not see that?" She said this gently, which made it all sound so much worse.

"You don't understand, it wasn't like that. It was me being hysterical and screaming and shouting at him. I really don't think he meant to hurt me. He just meant to…" I couldn't think of the right words.

"What did he not mean to do?" she said.

A beat stretched into a long silence.

"I don't know. I don't *know*."

"Do you have your own money saved? Your own bank account and your own financial independence?" she asked, seemingly out of the blue.

"What's that got to do with any of this?"

"Because you need to make a contingency plan to leave Ashton. You need a strategy. You need to find yourself an apartment, and that's why I'm asking you if you have savings and if you are financially independent. I guess you must be because you have a job."

"Actually, my job is… I don't get paid, it's voluntary. I just get given expenses."

"Oh, I see. Still, you have a certain skillset and lots of experience and a degree in, what was it again?"

"I majored in English Literature and Psychology."

"Okay, good."

Her words about leaving Ashton felt like a pitchfork prodding me. This was way too… *soon*.

"Our relationship is very… complicated, I can't just walk away."

Dr. Becker didn't reply.

"Our marriage is a journey," I said, filling the silence. "It's about karma, you know? I mean, I swear, Ashton is a *good* man. I feel like I've betrayed him. He's good. He's a kind person. This will never happen again."

Dr. Becker pursed her lips. She opened her mouth to speak, but I cut her short.

"I do have my own bank account. Ashton and I also have a joint account for household expenditure. I don't have a lot of savings, though. But, Dr. Becker, I don't *want* to leave him. I'm in love with Ashton."

For a long time she sat there in her chair silently, waiting for me to go on. When I didn't speak, she said, "I see how hard this is for you, I do. But the problem is, Vivien, he's violent. We're not just talking about marital problems here; we're talking about domestic abuse."

"But he's not *abusive*. Not really. It was more like an accident."

"You think you're the first woman who's made excuses for domestic violence? Excusing Ashton and trying to understand his actions will not make this go away."

She laid a hand on mine. I wasn't sure if it was a kind gesture, or if she was irritated by me fiddling with a stray pen I'd picked up on her desk.

She maintained eye contact, but I looked away uneasily. "And you think he's cheating on you as well with this woman Belle? It sounds as if you also have major trust issues."

She wasn't mincing words.

I lifted my chin. "I don't think so. I think it's just me being jealous and insecure. Ninety percent of the time—even ninety-*five* percent of the time he treats me like a goddess. So tender. So caring. He buys me beautiful gifts. Cooks for me. Calls me several times a day when he's at work. Pays for everything. I never dreamed I'd have this skyscraper kind of love. He's incredible in bed too. I mean, Ashton's a catch. He's so good-looking and charming and everybody thinks he's the most amazing man. *And* he's a great doctor. I'm just a girl from the wrong side of the tracks. People like me don't get men like Ashton Buchanan in love with them."

Dr. Becker shook her head sadly. "Ah, so this is the crux of the problem. You don't feel you're worthy. Don't you see that you're a beautiful young woman, Vivien? You're worth so much more than you think you are. Why would Ashton be worth any more than you? Just because he's a doctor and well paid and has a nice house, that does not make him superior to you in any way whatsoever."

I turned her words over in my head, savoring her compliments. "I have to make so much *effort* with myself," I said, with a groan. "It's like I'm living a lie. The person I present to him is not the person I am inside. It's hard work keeping it all going, being this special, sporty, cool girl, who's an amazing cook and a fabulous wife. I don't feel beautiful or special, however hard I try."

Dr. Becker scribbled something in her notepad. "Can you explain these feelings to me in more depth? Where does this stem from, do you think, this chronic insecurity? You told me you had a close relationship with your parents."

I shrugged. Picked up the pen again. After an elongated silence, while I gathered my thoughts and decided what I was willing to share with Dr. Becker, and what I could not reveal, I admitted, "Well, for one thing I had my nose fixed in my early twenties."

"Rhinoplasty?"

I nodded. "Ashton has no idea. Nobody does."

"And you feel this is in some way cheating? Cheating on beauty? Think of all the celebrities we all aspire to be like. So many of them have had cosmetic surgery. Even many men. It doesn't make them any less special."

A tear slid down my now elegant nose, which I still couldn't believe really belonged to me. I wiped it away with the back of my hand. "Once you've had a horrible complex about yourself, even if you change it, it sticks with you for life. Inside, I feel like this girl—this woman—with a big hook nose and ugly face. The teasing at school. The jibes. Because, once upon a time, my nose ruled everything. Like it was an entity, a personality in its own right. And, yeah, I guess I feel like I'm conning people. Tricking them into believing I'm someone I'm not. That's just how I feel. I try so hard to shake it but… it just lives with me… this feeling."

Dr. Becker handed me some tissues and tilted her head at an angle as if imagining me with a large nose. "I'm so sorry you feel this way. But you're not alone. I've come across this frequently with many women who once had weight problems, even after they lose the weight. But you're a very attractive woman, and this is something we need to work on. When you say 'wrong side of the tracks,' what do you mean by that? It doesn't seem to fit—"

"Ugh," I groaned, cutting her short. I felt a throbbing at the base of my skull. Delving into my childhood was the last thing I needed right now. I'd already gone into detail in previous sessions about where I was raised and had told her everything. We had discussed my parents' death at length. The fact that I felt lonely without brothers or sisters. "Listen, Dr. Becker, I'm really sorry, but can we take a rain check? I think I need to go home and lie down."

She got up, smoothed her skirt briskly and said, "Remember what I suggested about planning a strategy. Unless a miracle happens, sooner or later, you'll need to leave your husband. It sounds scary and it may be the last thing in the world you want to hear, but next time—and there will be a next time, I can assure you—things could get very dangerous with Ashton."

# CHAPTER ELEVEN

"How's the eye?" Ashton's gaze was all concern and brimming over with sympathy.

We were in the kitchen having breakfast. He had made kedgeree with fresh collard greens. He was doing everything he could to be sweet and loving and was lavishing me with attention.

"I'm so sorry, honey," he gushed. "That kind of accident is unlikely to happen twice. Did you ice it this morning?"

*"Accident?" Ha, it was no accident!*

I shook my head. "I iced it last night."

"Let me get you something to help with that nasty bruise." He almost tripped over himself rushing to the refrigerator and pulled out a bag of frozen peas. Strolled over to where I was slumped at the breakfast table, head in my hands, and he tenderly lifted my chin and put the bag to my eye.

"Hold it like this," he whispered, as if his voice alone could do damage. "That's right. Keep your elbow on the table and ice the eye for as long as you can stand it. I don't think you should go into work today with that bash, sweetheart."

"But they're waiting for me." I reluctantly pressed the bag on my eye.

"I'll call them and tell them you're sick, okay? Don't get your feathers ruffled about work."

"Okay. I feel bad about playing hooky though. I hate letting vulnerable people down. Those youngsters rely on me."

Ashton took my other hand, the hand that wasn't holding the frozen peas in place. "You never take a day off, Vivien. You've been so loyal and conscientious with that job. And they're not even paying you. Please. Just one day, sweetheart."

I took my hand away from his and listlessly put a forkful of kedgeree into my mouth, chewing slowly, while Ashton called Community Promise and told them I'd slipped down by the dock when I was feeding the gulls, but I was fine, that I just needed to take it easy today. The kedgeree he'd made was delicious, but I didn't feel like complimenting his cooking.

"What time are you leaving for work?" I asked. I was looking forward to some alone time. The minute he was gone, I *would* go down by the dock and feed the gulls. Everything seemed to be happening so fast all of a sudden. I was now regretting opening up to Dr. Becker and wished Lindy hadn't seen my arm. *What have I gone and done?*

"I should've set off ten minutes ago. But I hate to leave you like this, sweetie. And I'm sorry, but tonight I'm going to have to stay over at the apartment."

"Should I come and meet you later? For dinner?" I offered.

"You'd be having dinner all alone if you came, I'm afraid. I've got a late afternoon meeting and two operations back to back starting at six a.m. tomorrow morning. It's so much easier if I just spend the night rather than worry about the traffic hour tomorrow. It's too stressful. I've got a late shift tonight too."

Belle popped into my mind. Was Ashton telling the truth? "I get so lonely sometimes," I griped. "I guess I could see Lindy for dinner."

I pictured the scene. Lindy launching a verbal attack on Ashton. Perhaps I wouldn't go and see Lindy. Perhaps I needed to cancel the barbecue next weekend. *How long does a black eye last?*

Ashton stayed sitting next to me, his gaze still hovering over my eye with concern. "I'm sorry you get lonely, honey. It sucks being a doctor's wife sometimes, I know." He stroked my head with his softest touch.

It was on the tip of my tongue: the urge to ask Ashton if he had domestic violence abuse cases at the hospital. Kicks to some poor, long-suffering wife's head, concussion, even coma.

*If you don't have anything nice to say just keep your pretty little mouth shut.*

I stopped myself speaking by taking another bite of kedgeree. I swallowed and, suppressing the nattering questions in my mind, changed the subject. "You know how the guest house is empty?"

Ashton topped up my coffee and poured himself a glass of juice. "Yeah, why?"

The "why" was said in a suspicious tone.

"You seem pretty adamant you don't want your mother living there," I began.

He set his glass down in a decisive thump. "Absolutely not. My mother is staying right where she is."

"Well, it seems crazy that the guest house is sitting empty when we could get some rent from it." The guest house, which was a hundred yards or so away from the house, was a cute cottage, like a mini version of our house but all wooden and with a little porch in front. It had two small bedrooms, a cozy living room, kitchen and bathroom. Ashton had designed it, although it looked as if it had always been here.

"Honey, we don't need the money," he said.

I took the bag of peas off my face. The ice was giving me a headache. "I know, but it's just going to waste sitting there. There's this young girl who's been sheltering at Community Promise, and I spoke to her mom and thought maybe—"

"No."

"Ashton, honey, why not?"

"It's a dumb idea to mix work with our personal life. Those kids… those kids are in trouble. Often dysfunctional. They come from dysfunctional families, and I really don't want them hanging around here."

"This poor girl has nowhere to go."

"That is *so* not my problem."

"Cady makes her own money," I persevered. "She could pay rent. She's surprisingly grown-up for her age and even earns money doing drop shipping. I don't know exactly what that entails, but something to do with selling on Amazon. Anyway, she said she makes really good money. The guest house is far enough away from this house, we'll never even have to see her if you don't want to."

"You think I'd accept rent money from some *kid*?"

"Okay, no rent then. The guest house is just sitting there doing nothing. It needs to get aired once in a while. Lived in."

"Olive can do that."

Olive was the cleaner, although "Olive" was her nickname because she looked almost identical to Popeye's Olive Oyl, all skinny arms and legs and jet-coal hair, which she often wore in a bun when she was working. Her real name was Glenda, but she had lived with Olive Oyl since high school and hated it if people called her Glenda.

I gave Ashton a pleading look. "Honey, please. It's just for a few weeks, no big deal. Until Cady's mom can have her come live with her. Otherwise social services will get involved, and the whole thing could get really horrible for Cady. It's just a few weeks, nothing more."

"Why can't she stay where she is?"

"Community Promise is a *temporary* shelter. It's not a permanent place for people to live."

"You just told me the guest house wouldn't be permanent either."

"What I'm trying to say is we need to have space available at Community Promise if battered women or vulnerable families come in." The irony of my words rang in my ears. *Battered women.*

Ashton didn't flinch.

"Cady could help me in the garden, too. You know poor old John can't keep up. And, to be honest, I could use the company," I said. "How do you think I feel all alone in the house when you're working night shifts?"

Ashton pressed the heels of his hands on his forehead as if this conversation was giving him a headache. "I just don't get why you want to get involved with some kid from your work." He let out another groan. "Who is this girl, anyway?"

"She's a sixteen-year-old girl from a broken family. Actually, no, she's just turned seventeen."

"Shouldn't she be in school?"

"She is in school. I enrolled her in the local high school. A straight-A student. Our guest cottage would be a great halfway house for her until she gets settled with her mom. It's just a couple of weeks."

"We're not this girl's responsibility. We're not a charity, honey."

"But my work *is* charity. That's what I *do*! That's who I am. It's my life and it means a lot to me, and I wish you would support me in this."

I could see the cogs turning in Ashton's inflexible, neurosurgical brain. He raked his hands through his swathe of thick hair. He wasn't in the mood to discuss this. It was easier for Ashton to slice someone's head open and fiddle around with his brain-biopsy instruments and gray matter than discuss domestic matters with his wife.

He finally spoke. "Where are her parents?"

"She doesn't know her dad. I've already spoken to her mom."

"This is the kind of thing you need in writing, honey. She's a minor."

"I have emails," I told him. "Her mother's more than happy to let Cady stay here, under my wing."

He threw up his hands. Sighed dramatically. "If it means that much to you then we can give this Cady girl a trial run for a week. If there's any nonsense, any bullshit, she's out, okay? I don't want her anywhere near the house. I know what teenagers are like. I know what *I* was like as a teenager. No drugs. No male visitors. No smoking weed. No cigarettes. No drinking, not even beer. Period."

"She's not into any of that stuff."

"All teenagers are into something bad."

"I promise, you won't get any of that from her."

"How do you know?"

"Because I've spent enough time with her to intuit these things."

Ashton's gaze was fixed on the table and then his eyes were on me, his expression morphing from irritated to menacing. He held my gaze for a second as if my black eye had insulted him somehow. He suddenly sprang up, which sent his chair tumbling to the floor. He placed it back, grabbed the peas from the table and marched back to the icebox with them, shoving them in the freezer and slapping the refrigerator door closed. I wondered if he secretly thought I looked less beautiful with a bruised eye. Or if he pitied me and in turn found me distasteful—my "perfection" marred.

"'*Intuit* these things'?" he said in a thunderous voice, which was so unlike him. "Actually, you know what, Vivien? No. Just… no. Cady's flakey mother can deal with the girl herself. This teenager is *not* our problem."


I cleared the breakfast things away after Ashton had set off for work, considering everything he'd said. What I'd told them all at my dinner party about my parents dying when I was nineteen? The truth was I was only seventeen when I was lumbered with responsibility and all alone in the world. I'd had to fend for myself. Support myself financially. I was almost the same age as Cady now. I knew what it was like to be without a grownup in your life at such a vulnerable age. Without help, without any help at all. My moral compass and every muscle and bone in my body told me I needed to do right by her. I had to fix things.

I stared at my cell phone, my mind pushing and pulling me in different directions about Ashton, everything that had happened, the choices before me.

My fingers hovered over the numbers, twitching to call the National Domestic Violence Hotline. But I couldn't do it. I just couldn't bring myself to. I didn't want to waste some poor person's time. There were *real* victims out there. Women beaten by their husbands or boyfriends, even brothers or fathers, on a regular basis. Women with no money, trapped, not able to leave their abusers. I wanted to reach out to them and say, *I understand. I'm nothing like you—Ashton is not like them—but I get it.*

Instead of calling, I browsed through some of the statistics on various domestic abuse websites instead. *Twenty people per minute are physically abused by an intimate partner in the United States,* it said. *One in four women experience physical violence from a partner… seventy percent of women have experienced physical and/or sexual violence from an intimate partner in their lifetime. And men who have witnessed their fathers being violent with their mothers or have been raised in a violent environment are far more likely to continue the cycle with their own wives or partners in their own relationships.*

Ashton's father, Buck? I had a sneaky suspicion he had been a big drinker. After all, he'd initiated Ashton to Wild Turkey when he was only fifteen. No doubt wanting a drinking buddy. I remembered what Georgia-May had said to Mariama, that Buck had spilled bourbon all over her dress and she'd not been able to get the smell out. She'd said that Buck was a "mean son-of-a-gun," and a "brute."

It made me wonder.

My eyes flicked back to my phone.

*A gun in the house increases the risk of homicide by 500%.*

Goosebumps spread like pinprick warnings along my arms. Marching toward the living room, I found Ashton's shotgun that he kept "hidden" behind a bookshelf. Olive and I were the only people that knew about this gun... or not? It gave me the spooks. But what was I supposed to do? I couldn't unload the thing; I had no idea how—it was too risky. I caught a glimpse of my face reflected in the window as I passed. Everyone would ask questions about my purple eye. I thought of all those domestic violence victims again and felt a whoosh of shame. Living in this grand house with all my privileges, I couldn't even begin to know how they felt. I reflected on everything Lindy had said. The look of pity on her face.

Lindy... that reminded me, I needed to cancel her barbecue. I wasn't up for a big song and dance about how awful Ashton was. I sent her text message, along with a sad emoji face:

*Ashton too busy at work for the barbecue. So sorry but have to cancel.*

Lindy immediately called back, but I didn't pick up and let it go to voicemail. I had such an urge to go to the club and play tennis and let off steam, but I knew that too would incite questions. Everybody staring at me in hushed whispers? The gossip would be out of control. And I couldn't play a decent game of tennis with sunglasses on.

It was a whole new ballgame being the person I was now. I felt like one of those butterflies Georgia-May told me about... the butterflies Ashton had collected as a child.

Mrs. Ashton Buchanan in her beautiful home in her beautiful outfits hiding from friends.

Hiding the truth.

*

I walked down to the end of the dock (where my supposed "accident" had happened), carrying some scraps from breakfast and bits of old bread I'd stored up. Ever since I'd read that book *Jonathan Livingston Seagull*, I got a kick out of hearing the gulls' cries and watching them catch tidbits I threw for them on the fly.

I arrived later than I usually did most mornings, and the gulls must have given up on me because they weren't there. Just a still heron fishing in the water amidst the pearly tendrils of morning mist. I took off my shoes and sat at the tip of the dock, my bare feet dipping in the deep water—the tide was up. I felt as solitary as the heron.

I stared out at the creek, my thoughts crashing into each other. My purple eye, Ashton's feelings about having kids. Cady—who I felt had barreled her way into my life before I was ready, yet I couldn't turn her away. My old nose that lived forever on my face—a reminder that I was a fraud, that I wasn't the person I pretended to be. Belle, Ashton's first love.

*First love never dies.*

I thought about how Ashton had robbed me of real, uncensored, carefree happiness. And how painful being in love was. It made me furious I had such deep feelings for him that I couldn't suppress, whatever my left brain—the voice of reason—told me. Or was it the right brain? I didn't dare ask Ashton for details. He was always talking about brains. I didn't want to sound stupid by asking something I should know.

Each of my problems clamored for attention as the peace of the wind rustled through my hair and the white sun climbed higher and higher into the sheer blue sky. An osprey hovered above, its slender body and long legs set off by its massive wingspan, waiting to swoop down on its prey. I waited to see if it would plunge into the water. Nature didn't care about me. It just carried on, oblivious, steady in its beauty and rampage of destruction and re-creation. Every hundredth of a second, I supposed, something or someone was born and something died.

I needed to be strong. To dig deep inside my battered soul and pull out every scrap of strength and filament of determination to re-create the life I knew I deserved. Yes, I was in love with Ashton Buchanan, despite everything. But he'd stolen the shine from my love.

*Time and tide wait for no man.* A quote I'd heard somewhere. I had to put myself first, however harrowing. Hope and dread, misery and excitement; all these emotions rolled in on themselves, merging into one great big decision.

A breeze murmured in my ear: "*Forgive Ashton for what he did. What you're doing is wrong.*"

But I made a wish in that moment, anyway, under my breath. The marsh caught it like a secret. It rippled along the gilded water, traveled through the grasses, and evaporated into the steamy, Carolina heat.

*Be careful what you wish for because it may come true.*

Too late, the wish was done.

# CHAPTER TWELVE

When I came back from the dock, I noticed something eerie. A jug of iced tea I had made earlier was empty, a dirty glass by its side. I had definitely not drunk all the tea! As I was running through the possibilities of who had slipped into the house, I heard shuffling from behind the kitchen screen door. My heart leapt into my throat.

"You-hoo! Is anyone ho-o-ome?"

The door opened with a little shove and a creak. It was Lindy.

"You scared the living daylights out of me," I exclaimed. It was as if Lindy had come out of nowhere. I hadn't heard the tires of her car scrunch on the driveway, or even her footsteps.

"Oh Lord, Vivien, I'm so sorry, I didn't mean to scare you. I did call your cell and the landline, but I didn't get an answer."

"Didn't hear you call and I didn't hear your car," I said, realizing I'd left my cell phone in the house when I'd gone down to the dock. "Did you come in earlier? While I was out?"

"No, I just this second arrived."

"Oh, just… never mind."

"You must be… hey! What's that on your eye?" Lindy flung her purse down on the kitchen island and came rushing over. "Oh my Lord! Oh my goodness, what in the heck *happened* to you?"

I didn't know what to say. If I'd known she was coming I would've worn my shades. "Nothing, I'm fine, honestly. It doesn't even hurt."

"*Ashton* did this?"

"No, no. I slipped. On the dock. Last night it was getting dark and I went out to feed the gulls and I slipped and knocked my eye on one of the boat posts."

Lindy looked skeptical, squinting at me suspiciously. "Did you ice it?"

"Yeah, of course. But I'm getting bored of icing, it gives me a headache. Time will heal it, don't worry, I'm fine. Really."

Lindy pulled out a chair for me as if I were an invalid and ushered me to sit. I plopped myself down.

"Where's Ashton?" she demanded.

"In Charleston, at the hospital. He had a ton of meetings, and tomorrow back-to-back operations really early in the morning."

"Of course. He works like a dog." Her tone was sarcastic. The word "dog" came out as "dawg." She stroked my hair gently and didn't say anything more. My fib made me feel guilty for some reason, as if I were betraying her.

"You don't have to lie to me, you know," she said. "You can trust me."

"I have a… plan," I offered, as if by way of revealing the truth. "I'll be okay."

Lindy grabbed her purse from the island, took out her phone, and clicked some photos of my face. "I'm doing this for good measure, honey. Whatever you decide to do is your own business, but here and now I am your witness and these photos might be useful sometime down the line, okay?"

I touched my purple eye, wondering if I looked laughably ridiculous.

"I know how tough this must be," she said. "And please don't think I'm judging you for not being tougher with Ashton. I know how it goes and it isn't easy. This happened to me once."

I looked at her in surprise. I couldn't imagine anyone being violent with tough-cookie Lindy. "Really? With Richard?"

"No, not Richard. Richard would never lay a finger on me. It was Tony, my boyfriend, actually my fiancé, a few years before I met Richard. I was desperately in love with the guy, and we were all set to get married. We even had wedding invitations made up, everything. My parents adored him. But then, I discovered his true colors. He was so jealous and insanely possessive and turned out to be a hitter. Oh, and guess what? At the same time, he was cheating on me with his ex-girlfriend! It broke my heart to break up with him, but I did. I never stopped loving the bastard, even to this day. How crazy is that?"

I blinked at her, surprised. "I always think of you and Richard as really happy together."

"We are. But my feeling is… if a man loves a woman at least ten percent more than she loves him, it makes for a good, working marriage. The woman has always got to be a little bit on top, in more ways than one!" She laughed. "Excuse my potty mouth. But you know what I mean? When you're desperately in love with a guy, it hurts. Believe me, I know. Better that he's the one who's in love with you."

I could feel my eyes misting. "Ashton's my world, he… he… I wish he hadn't hurt me."

She tucked a loose tendril of my hair behind my ear. "I know, honey, I'm so sorry."

"Does this ex of yours live round here?"

"No, he lives in Richmond, Virginia. It looks like everything turned out perfect for him. He and his wife have four kids. I've seen her Facebook page—she has zero filters in place. She's madly in love with him—happy as a pig in mud—and it makes me jealous. Which is crazy, I know. She's probably just putting on a real good act, but of course it makes me wonder if there was something about *me* that made him hit me. Logically, I don't think that, but in my heart, I can't help it."

Lindy had social-media-stalked this woman the way I had stalked Belle! It made me feel a whole lot better that I wasn't the only freak around.

"You know Belle?" I asked. "The girl Ashton dated when they were teenagers? Now married to his ex-best friend Bradley?"

"No. But I did hear from someone at Sea Oats—I can't remember who—say that Belle was, you know, a little bit slutty in her day, not to bad-mouth her or anything, bless her heart."

"To be honest, I don't like that word 'slutty,'" I said. "It's so unfair. Men can do anything they like, but women? Women get labeled. But it's never the woman's fault. It's *them*, isn't it? The men."

"Men are stronger than women so it's not fair, you're right," Lindy agreed, thinking I was referring to my black eye. "But the illogical side of you can't help questioning yourself," she went on. "I'm saying this to you in private, honey. Sharing my thoughts, so you don't feel alone. I just want to let you know that it's normal to feel this way, even though what Ashton did is *not your fault* and it is *not* okay."

"Thank you, Lindy. But he didn't—"

"No more buts or excuses," Lindy said. She sashayed toward the fridge. Today she was wearing a tight pink and orange leopard-print dress, which showed off all her curves and then some. "Can I get a beer or something?"

I jumped up. "Sure, I'm so sorry, I'm so bad-mannered, to forget to offer you a drink."

"Stay where you are, I'll get it." Lindy opened the fridge door and pulled out a couple of beers. She unscrewed the tops using the hem of her dress and handed me one. "It's hot, isn't it?" She wiped some jewels of perspiration from her brow. "Excuse me, darlin', I'm sweating like a sinner in church."

I laughed. I loved these Southern expressions.

She took several gulps then breathed out a sigh of satisfaction. "Have you gone through Ashton's bank records? Made copies of all his bank statements?" Her question came out of left field.

"No. Why?"

"'Cause, when the shit hits the fan, he'll hide his money, you can bet on it. All men do that when they know a divorce is pending. Does he have any idea that you're thinking about leaving him?"

"No, none. I mean... no. I'm not ready to do it right now, anyway, I need more time."

Lindy raised an eyebrow. I had always wanted to do that: raise just *one* eyebrow. I'd practiced half my childhood but had never been able to isolate that eye muscle. I wondered if Lindy would also be able to do one of those finger-in-mouth wolf whistles.

"Please don't think I'm pathetic for saying this," I said, almost like an apology, "but I do want to give Ashton another chance."

Lindy didn't react, just answered coolly, "Where does he keep his bank statements?"

"In the filing cabinet in his office, upstairs."

"Office locked?"

"No. He would never do that."

She nodded. "Does he hide 'em from you?"

"No, he trusts me."

Lindy raised that russet eyebrow again. "Well I do declare!" she said with her Southern twang. "Let's go take a look."

"What? Now?"

"Is there a better time? You got a scanner, right?"

I chuckled nervously. I couldn't believe how brazen Lindy was being—she was really taking liberties.

She took my hand in hers and yanked me out of my chair. "Come on, what are you waiting for?"

We climbed the stairs, and I guiltily led Lindy into Ashton's office. I hardly ever came into this room, unless to get some writing paper or a stamp. I always felt it was his private space. Ashton never set foot in my walk-in wardrobe. There were unspoken boundaries between spouses, weren't there? I had never snooped in his computer or phone either. This place was his sort of sanctuary, and I had always respected that.

It had never occurred to me to look at Ashton's bank statements. He was so generous with money, never questioning credit card bills or household expenditure. He bought me my beautiful car, and he paid all the bills without question, always on time. We *never* had disputes about money like many couples. Ashton was meticulous about paying his taxes, and very honest, as far as I knew. He didn't have offshore accounts, either, as far as I knew. But the truth was, I had never *asked* him. Always being financially independent myself—up until this marriage—I somehow didn't think it was my business. I had offered to contribute from my paltry savings, but he insisted upon paying every single bill himself when it came to running the house: the heat, air-conditioning and electricity. He took care of the gardener, the cleaner, he even paid for my car to be serviced. Everything. Why would I need to question him about his financial affairs?

His office looked onto the wrap-around porch. It had a beautiful view over the garden and the creek beyond. His imposing, Victorian campaign desk, the top leathered in black and gold detail, faced the view. Sunbeams streamed in through the windows. There was a leather Chesterfield and a big set of old wooden filing cabinets from the last century. None locked. I started sifting through them, feeling like a spy.

"Don't hold back," Lindy instructed, with a rebellious, cat-ate-the-cream smile, lopsided and irreverent.

My fingers flitted through the paperwork, all vertically stashed. Ashton had three bank accounts. In his savings $258,000. In his checking $11,300. And in a money market account there was

$59,000. Everything was filed meticulously in alphabetical order. From Ashton Personal to Water Bills.

"Ashton's not about to arrive home right now, is he?" Lindy let out a raucous peal of laughter. "How embarrassing that would be if he caught us red-handed!"

I shook my head. "No, definitely not."

Lindy's voice turned whispery and conspiratorial. "Scan what's important and then send them in emails to yourself so you have the send dates recorded."

"Really?" I began to scan the latest bank statements, still feeling terrible about it. Meanwhile, Lindy was going around the office opening drawers. I was shocked by her behavior, although I couldn't stop myself from joining in. She was just being a good friend to me and on my side, which I was grateful for. Yet I was secretly appalled at how little respect she had for someone else's property. Ashton was my husband, so at least I had a legal right to look through his things in my own home. But Lindy was dyed-in-the-wool outrageous!

"Hey, for crying out loud! This drawer doesn't open, Vivien. It's locked. You got the key?"

It was the bottom drawer of Ashton's vintage campaign desk. I had no idea where the key might be.

Lindy got down on her hands and knees and started brushing her hand under an old Persian rug—her feral red hair covering half her rebellious green eyes.

I giggled at the scene, despite myself. She was like the bad girl at school who leads others into trouble. The "ringleader."

"It won't be far," she said, scrambling around the room. "When people hide keys, they usually stash 'em somewhere nearby, in a pretty obvious place, because otherwise they forget where they are."

She heaved herself up, rummaged around the bookshelves, under another carpet, under ornaments. She approached the hearth, her eyes darting around wildly for a clue. There was a beautiful model boat above the fireplace. It was a museum-quality model ship of the American frigate U.S.S. *Constitution* that Ashton had proudly told me he had bought in an auction at Christie's. It was one of his absolute treasures. I saw Lindy's great hand reaching for it like a child's sticky fingers for candy on a top shelf.

I screeched, "Please be *careful*, Lindy, that thing's incredibly delicate and Ashton will freak if it gets broken."

But she was unstoppable. She took off her shoes, pulled out a chair and climbed on top of it so she could get a better view. "I knew it!" she squealed. "There's a key right here!" She seized the key with her cumbersome fingers—I winced as she did so—then clambered down from the chair. The key fit beautifully into the drawer.

Lindy's grin lit up her flashing green eyes. "There'll be something juicy in here, you can bet ya!"

I started to rifle through all the paperwork. Nothing was filed but neatly stacked in a pile. There was a huge brown envelope marked HOUSE. I gingerly pulled it out, careful to remember where in the pile it had been.

Deeds to a house I had no idea about. A house in the Bahamas. On Harbour Island. Any house on Harbour Island had to be worth millions. The place was beyond exclusive. Beyond gorgeous. No cars. Just golf carts. Zillionaires and their winter homes. Pink sand beaches. Ocean the brightest turquoise, so blue it looked fake. I'd seen this paradise online. Why had Ashton hidden this from me?

"Tell, tell, tell!" Lindy squawked.

My eyes ran over the deeds, flitting through the pages for numbers. It was worth plenty. Ashton had bought this two-bedroomed, two-bath house three years ago for $3.8 million. Who knew what it was worth now? Why had he not told me that he owned a house in the Bahamas? I showed Lindy the paperwork, then scanned each and every page.

She splayed her hands either side of her leopard-print hips and said, "Obviously Ashton wanted to hide this house from you, or the deeds wouldn't have been locked up."

"But why? He knows I didn't marry him for his money."

Her face pulled itself into seriousness, the fun and games over. "Looks like he doesn't trust you."

I continued scanning the deeds methodically. "The Bahamas is tax-free, isn't it? A good place to launder money, if that's what this is all about."

The idea that it was personal on his part, that he didn't want *me* knowing, did hurt. I glanced at Lindy. She seemed to know more than I did about how men's minds worked. She gazed back at me with a strange glint in her eye.

Tightening her red lips, she said. "You need to see a divorce attorney. Fast. I have just the person."

# CHAPTER THIRTEEN

The more I pondered over everything in bed the next morning, the more chaotic my mind became. I wanted things to slow down.

The *LEAVE ASHTON WHILE THE GOING'S GOOD* note.

The Harbour Island house.

Ashton spending nights at the apartment in Charleston.

Belle.

Especially Belle, his cheerleading ex, who supposedly had the perfect life, according to her Facebook page. The whole darn lot was sifting through my brain like ingredients for some cake which it was better not to eat because it would ruin you. Belle thrown into the mix. That's how crazy and jumbled my mind was when I awoke with a jerk in a horrible sweat, half dreaming, my breath hot on the pillow, my throat parched with thirst.

It was after Ashton had called me last night to say he was staying on in Charleston a couple more nights that put my suspicious brain into overload. He told me an emergency had come up: another shotgun wound, and he just couldn't face coming home because he was "too dog-tired." Belle lived in Charleston. Was I being paranoid to imagine the worst?

All last night I had tossed and lobbed myself around in our king-size bed, alone. I hated being alone in this house—I'd move into the guest cottage. This place was so big, so eerie. I didn't feel safe. I felt like someone was hovering around, watching me through the big windows. I had briefly considered driving to Charleston last night, but I'd had those beers with Lindy. The mad idea came to me to watch his apartment to see if anyone came in or came out. I couldn't believe that I was entertaining the idea of stalking Ashton, my own husband. Eight hours of bad sleep, fantasizing about Belle and her cheerleading smile had done my head in. I knew what it was like to harbor love. Was something going on between them? I mentally pressed replay: Ashton talking to her on the landline when she'd called the house, supposedly offering him a bunch of old photos. Ashton walking out of the room with the phone, breathing into the receiver quietly: "I'd rather she didn't know about that."

*Didn't know about what?*

Now fully awake, I dragged myself to the bathroom feeling like a headache was blooming. I looked in the mirror at the ridiculous color of my eye. Took a shower, drank a whole bottle of water, and then I did my makeup, concentrating on fixing the purple. I needed to call Belle myself. Talk to her in person. How to find her number, though? I was hardly about to ask Ashton.

I remembered there was a way you could recall numbers... what was it? I hadn't used the landline for so long I'd forgotten how to do that. I looked it up online. Had anyone else called our number since then? I didn't think so. I pressed *69 on the landline phone. It began to ring. I crossed my fingers the number was Belle's and not some robot call about voting or something.

That house in Harbour Island made me feel suspicious about everything now. If Ashton was capable of hiding that from me, he could hide anything. And who wrote the anonymous note? The same person who came into the kitchen and drank the tea?

A female voice answered. I was tempted to hang up.

"Hi, Ashton," she said. It was Belle.

"How did you know what number this was?" I asked.

"Who is this?"

"Who is *this*?" I shot back, shocked at how rude I sounded.

She laughed, incredulous. "Excuse me but you called *me*."

"Sorry but this is a last number recall and you called this number the other day, so I'm simply returning the call."

"Am I speaking to Ashton's wife?" She had a slow, lazy pliability to her voice that conjured up long, hot summers.

"This is she," I said, with a sliver of Katharine Hepburn to my tone. What made me want to be unfriendly, I wasn't sure. I knew I was being rude but just couldn't stop myself. Jealousy?

"Oh yeah, I did call you the other day," Belle remembered.

"I think you called *Ashton* the other day?"

"Look, would you like to meet for a coffee or something?" Belle suggested.

Her invitation stunned me into silence. *What does she want?*

She spoke again in her unhurried, sexy voice. "Hi, are you still there? I'm sorry, I don't even know your name?"

*Hitting below the belt.*

"Vivien," I said.

"Pleased to know you, Vivien. You want to grab some breakfast? It's only eight-thirty, people don't usually call this early, I haven't even had a coffee. You want to meet up?" Her little dig at how impolite I was for calling so early did not go unnoticed. Yet her tone was sweet.

"Coffee's a bit far for me," I said.

"Far? You're around the corner."

"But aren't you in Charleston?" Her Facebook pictures rolled over in my mind. The barbecues, the perfect children with gaps between their front teeth—the girl all tutu-ballet-pink, the other a cheeky-looking little boy dressed in a firefighter's helmet.

"No, we moved back to Beaufort last year," she said languorously, on a yawn. "We don't live in Charleston anymore. Bradley got a job teaching at the local school here. He's the new football coach."

"Oh, I didn't realize you were back."

The note loomed into my gallery of images. Someone who knew Distant Sands well walking nonchalantly into the kitchen, helping themselves to a glass of iced tea and casually walking out again. Whoever it was had to live nearby. I added Belle to my list of suspects.

"Vivien, are you still there?"

"Yeah, I'm still here."

"You wanna grab a coffee?"

"Sure."

"Let's meet at the Dock Café, that new place at Waterfront Park, should we say, twenty minutes?"

"Sure," I said. "Looking forward to it." My curiosity made me say yes, but the fact Belle wanted to meet in person, woman-to-woman, made me edgy. Was she going to spill the beans about her and Ashton?

Twenty minutes later, I arrived at the cute café by the waterfront. I parked and waited for Belle. Checked my makeup in the car. Reapplied my mascara. Just a dash, so I looked natural, yet appropriately freshened up for eight-fifty in the morning. I didn't want to feel eclipsed by her.

*Belle.*

Belle: "beautiful" in French. Her parents must've really adored her to call her such a pretty name.

I walked into the Dock Café and told the hostess I was waiting for a "friend," doubting very much that Belle and I would ever be friends.

Belle glided into the café, and did look as beautiful as her namesake. Just like her Facebook profile, yet a touch mother-of-two-disheveled. She had long dark hair and was pencil thin. Actually, she looked a lot like me. We both had that Irish look: blue eyes and dark hair. Pale skin, a sprinkle of freckles. Our noses were very similar, hers, of course, being what God had given her. We were about the same height, too.

"Hi, Vivien, how do you do," she said, a huge grin sweeping across her face. Her teeth were sparkly white. "I won't shake your hand—I've got popsicle stickiness all over me. Sticky car seats."

Belle asked the waitress if we could sit outside on the patio. We took a table with a view to the waterfront, replete with an array of elegant yachts of all sizes and denominations. I say "denominations" because boats can do that. They tell their story. "I fish and work for a living" or, "I have an asshole boss, look at me and my ostentatious black trim," or, "I'm elegant and understated, I come from *old* money." In Beaufort, there was room for all sorts of people. *If I were a boat,* I thought, *what would I be like?*

Belle and I sat down at a table for two, looking onto the waterfront. The breeze picked up, and I made out the soporific sounds: the jingle of the boats rocking gently in the harbor. The plopping waves lapping against the hulls.

"Nice you can have breakfast with me," I said. "You didn't have to take your kids to school?"

"No, Bradley does that."

She shed her jacket and hung it on the back of the chair. "How do you know I have kids?"

"Um, the popsicle?"

She laughed. Her smile was bright and pretty, with one tooth ever so slightly overlapping the other, which gave her a cute, girlish charm. She ordered a black coffee and some muesli with berries and Greek yogurt. *Healthy.* To hell with any kind of diet; I'd order a latte and some shrimp 'n' grits. But then, looking at her svelte figure, I quickly changed my mind. I ordered the same as Belle.

Belle looked like a yummy-mommy hippie, in a pretty flowery dress and lace-up boots. I felt almost preppy next to her, and boring, dressed in my jeans, sneakers, and cashmere sweater. An unbidden wave of envy washed over me—I couldn't help it—remembering that Belle had been Ashton's first love, and maybe, despite Bradley, he was *still* in love with her? I decided to come straight out with it. No point nurturing my paranoia and dragging out my mistrust any longer.

"Is this meeting about you and Ashton?" I said, my tone a little brusque.

Belle spluttered her coffee mid-sip. "*What?*"

"I thought maybe something's going on between you," I said.

"This is *crazy*! No, you don't understand, it's not like that at *all*."

I said nothing.

Belle burst out, "The reason I asked you to meet me is… look, Vivien, I haven't seen Ashton for years… I don't *want* to see the guy. We didn't end on a good note. It's just sad. Sad that he and Bradley never get to hang out anymore. I thought it would be nice if they reconnected. Here," she said, pulling out two big piles of photos from her bag. "There are some cool photos of us as kids. Some really nice ones of Lily. When I called Ashton the other day, he said he didn't want them, but that doesn't make sense. Why wouldn't he want photos of his sister?"

"Sister? Ashton doesn't have a sister."

The waiter came with our mueslis and did the usual interrupting thing that waiters tend to do, always right in the middle of a piece of gossip or some huge family secret. I smiled at him as he hovered there, oblivious, telling us about the specials and what his name was, *et cetera, et cetera.* "Thank you, everything's great," I said, desperate to get back to my conversation with Belle before she lost the thread.

Belle picked a berry off the top of her muesli and popped it into her pretty mouth.

"No, he doesn't have a sister, but he *did* have a sister," she said.

I gazed at Belle, baffled.

"Lily, his *sister?*" she enunciated. "His sister who died? You didn't *know* that?"

"Are you sure? Ashton has never mentioned a sister to me!"

"Course I'm sure. We hung out together our whole childhood. Here, look at the photos." Belle picked some photos from one of the piles and fanned them out on the table.

I remembered Ashton's low voice hissing into the phone, "*I'd rather she didn't know about that*." Why didn't he want me to know about his sister? What was he hiding?

I pushed my sunglasses onto my head, to get a better look.

Belle gawped at my face. "Oh my God, what happened to your eye? You okay?"

"I'm fine," I said quickly. "Bumped my eye on a boat post. Sorry, I meant to keep my shades on."

"Right," Belle said, unconvinced. "Keep your shades on to keep up appearances, right?"

I ignored her remark, and ran my gaze over the pictures. A cute, skinny-legged girl, all smiles and long, blonde hair grinned at me. She looked a lot like Ashton. I felt a horrible pang of sadness. Swimming in a blue, polka-dot bikini. Diving off the dock. Steering the boat. The ages varied. The photos were jumbled. Some with Lily and Ashton, arm in arm. Others with Lily and a golden retriever. Christmas with the whole family, the decorated tree in the background. Their dad Buck was handsome, just like Ashton. But rougher, coarser, his forearms like a true blue-collar worker who had to use his physique all day long, his face broader, his body chunky like a heavyweight boxer, with a nose to match. But good looking, nonetheless.

Ashton looked the same in the photos, just younger and less developed. Still the signature soulful eyes. The thick, mussed-up hair. That same irresistible Ashton smile, although the smile looked cockier in these photos—the self-assuredness of a teenager who ruled the world.

Who was the Ashton I'd married? His lies—or omission of the truth—were catching up with him. His sister, his swanky Harbour Island house. *How could he not tell me about his sister?*

"How did Lily die?" I asked Belle, flicking through some more photos: one of Belle, arm in arm with Ashton.

She regarded me a long while as if deciding if she should confide in me or not. "Suicide," she said, finally.

My heart rate picked up.

"She drowned in the creek. She tied a rope around her ankle with a sailor's knot, with an old anchor attached. The weight of it pulled her down."

I held Belle's gaze, before she looked away. "How come I didn't know about this?"

She gave me a tiny smile. "I guess your husband didn't want to confide in you." She said this with a tinge of relish. Or was I imagining it?

I said, "But why didn't anyone ever tell me? The guests at our wedding, the people we know?"

"Suicide's not the kind of thing you chit-chat about at a party, now, is it? That's not the Southern way."

She was right, but I wondered why Lindy hadn't let me in on this integral piece of information. Or maybe she assumed I knew and was too polite to bring it up?

"How old was Ashton when this happened?" I said, a little roughly. Belle's voice was like whipped cream, all soft, slow, and dreamy. With a cherry on top. Mine, I felt, was more like a martini with an olive. Belle took a mouthful of muesli just as I asked the question.

She answered, her hand covering her mouth. "Eighteen. Lily was seventeen. There was no proof, of course, but something wasn't quite right." Belle washed her food down with some coffee. For such a skinny thing she wolfed her breakfast like there were two of her. I wondered if a baby was on the way.

I sipped my coffee. My muesli practically untouched. All this was taking away my appetite. I thoughtfully swallowed a berry, mulling over Belle's insinuations. "What are you saying?" I whispered. "That Ashton killed his own *sister*?" I pictured the perfect sailor's knot that Ashton had tied when we'd had our picnic.

Belle focused on my bruise. Which now had golden tinges, the color of overripe pears.

"I'm not saying anything," she said. "Ashton just changed overnight. One minute he was this great guy, but after his sister died, he turned into this crazy maniac. Drinking himself silly every day, partying, screwing every girl he could lay his hands on. His whole personality changed."

"Maybe because he was so unhappy," I said, defensive.

"Or guilty," she drawled. She took another gulp of coffee. Her dark hair flopped over her face like a curtain, like she was trying to hide.

"What makes you think Ashton had anything to do with the accident?" I said.

"I don't know, it's just a hunch, I guess. They'd been fighting like Tom and Jerry, he and Lily."

"How come I didn't read about this in the papers? How come it's not something that's common knowledge?" I asked again.

Belle took out a scrunchie and scooped her thick hair into a ponytail, all shine and gloss. "It *is* common knowledge if you dig deep enough and know the right people. I'm sure you'll find the story in the library, maybe even online. But I guess the 'right people' must've been hushed up. Ashton's family has contacts. Old friends, you know. Judges. Attorneys. The local newspaper. That kind of shit. Small-town stuff."

I conjured up the scene in my mind. Georgia-May flouncing around in pink chiffon, trying to hush things up. Buck, the brutish father.

"But Buck wasn't rich or influential," I said.

"Mr. Buchanan had his friends."

"So what happened with you and Ashton?" I asked.

"Ashton was like a different person, like Jekyll and Hyde."

"That's when you started going out with Bradley? When Ashton and you split up?"

"Yeah, I guess you could say that's what happened."

"How come, then," I said with confusion, "if he was drinking and partying like crazy, and being such an ass, he managed to get into the top medical school in the country and pass all his exams with flying colors?"

Belle wrinkled her brow as if summoning forth a possible reason. "I have no idea, he's just one of those natural geniuses, I guess. The kind of guy who can study and do an all-nighter and ace exams. Ashton was kind of born with a silver spoon in his mouth, ya know? There's no denying the guy is super intelligent." She pulled a face and suddenly looked like her sixteen-year-old photo again. "Or maybe, come to think of it, he'd already been accepted at college before Lily's supposed 'suicide.'"

"You sound a little bitter," I said.

She shrugged. "I am so *over* him, believe me."

I looked at my watch. A beautiful Tank Cartier that Ashton had given me for my birthday. "I need to get going, Belle. I'm late for an appointment. It was nice meeting you." I got up from my seat, my breakfast unfinished. Gathered together the photos and put them in my handbag. I picked my sunglasses off my head and slid them back onto my face. "Thank you for these photos, I'll pass them along to Ashton. Breakfast's on me, by the way."

Belle drained the rest of her coffee. "Ashton doesn't want the photos—he made that clear on the phone when I called."

"Then, to be honest, I'm a little confused as to why you invited me here?" I said, opening the café door to go pay inside.

"You know what? Me either. This whole idea was fucked up. I don't know, I felt kind of nostalgic for the old Ashton, and thought he and Bradley could make up or something, and you could bridge that gap. But seeing your black eye? I never want to see the guy again. Thanks for breakfast, Vivien. See ya around."

Her comment about my eye made my face heat up in a beetroot-rush of shame, wishing I hadn't taken off my sunglasses. But so much worse were the revelations about Ashton's sister, Lily.

If only I trusted Ashton. But I didn't. Marriage without trust is like rain without clouds… it simply doesn't make sense.

Ashton was a dark horse. A horse that could throw me to the ground and trample me down.

# CHAPTER FOURTEEN

I moved Cady into the guest house. I'd deal with the consequences later. I couldn't leave the poor thing stranded with nowhere to go.

When I arrived with a big box of groceries, Cady was busy organizing herself. Dressed in overalls, her spiky hair now dyed ginger, she was cleaning the windows.

"Hi, Cady hon, I brought over some things for the kitchen. Olive oil, stuff for making salads, salt and pepper, pasta, things to get you started."

Standing barefoot on the kitchen countertop, she replied, "Cool. How about we make lunch and eat it here?"

I set the box down. "Well, I suppose we could do that. Why not?"

"And we could watch a movie together?"

It was raining outside and the idea of a movie and lunch was really appealing. Her invitation was sweet and Ashton wasn't home yet.

I sat on the sofa, took off my sneakers and put my feet up on the coffee table. Something I never did with Ashton. Cady and I needed to talk. After her humdinger revelation when I last saw her at Community Promise, I was worried about her. "How are you getting on at school?" I asked, easing into the conversation.

She took a fresh cloth from the pocket of her overalls and dried and polished the window to a shine. "Okay, I guess."

"Fun classes? New friends?"

"I'm really enjoying the environmental science class we're doing. It's pretty cool. We saw this film, *Breaking Their Silence*, about these awesome women in Africa on the frontline of the poaching war, protecting mainly elephants and rhinos. These incredible women are risking their lives. The film crew couldn't even mention where they were 'cause they'd be attacked and poachers would come kill the elephants. It's so nasty. You know, a hundred elephants are killed in Africa? Every. Single. Day. For the ivory and even body parts. Did you know that?"

"I didn't know it was that bad! How awful."

"Me either. And five rhinos every day are also poached. It's horrible. The horns get ground up to powder for some 'medicinal' cure and sold in Asia. It's gross. It makes me so mad."

I grimaced. "It's so horrible, it's hard to think about."

Cady polished the same window in a riled-up frenzy of nerves. "Yeah, well, we're all linked. Without these animals the human race will die. Like bees, you know? They may seem unimportant, but they're essential. Anyways, I'm like, pretty sure that's what I wanna do with my life, I wanna do something for ecology… something for the planet."

I had tears in my eyes. Her speech moved me. How many teenagers even cared about this stuff? "You're such a cool kid, you know that, hon? I'm so proud of you. So impressed."

Cady grinned. "Thanks. Truth is? I care more about animals than humans. Humans suck."

*Poor thing*, I thought. No wonder she felt that way. "Listen, Cady, what you told me about being sexually molested, was that true?"

She stopped polishing the window. "Yeah. And I don't like that word, 'molested.' It's like 'assaulted.' They're bullshit, cloudy words. The word we need to use is 'rape.'"

I nodded in agreement. "You're right. Do you want to talk about it?"

"No."

"Why not?"

"I told you everything already." She started giving the window another high shine.

"I'm not talking about details, I'm talking about your feelings. That kind of stuff runs deep and it follows you through life; you know that, don't you? You can't bottle that stuff up."

"I'll be fine."

"Would you like to see a therapist about it?"

"Hell, no."

"Why not?"

"'Cause I can deal with this shit on my own."

"You need to talk to someone."

"No, I don't."

"Please think about it, Cady. Do you want to talk to me?"

"I already said no."

"Well, I'm always here if you need me."

All I could do was my best, given the circumstances. I remembered how I felt at her age. I cooked up some pasta with pesto and tomatoes, and we watched a romcom to lighten the mood. It felt good. Relaxed. I hoped at some point Cady would open up to me about her terrible ordeal. I couldn't even imagine what she must be going through. I wanted to be there for her, and whatever Ashton said, I had the right to make choices too in our home, and this was my choice: to set Cady up in the guest cottage temporarily.

A couple of hours later, I heard Ashton's car roll into the driveway. I left Cady with the TV on softly, slipped out the door and ran to the side of the main house, remembering I hadn't locked the doors. Again. Luckily there was no sign of any visitor. It was a bad habit Ashton had gotten me into; he rarely locked the doors either. Distant Island was that kind of place. At least it used to be. Who knew now? Wandering into an unlocked kitchen and drinking someone's iced tea... was that a crime, or just creepy? I waited for Ashton, fixed him a chicken sandwich and made a fresh jug of tea. I didn't hear him come in at any point, so I went outside to find him, wondering if I should bring up the subject of his sister's suicide. Was that why he had lied about being an only child? Because her suicide was so painful for him?

He was sitting under the oak tree, almost as if in meditation. Lost in himself, his knees bent, drawn up to his chest. The oak's gnarly girth and twisty limbs swept the ground in a diameter of more than a hundred and fifty feet—roughly half a football field. These unusual proportions meant it was unlikely to topple even in the strongest hurricane.

*And I,* I wondered, *will I survive my own personal hurricane?*

Tiny pearls of raindrops plummeted from some leaves above and plopped on Ashton's shoulder. He didn't notice. I was going to mention the ice-tea theft, but judging by his apparent mood, I decided to leave it. I didn't want him getting angry with me.

"Hi, hon," I said. "I made you a sandwich. It's in the fridge. You hungry?"

He looked at me as if I'd shaken him from a dream. "Wow, you took me by surprise!"

I smoothed a wayward strand of hair away from my mouth. "Sorry, I didn't mean to startle you. Everything okay?"

"Yep. Just thinking."

Ashton gazed up into the boughs of the tree, dappled sun catching his face and eyes. He looked so handsomely boyish in this moment. I snapped a mental shot of him with the lens of my eye and remembered his dead sister, who looked so like him.

"This tree has always been my guardian. I used to play in it as a boy, for hours and hours and hours. All my friends were envious because nobody had a tree like this in their backyard. You know, we have a lot of these trees in South Carolina—these Southern live oaks? The beauty of this species is that live oaks are not deciduous like regular oak trees—or they are, but they behave more like evergreens, because they only lose their deep green waxy leaves for a brief period—a couple of weeks in early spring—and quickly replenish 'em again, giving the impression they're evergreen. But technically they aren't. They're actually deciduous, but few people know that."

His manner was different, like a teacher speaking to a student, not a man to his wife. Ashton usually embraced me when he got home. This was the first time he hadn't stood up for me, or greeted me with a kiss. Perplexed, I let him carry on talking.

"Strange everybody calls it Spanish moss," he continued, almost to himself, his eyes roving across the damp, moss-draped branches, "because it isn't Spanish, nor actual moss, but an epiphytic herb."

"She's beautiful," I said. "This tree's very special to me too."

"She?"

I shifted my weight, causing my elongated shadow to darken him in the late afternoon sun. I was stealing his light.

I said, "I named this tree Eve, because it feels like she was here from the beginning of time."

Ashton had a sad look in his eyes. It just wasn't like him not to jump up and kiss me hello. *What does he know? Has he got wind of something? Can I trust Lindy?*

Earlier I had made up my mind not to mention his sister Lily, but it just popped out. "Thinking about Lily?" I said, keeping my voice airy and light.

There was a prolonged silence. He didn't reply.

"I had coffee—actually breakfast—with Belle," I told him.

He flicked me a glance. "I know."

"You *know?* Boy, news travels fast around here!" I remembered Belle saying how she never wanted to see Ashton again. And she'd *called* him?

"I knew it was only a matter of time before Belle contacted you, too," he said. "It's the kind of thing she does. But I spoke to Bradley—he called to give me the heads-up. We talked about old times. It was weird, like no time had passed at all, like five minutes, not twenty years."

I was still standing, not sure where to put myself. "That's what it's like with true friends, isn't it? Or close members of family? A real connection can never be broken. Or forgotten."

Ashton continued with his taciturn daydream, now looking out to the water. Moody. I felt so rejected. Some birds flittered and chirped in the tree. Ashton blinked at the view.

"Do you believe that once you've made a connection with someone, it's there for life? A friend? A sibling?" I pressed. "I do."

He picked up a twig and drew circles in the earth, still wet from the rain, earlier. "If it's a real connection, sure. You never forget someone who was special to you."

"You don't have anything to share?" I persevered. "Maybe something you haven't told me?"

He shrugged again. "Don't think so."

I had looked up Lily's suicide online and hadn't found anything. No news of any suicide in Beaufort, except for one seventeen-year-old boy. Nothing about a Lily Buchanan. I wanted to ask Ashton directly, but it felt cruel to pick and probe into something so distressing. I guessed we'd talk about it when he was ready.

Ashton remained silent. His eyes had a watery glare.

"If you ever feel the need to share stuff about your family," I said. I sat down beside him, giving him the chance to reach out. The ground dampened my jeans. It was weird that he and I didn't touch, that we both sat there in silence, the wind rustling through the trees, great shadows of the oak casting chiaroscuro patterns on the lawn. Any outside observer would've thought how romantic we looked, the two of us sitting under this tree.

"Taking the boat out was…" He didn't say more.

"What were you about to tell me?"

"Nothing. I just had a patient die on me. I feel very drained right now, feeling a little, you know… sad. I did my very best but…"

I said, in a soft voice, "I'm so sorry, hon. You probably picked the hardest job in the whole world."

"The lows are really low, but the highs are worth it," he answered, giving me a weak smile. "We had a couple of successes in the last few days, too. I guess you never think about the successes but only focus on the negative. You know, sometimes we work miracles, but not always."

I didn't want to ask him about the patient dying, and I wasn't about to grill him about Lily, tempting though it was. It didn't matter anyway. I'd find out from Lindy or go to the library and search through records.

"I have something to tell you," I said.

"You've moved that girl in."

"How did you know?"

"I saw the windows open to the cottage when I drove up to the house. If you think I'm going to fight you on this, you're wrong. I just don't have the energy right now."

I responded brightly, "You'll like her, she's a good kid."

Silence.

I touched his shoulder. "You aren't pissed?"

"I'm not gonna argue with you, okay? Whatever you say or do is fine. Do whatever you want. I just want to have five minutes here under my tree, take a nap in my bedroom, enjoy a big glass of wine and then take you to bed. That's all I ask, nothing more, nothing less." He smiled at me briefly. Flashed his Ashton smile for a nanosecond and then it was gone.

This hot and cold treatment from him was disarming. I still wondered if Lindy had said something to her husband. If so, why didn't Ashton just come out with it? I hated this silent tension, the buried secrets. I wished I could rewind the clock. I felt like I had created chaos in our relationship, but now it was all too late. Something was up, for sure. His mood had changed so radically.

"You can talk to me, you know, Ashton. You can trust me." Silence. Today I certainly wasn't having any luck with people opening up to me. Ashton. Cady. I persevered. "You know, if you want to share stuff about your past, I understand. Some of your friends say that you went on a drinking spree and slept with lots of girls?"

He closed his eyes and sipped in a deep breath, inhaling the sweet, rain-scented air. Then let out a groan. "Smells good, doesn't it? After a bout of rain?" He looked back at the water. "Truth is, I don't remember anything I did back then. It's like one big, black cloud."

I lifted my brows. "People always talk about blacking out when they're drunk, but maybe that's an excuse to behave badly? An excuse so people will forgive you." I tried to make it sound jokey, not accusatory, but Ashton didn't smile.

"Maybe because you've never gone off the rails like I have. I don't even know what I did. Like I said, it's all a haze. Guess I must've been drinking a whole darn lot for me not to remember that period in my life."

I felt the damp of the ground seep into my skin but remained sitting. Anything Ashton shared about his past might give me some insight, some clues, but he still wasn't saying anything about Lily. "How did you manage your exams at Johns Hopkins?"

"Guess I have a kind of photographic memory for textbook stuff. Words, numbers, facts, learning by rote. Some people might call it intelligence, but I call it luck. I was born that way. I aced my exams—a miracle, really. But don't ask me to remember those years. I mean, don't get me wrong, I know what I'm doing now. My neurosurgical internship, that I also did at Johns Hopkins, was like a cold bucket of water thrown over my head. Dr. Daniel Gates was my mentor and he sure as hell knocked some sense into me." Ashton crossed his arms. "And you know I never drink on duty. Not even a beer. I need my hands steady and my brain sharp."

I touched his knee. "I know," I said. "I know what a good doctor you are and how seriously you take things."

Ashton breathed in the rainy aftermath again and surveyed the view. The sultry gray clouds held the humidity in the air. I followed his gaze. A pod of pelicans flew over the water in the distance, their bills impossibly long, cruising the coast for prey.

I shuffled on the ground, my butt damp and acorns sticking into me, but I felt it necessary to hold onto these straws of conversation while I could, before Ashton shut down completely. "Tell me about your family. Were you close?"

"Honey, I really don't want to dredge all this up right now. My past seriously doesn't interest me. There's nothing I can do about any of it. I moved on. Look, it's a long and complicated story, and someday soon we can talk about it. But right now's not the moment, okay?"

I had a feeling it would never "be the moment." I'd find out, though.

I'd find out.

# CHAPTER FIFTEEN

Over the next couple of days, I searched everywhere for information about Lily Buchanan. Nothing. In the library, online. I knew that the Internet was in its infancy when she died, and not every single thing someone ate for breakfast was reported in those days. But death? It was weird. Nowhere did I find any hint about the suicide of a Lily Buchanan. There was only so much a newspaper would hush-hush, however many contacts you had. Something was off.

I decided to pay Georgia-May a visit, and not just for altruistic reasons. This time I didn't call ahead, but decided to just turn up. It was not the best idea, as I discovered afterward.

As I was about to get out of my car, in the parking lot of Heritage Park, Lindy called.

"Vivien, hi, everything all right? I've been thinking about you. Thought we should catch up and have lunch sometime."

"That would be lovely. Everything's fine, I'm about to visit my mother-in-law."

"Oh, that's so good of you, she must adore your visits. I was just wondering if you'd called Silverman? To make an appointment?"

"Silverman?"

"Noah Silverman, the divorce attorney."

I closed the car door and walked toward reception "No, I haven't had time."

"You need to prepare yourself, just in case, don't you think? Ashton has hidden his assets from you. Don't you want to know where you stand legally? Get your ducks in a row?"

"It seems so precipitated. Shouldn't I talk to Ashton first about this?"

"Honey, he's hiding stuff from you for a reason. If you let him know you know, I don't think that would be very smart, do you?"

"Maybe you're right. Listen, I need to go. I'll call you back later, okay?"

"Okay, but don't be nervous about seeing Silverman, he won't bite."

"Okay, thanks for looking out for me, Lindy. Bye. I'll call you about lunch."

Georgia-May was not dressed in her usual garb of double-pearls and pink. Today she looked a little unkempt. And I could tell I had embarrassed her by not giving her time to prepare for me, by not calling in advance. She was all about appearances, and I remembered that the pearls were part of her reinvention of herself. She was a shrimper's wife, nothing fancy, not this "old money" act that she put on for strangers—and for everyone, even me. Georgia-May was just a regular woman, but she behaved as if she was from high aristocracy.

A new nurse, not Mariama, stood by us as we had a cup of coffee together in the cafeteria. The nurse was young, slim, and edgy-nervous, with white skin that looked as if she suffered from some kind of skin disorder like psoriasis. Her name was Lucy. On the way here, I had stopped to pick up a pretty frame and picked the nicest photo of Lily from the pack of photos Belle had given me. I thought Georgia-May might like a memento, but was a little wary of how she might respond.

Lucy, after introducing herself, said to me, "I'm sorry, Mrs. Buchanan, but this is highly unusual to just drop by like this, so Mrs. Buchanan Senior can only give you five minutes of her time."

My mother-in-law stared at me, her eyes glazy and bewildered. "This lady should never have come here if she knows what's good for her," Georgia-May called out, turning to Lucy. She fluttered her hand to gesture me away.

"It's me, Vivien, your daughter-in-law, Ashton's wife."

"It's too late, young lady, too late! Get out of here, keep away from my son!"

Her words sent a shudder through my body.

"I was a fool to have opened my arms to you. Stay away. Stay away!"

What she said stunned me into silence. Such a one-eighty from the last time we'd met.

I persevered. Brought out the framed photo of Lily from my purse. "I brought you something." I handed it to her.

She stared at it for a long while then gave a little yelp. "Why are you giving me this picture?"

"It's Lily when she was about sixteen."

"I don't know who this is. Why are you showing me this photograph?" She handed me back the frame.

"Because I thought you might like a picture of Lily. Your daughter."

"I don't have a *daughter!*"

"Ashton's sister, Lily. Your daughter," I said again, but then realized too late that in her condition I might have done the worst thing possible by showing her this photo.

She turned to Lucy. "Why is she insisting? Please make her leave."

Lucy shrugged, making an I'm-sorry face. "I really think you should leave now. Mrs. Buchanan is very upset. I really don't want her to have a relapse."

"I'm so sorry, I really didn't mean to—"

"Please leave," Lucy said, stern now. "I don't want any trouble. This is just my second week here, and I can't afford to have any problems. I'm so sorry. That photograph is upsetting her. Best if you take it with you."

Georgia-May pointed a finger at me. Her pink nails long and curly. "It's the duet, isn't it? Are you part of this now?" A scowl clouded her face. "Twisting the truth, pretending things happened when they didn't. You should never have gotten involved with my family."

"I'm so, so sorry. I—" I mustered up a small smile.

"Oh, so you're laughing at me now?" Georgia-May scoffed. "Think this is funny?"

"No, God. No, I—"

"Best be on your way now," Lucy said. "And make sure you call next time."

I left. Flabbergasted. *The duet?* What was that? She was talking about classical music or something?

As I drove away from the clinic, I felt just awful about what had happened. But curiosity was nipping at my heels too. I considered calling Belle again to grill her for the truth. I didn't know any other old-timers here. I'd press Lindy, just in case Richard knew something.

Ashton—and maybe Georgia-May too—were harboring shady secrets.

Who *was* this man I'd married?

# CHAPTER SIXTEEN

Dr. Becker looked drained. Even through her glasses, I could detect she had tender dark pillows under her eyes. I had no idea how many patients she saw each day.

"Good morning, Vivien. Please sit down." She didn't get up to greet me this time, the way she usually did.

"Good morning, Dr. Becker, how are you?" I wanted my voice to sound chirpy and bright. But I was worried and stressed. Ashton had turned cold on me. I had ruined our marriage. Like a ball rolling down a hill that you can't stop, or a paper flying along the ground in the wind that every time you try to step on flies off just a bit further and then eventually ends up in a puddle or worse, a drain. I kept having to remind myself that Ashton was not the innocent one here, and that I wasn't a bad person. *I am not a bad person!*

"I'm just fine, thank you, Vivien," Dr. Becker replied. "Tell me about your week."

I sat down on my usual chair, opposite her. "Well, I moved that teenager, Cady, into the guest cottage."

"My word, that was pretty quick. And what did Ashton think about that?"

"He was against it and told me not to."

"But you did it anyway?"

I bit my lip. "Yes."

"Overruling him. Interesting. And did this cause any kind of scene?"

"Strangely, no. He took it with resignation. Like he was tired and couldn't face arguing with me. He said as much."

"Any more signs of violence?" Dr. Becker poised a pen above her notepad.

"No, not at all."

Dr. Becker nodded again and scribbled something down. "Are you and Ashton still tactile, intimate?"

Her question took me by surprise. I felt so uneasy, like she was prying too much. Of course she was... it was her job. "That part of our relationship's still very good."

"It hasn't been affected at all with... what happened?"

I hesitated before I spoke. "Lately he hasn't been very cuddly or affectionate. But we've been having sex. It's different from usual."

She peered at me over her glasses. "How so?"

"Animalistic. Like a kind of craving. It's disconcerting. But it's... look, I don't want to talk about that, I'd rather talk about his sister, Lily. A new discovery."

"Ashton has a *sister*?"

"His ex-girlfriend, Belle, called me with a bunch of photos. We had coffee, and I discovered Ashton has... *had* a sister, who died at the age of seventeen. Belle said she 'supposedly' killed herself. But I can't find anything in the papers, or on the Internet, or in the library, nothing about her death. And Ashton won't talk about it, and his mother pretends like she never had a daughter. But I know that there was a daughter and a sister because I've seen the photos and the photos look just like Ashton. I mean, it's definitely his sister."

Dr. Becker frowned. "What is it exactly you're worried about?"

"I'm thinking maybe there was some kind of accident and she was killed. Maybe manslaughter. Belle said that she and Ashton had been fighting. And then Lily supposedly took her own life, but it wasn't suicide according to Belle, reading between the lines."

Dr. Becker blinked at me then said somewhat sternly, "Vivien, suicide or not, sister or no sister, it doesn't sound as if you trust Ashton at all. Is that really the kind of marriage you want? I very rarely tell clients want to do. I need them to come to their own conclusions. But in your case, you are stalling even though you're frightened of Ashton. And with good reason. He has a track record of violence, and he could hurt you. And everything you're telling me is compounding this. Even if Ashton is innocent of hurting his sister, *you* feel threatened. And *that* is what is paramount."

Again, I felt that desperation to turn back the clock. I wished now that Dr. Becker had never seen my black eye. Or Lindy the bruises. Everything felt like it was spinning out of control, moving way too fast. "I know, I know. I just need a little bit more time. My friend Lindy recommended a divorce attorney, and I have an appointment lined up, actually." It was a lie. I hadn't yet called the lawyer.

Dr. Becker nodded sagely. "That's great to know."

"As you know, I don't have much money. I love my job so much, but the idea of paying for everything myself, finding an apartment, setting out on my own again… it scares me."

"You're young, Vivien, you have qualifications, you have skills. You'll find a new job. A paying one."

"You make it sound so easy. And the question of where I should live has been weighing on me. I find it hard to get to sleep for the worry. Obviously, I wouldn't be able to stay here. This is Ashton's territory, and I don't think I would be very popular after divorcing him. I know you think I'm weak and pathetic and making excuses—"

"I never said those words," Dr. Becker broke in.

"I know, but I'm sure you're thinking them because I haven't left him already and I haven't dealt with this. But I just need a little time. I don't feel ready. Not even close."

Dr. Becker sighed quietly. I could tell something else was on her mind.

"Oh, I forgot to tell you about an anonymous note in my letterbox, which felt really threatening. It said, in capital letters, *LEAVE ASHTON WHILE THE GOING'S GOOD.*"

"Did you report this to the police?"

"No, it seemed too… well, nobody was threatening my *life*. The police would think it a waste of their time."

"You think a man wrote the note? An admirer?"

"No. Definitely not. I think it must be a woman."

"Why?"

"I don't know. The nice writing paper, the expensive envelope? Men don't really write notes, do they? Unless someone's trying to put me off the scent. You think that's possible?"

"When you say the note was threatening, do you think it could be a friendly warning?"

"Maybe. But I took it as a threat. You think I'm being too suspicious?"

Dr. Becker made a hmmm sound and then said, "It seems to me as if everything about your surroundings, your family life, your home… is threatening you. Ashton, the note, the fear of Lily having been killed."

"You think I'm being paranoid, don't you?"

"What *I* think is unimportant. It's what *you* think and feel, Vivien. With all this going on, I'm surprised you're still living in that house, with a man who has shown he's violent, in a home in which you feel threatened."

"I need to find out who wrote the note. And about Ashton's past." I could hear my tone warble—a feeble, reedy voice. *She probably thinks I'm weak. Indecisive. Stalling.*

Dr. Becker took off her glasses, rubbed her eyes, then said, "Instead of focusing on these things that make you fearful, wouldn't it be a better use of your time to concentrate on finding a new job? Of making plans to leave your insecure environment? The beauty is you don't have children, you're free to start fresh. Look in the papers. See what kind of jobs are on offer for which you're qualified. I'm sure there'd be lots of things suitable for you. You could move to another state if you wanted. Remember, the world's your oyster. Most women aren't in your position of being able to start again."

I gave her a small smile. "I guess."

"Meanwhile, you have your appointment with the divorce attorney. That's a great start. Have you decided to talk to the police? And press charges against Ashton?"

I shook my head. "I haven't thought about pressing charges, no. I thought I should just touch base with the attorney. I don't *want* to press charges. No way."

"The strength is within you, Vivien. Anyone who can deal with their parents dying at the age of seventeen and set out on their own is a strong person. You *are* strong. This will pass, believe me, and you'll look back at your marriage with Ashton as just one little chapter in your life. Don't let it define who you are."

After I left our appointment, I mused over everything Dr. Becker had said. I sat in my car, crying and bingeing on candy bars. What she told me was not true about Ashton not defining me.

Ashton defined everything about me.

Everything I was, what I stood for, and my worth was because of Ashton Buchanan.

# CHAPTER SEVENTEEN

I stopped at the grocery store on my way home, simultaneously looking up a recipe online. I wanted to smooth things over with Ashton, keep things on an even keel. What if he got wind of the fact Lindy and Dr. Becker were pushing me into leaving him and seeing a divorce attorney? I needed everything to appear normal. I decided on caramelized red-onion tarts. Nothing like cooking to banish problems from the mind. I'd surprise Ashton with something delicious.

Busy in the kitchen, I chopped the onions and heated the olive oil and butter in a large iron skillet until it sizzled, added the onions, some fresh rosemary from the garden, a dash of vinegar and some sugar. I rolled out the pastry on a lightly floured surface and cut it into rounds. Prepared a mixture of goat's cheese and parsley and cooled the pastry in the fridge. It wouldn't take long to cook—I could do it when we were having our wine. All the while, I rewound the pros and cons of leaving Ashton in my head. The reality of it was daunting, however much my feelings of injury and hurt simmered on the back burner.

I pushed my negativity out of my head and continued on my quest: to impress my husband with a fabulous meal.

For the main course, I prepared a chicken pot pie with oyster and chanterelle mushrooms, fresh sage, butternut squash, all topped with a flaky puff pastry. I stuck it in the oven with some baked sweet potato halves sprinkled with rosemary and sea salt and drizzled on some fresh lime juice. But then it occurred to me I had too much pastry going on, so decided that for hors d'oeuvres I'd do herb deviled eggs with some local, organic eggs, and a big green salad with roasted pumpkin seeds.

*Ha! Ashton will be sorry for treating me the way he did!*

Once all was tucked into the oven, the concoction basking in its heady aromas, I moseyed down to the dock and sat there contemplating my life and my future. The sound of cicadas and the lapping waves told me how good I had it and what a fool I was to even entertain tearing it all apart. I still felt confused, so torn in two. I wished that Ashton and I could live a perfect life.

That's all I had ever wanted from him from the second I met him: a happily ever after.

But his lies and deceit had made that impossible.

When I got back to the house, the door to the kitchen was unlocked. I knew I had remembered to lock it. The key was in my shorts pocket. Maybe I hadn't locked it and just thought I had. The fear of me getting early Alzheimer's like Georgia-May bubbled up inside me. Sometimes I'd come into a room and couldn't remember what I was looking for. *Why am I here?* I was *sure* I'd locked the door this time, though. Then I heard voices. Cady? What was *she* doing here?

I found her in the kitchen nonchalantly swiveling on the barstool by the kitchen island, nursing a beer. Chatting with Ashton! I couldn't believe it.

"Hi, Cady," I said, glowering at her.

She sat there as if it were the most normal thing in the world. "I got tempted by the amazing smell coming from the oven, and I found Ashton here."

"Mr. Buchanan, you mean." Her gall prickled me all over. Her lack of respect for someone double her age.

"Hi, honey, what you got cookin'?" Ashton said. "Cady and I were sharing a beer."

"She's seventeen, Ashton."

Cady giggled and shot Ashton an almost flirtatious glance. "It's non-alcoholic. Besides, I'm allowed to drink in the presence of grownups, here in South Carolina, didn't you know? That's the rule, as long as I have an adult present and drink in my own home."

*In my own home.*

I couldn't believe her nerve. "In your own *home*?" I echoed.

"It smells so amazing. Ashton's invited me for dinner."

"Has he?" I turned to Ashton, my eyes a pair of darts. "Did you invite Cady for dinner, Ashton?"

"Why not? The girl needs fattening up. Looks like she needs a full square meal."

How had he even noticed that? He had appraised her body, noticed she was thin? I felt a vein throb in my temple.

"I made the meal for *my husband,* Cady. This was not supposed to be a group dinner. Besides, dinner won't appeal to your vegan taste, as I'm cooking chicken pie."

"I can eat those yummy sweet potatoes. And the salad. I'll help set the table," Cady offered, ignoring my remark. "How about that?"

Ashton said, a hint of a smile twitching on his lips, "I thought we could eat in the dining room tonight instead of the kitchen; that sound good?"

It was as if a rug had been ripped from underneath my feet and I had tumbled, or when someone knocks you at the back of your knees and you crumple to the floor. This one hundred and eighty-degree change in Ashton's attitude toward having Cady around flummoxed me. Inviting this teenager into our inner sanctum? I couldn't work him out. I couldn't understand what his game plan was. It was as if he was testing me.

As I prepared the onion tarts and some panna cotta with balsamic raspberries for dessert (too bad, Cady, if you don't eat dairy), another interesting thing occurred to me. Ashton seemed to be in a good mood, smiling, and the taciturn silence I had been used to for the last couple of weeks, ever since the bruise on my eye, was suddenly lifted by Cady's presence. For the first time in my life, I felt competitive. It was crazy! I shocked even myself.

"The flatware's in the bureau in the dining room," I said stonily. "Hey, we might as well go all-out and use the silver candlesticks too."

I was being facetious, but Cady had a big grin on her face, and Ashton didn't say a word. This girl was seventeen and had barged her way into Ashton's house! *Our* house.

Cady, oblivious, was fiddling around with her phone, sending and receiving text messages, no doubt. I wondered what Shakespeare would think if he could jump into a time capsule machine. The young taking to writing like this. The number of messages these kids sent each other could fill great tomes.

I caught Ashton, a tumbler of Scotch in his hand, raking his gaze up and down over Cady again, studying her with fascination. She was wearing tight skinny jeans, but instead of one of her usual baggy T-shirts that swamped her body with some message like GO GREEN OR DIE, she was wearing a crop top that showed a sliver of stomach, lean and pale, including her navel piercing, which sported a little ruby. I noticed she had applied more makeup than usual. Her skin the usual creamy translucence but her eyes laced with thick mascara that made her less Bambi and more baby doll. I didn't like it one bit.

"You're wearing way too much makeup," I hissed at her as we passed each other at the dining room entrance. I opened the bureau and pulled out some plates.

"Whatever," she said, brushing past me with disdain, skipping straight back into the kitchen to be with Ashton, leaving me with the plates. My blood was simmering.

I heard them talking about sharks. Ashton telling her all about his diving excursions. Cady telling him how much she'd love to come along some time.

"Can you please come in here and *help* me, Cady?" I yelled through the door.

"Sure. Be right there." She swaggered into the room, her skinny little hips swinging from side to side as she walked.

"I don't like your attitude, missy," I whispered to her. "This is going too far. You have a perfectly good kitchen of your own next door in that gorgeous cottage. You're really pushing things too far, young lady."

"But Ashton says it's fine."

"I don't care what Ashton says. And by the way, it's *Mr. Buchanan* to you, got it?"

She stuck out her bottom lip. "Soreee. Just going with the flow, you know? Lighten up." She spun around in a circle, swinging her arms. "This house is so swanky, I love the silver candlesticks. I've never had dinner by candlelight before."

"Oh, haven't you," I said. Cady was really pushing her luck. I couldn't believe what a fast worker the girl was. As if this were *her* house. This dinner was supposed to be a private kiss-and-make-up meal between Ashton and me, not a free-for-all!

We set the table in silence. I showed her which way the knives should be set, with the blade pointing inwards toward the plate. Something I had to learn by rote from one of those etiquette books. The dining room was a piece of art in itself. The long Chippendale table in the center of the room, with chairs to match. A bureau, with inlaid cherry wood. French doors with a view to the water. Paintings on the crimson damask wall, of old English hunting scenes—horses and hounds, men in "pink" coats, which weren't pink but red. Not to my taste, but gallery-worthy. Polished silver tea and coffee sets, whose reflections shone in the gleaming dark wood of the furniture. Silver trophies that Ashton had won over the years. Football. Golf.

Personally, I didn't like this room. But it was impressive, if you were into this sort of thing.

"Is this some kind of trick?" I questioned Ashton quietly, back in the kitchen. I got out the salad bowl, ripped the lettuce furiously and chopped up some herbs. I counted to ten under my breath to stop myself lashing out at him. What was he *up* to?

He laughed. "Why would you think it's a trick?" Then he held his eyes with mine, hazel highlights in his irises glittering with mirth. "Takes one to know one, huh?"

My nostrils flared. "What the heck are you talking about?"

"You're the one who invited Cady here. I'd be interested to see where this goes."

"I hadn't imagined she'd barge her way into this house and expect dinner. I didn't expect my husband to invite a seventeen-year-old into our home when she has her own kitchen, in her own guest house. From *my* generosity, I may add."

"Not mine?" he challenged.

*Touché.*

A weighty silence filled the space between us, then I said, "This dinner was meant to be something special for *us* this evening, not a spoiled teenager. The last thing I expected was for her to gatecrash my—"

"It'll be fun," Ashton broke in. "Don't you think? *You* were the one who invited Cady into our life—you've made your bed, honey, so now you can lie in it."

I could feel my eyes sting. I wasn't sure if it was chopping the onions earlier, or tears threatening to brim over.

"Cady?" I shouted for Cady but didn't get an answer. I marched into the hallway, then heard her upstairs in one of the bathrooms. Wow, she was really taking liberties. I raced upstairs and knocked on the door. "Cady? Cady, are you in there?"

"I'll be out in a sec."

I waited for her until she emerged. My hands were shaking. My breathing like a dragon's—invisible steam coming out of me in hot bursts. "You were meant to use the bathroom *downstairs*. Who said you could come up here?"

"Nobody."

"Exactly! Nobody. This is the last time you're coming into this house, do you understand? You'll behave yourself at dinner, and then I never want to see you here again, have I made myself clear?"

"But Ashton invited—"

"Do I make myself clear?" I yelled. I was aware that Ashton could hear me. I wanted him to. "Now get downstairs, and busy yourself in the garden while I have a word with my husband."

"Garden?" she mimicked.

"The backyard. Come back in ten minutes, wash your hands again, and we'll all have dinner together."

Cady bounded down the stairs, jumping three steps at a time, and tore into the kitchen. I heard her go outside. I went downstairs slowly, turning everything over in my mind; everything felt like it was inside out, upside down.

Ashton was standing in the doorway, a smirk on his face. "I warned you not to mix pleasure with work. I told you these kids from Community Promise were from dysfunctional homes."

"Let's just have dinner and get it over with," I snapped.

"Well, it smells incredible." He surveyed me again, cocking his head to one side as if seeing me for the first time. "Was marrying you the greatest thing I ever did? Or the dumbest?"

# CHAPTER EIGHTEEN

Lindy and I met for lunch at the Sea Oats Country Club, the place her husband owned. The dinner that Cady had gatecrashed last week was still rolling over in my mind. The welling feeling of betrayal, the realization that things were beyond my control. Should I share this with Lindy?

The club was a pretty clapboard Colonial surrounded by great swathes of land, a winding driveway leading up to the clubhouse, flanked with magnolias. Some majestic oaks peppered the land. An indoor and outdoor pool, three tennis courts, and, of course, their famous golf course. It screamed "chic," because the place wasn't ostentatious or glitzy, but old-worldly, and you had to be a member. I never forgot how privileged I was to be accepted by places like these. Some people took membership in their stride as if it was their birthright. Me? I had had to earn my place here—I was all too aware.

I had no desire to play tennis today or swim. We had just come for a "ladies' lunch." I hadn't seen Lindy for a couple of weeks, only spoken on the phone. I needed to get out of the house, away from Distant Sands. I wasn't the only one not taking any exercise today. A lot of the women came here to relax. There was a dietitian, a beautician, and a masseuse, amongst other services. Many of these women here were on their lunch breaks, others *were* ladies of leisure or retired, yet the less they worked or had jobs, the busier they often pretended to be. Being a lady of leisure was not me, sadly, despite Ashton's ongoing suggestion that I give up my job.

Lindy and I had nearly collided into each other in the car park. She was reversing her sports car, roof down. It was fall now, but a beautiful, sunny day, the sky a sheer, sharp blue, not a cloud in sight. But the air cool. Lindy wore a silk scarf, 1950s style, her wild red hair tamed beneath. She laughed when she almost reversed into me.

She shouted out the window, "What is it about parking lots that's so dangerous? I swear to God I've had more accidents in parking lots than anywhere else. People drive like lunatics, me included!"

We both got out of our cars and walked into the club, arm in arm, the sweep of verdant lawn fringing the path to the entrance, the roll-perfect golf course stretched beyond us, almost as far as the eye could see. Ashton would often come here to play golf.

"Your eye," Lindy said. "There's no trace of color anymore. All gone."

"Makeup," I said. "The yellow's easy to cover up."

"How are things with Ashton?"

"Good," I lied. "Much better, thanks." I didn't want to go into detail about how Ashton and I had become virtual strangers lately. Like passing ships in the night except, of course, when we were in bed together. Things were civil but quiet, no arguments, no scenes. But I didn't share this with Lindy.

*It's weird*, I thought to myself, as we walked through the main entrance and toward the clubhouse dining room. *That ever since the "accident" to my eye Ashton has completely changed.*

"You think it's going to happen again?" she asked.

"What?" I said.

"Your eye?"

"No."

"You seem very sure about that."

"I am. Nothing like that will happen again," I said, upbeat.

We took a discreet table by the window and both ordered white wine spritzers and the fish special of the day with new potatoes and a dill sauce.

"How are the kids?" I asked.

Lindy unfolded a linen napkin and placed it on her lap. "Fine, but I really don't want to talk about them right now. I feel so housebound at the moment. My life is *very* uninteresting. I'd rather talk about you. What's going on in *your* household? I'm worried about you, honey."

"Well," I said, not sure of how much I should reveal or hide. "You remember Cady? The teenager? The one who moved into the cottage? She's taking liberties, and I realize I might have made a big mistake inviting her to stay."

Lindy sighed as if she knew what was coming. "Why?"

"She and Ashton seem to be kind of hanging out together, when he gets home from work."

"But she's only sixteen!"

"Seventeen now."

"Wow, like that really makes a difference!"

"Ever since she barged in on our dinner last week... well Ashton invited her, so I couldn't say anything. Cady... anyway, she now hangs out with him in the kitchen, you know, they *talk*. They chat about ecology. Saving sharks, in particular. She asked him to help her get a petition together to free sharks and dolphins and orca whales from aquariums. He seemed excited about her being so interested in marine life and environmental issues and told her all about this shark conservationist called Alex Leader whom he donates to. Cady keeps asking Ashton to help her with her homework too. He says he likes her, that she's funny and makes him laugh and feels like they have a good rapport."

"You're kidding me? A good *rapport*? That's crazy."

"I know. I'm not sure what to do."

Lindy was about to take a sip of her spritzer but stopped mid-action. "Wait a minute, I thought you said Cady has a mother who's waiting for Cady to come and join her?"

"Yeah," I said, "that's true. But, oh, things are so complicated... her mom says she's not ready yet. I feel responsible. But I want to get that girl away from Ashton, because I don't trust them together."

Lindy raised an eyebrow. "He lied to you about the Bahamas property, he hit you so hard you got a black eye, and now this. What's the next step? Are you planning to divorce him or not? You *must* go see Silverman, the divorce attorney. Did you call him?"

"Ssh, let's keep our voices down, I don't want anyone to hear you say the D word."

Lindy shook her head. She was disappointed in me, I could tell.

"There's something I want to ask you about," I said, changing the subject.

"Fire away."

"Ashton's sister."

"Yeah, you mentioned that, and I told you I had no idea. I didn't know he had a sister, and I've never heard anything about a suicide, so I'm sorry I can't help you there."

"Did you ask Richard?"

"I did, actually, and you know what Richard's like. He doesn't share much with me, but he did tell me that he didn't know anything about a sister either. You know how it is. When he and Ashton get together all they do is talk about hunting and fishing and sports and shit like that. Man-talk. They never gossip or get personal or ask each other about their wives or anything. They keep it very light. Didn't you ask Ashton yourself?"

"Sure I did. But right now, I don't want to rock the boat."

Lindy shook her head. "Listen, I think you're focusing on Ashton's sister because you don't want to face the real issues, like the state of your marriage and what you're going to do."

"Maybe," I said despondently. "What I need to do first is move Cady out the guest cottage and make sure she never comes back to our house again. I have a weird feeling. Like a premonition. Something bad could happen, I can feel it in my bones."

As I was driving back after lunch, just two miles from home, I spotted Cady and Ashton riding side by side on bicycles. I couldn't believe my eyes. I slowed the car down.

Buzzing the window open, I shouted out, "You know how dangerous it is to be riding side by side like this? No helmets?"

Ashton stopped his bike. Cady pedaled on ahead. He leaned in through the window. "Come on, honey, we're just tootling along, no harm done."

"I want you to stop hanging out with that... that *child*," I hissed at him.

"It's a harmless bike ride. Cady wanted me to show her the neighborhood."

"I bet she did."

He made a face. "You're overreacting, Vivien."

"What am I meant to tell her mother," I said, "if something happens to her? *I* am responsible for that girl."

"No denying that," he said.

"Well then."

"See you back home." He rode off, pedaling like crazy to catch up with Cady.

I overtook them and after I passed, I saw in my rearview mirror how they were hooting with laugher and joking. It even looked as if they were making fun of me.

Back home, I waited for Ashton in the kitchen. I even poured myself a Scotch and swallowed half a tumbler. I waited. And waited. After twenty minutes, he still hadn't arrived. I stumbled outside and found the bikes in the driveway. Where were they?

I checked the guest cottage… nobody. I marched down towards the dock and saw two figures getting into the FlatsMaster. I waved and shouted, but they didn't hear me. By the time I reached the end of the dock, they were well on their way out to sea.

I could feel it in my bones…

This was the tipping point.

# CHAPTER NINETEEN

Mr. Silverman must have been in his early forties. He was one of those men who had lost his youth early in life; a receding hairline followed the slope of his forehead revealing a sun-bronzed patch where his hair was thinning. Yet he was still very attractive and sporty looking. Clean-shaven. He had a friendly smile but got straight down to business. Lindy had told me that he and Ashton disliked each other.

"So, how can I help?" he said, after shaking my hand, his inflection very don't-waste-my-time. "Please do sit down."

I sat down, took off my sunglasses without thinking.

He stared at me. I quickly put my shades back on. The golden remnants of my bruise must have showed through the makeup. He raised his eyebrows as if to say, *Too late… I've got your number.* He said, "Marital problems? Lindy already filled me in."

My mouth hung open, but instead of walking out the door, I sat there stupefied. Lindy's indiscretion was quite something. I wanted to tell this lawyer that I was only here because of pressure from her and my psychotherapist, but that would have made me look ridiculous. What I said instead came out in a garbled rush. "I still love my husband. I mean, I'm not even sure why I'm here. Really, I should go. So sorry, I shouldn't have come, I'm not ready for this." I got up, but he motioned me to stay sitting.

"You don't have to explain, Mrs. Buchanan." He furrowed his forehead, eased himself down but then stood up again and paced around the room. There were family photos on his desk in big silver frames: a happy man himself, by the looks of the pictures of him kissing his wife. Yet he was embroiled in this messy business of divorce. His bread and butter. I supposed he was able to feel impartial. Photos of him playing golf, scuba diving, a beach vacation with a kid on either arm. Twin boys. By the way Mr. Silverman was striding around, chin in hand, he looked like the type to have a lot of excess energy he didn't know how to expend. But no bitterness, no axe to grind. Just a friendly guy who knew his business, which happened to be tearing families apart.

He suddenly swiveled on his heel and said, "So, Mrs. Buchanan, you've only been married for six months?"

"Please call me Vivien," I said. "Yes, just six months." Lindy had obviously told him everything.

"What's your goal here?" he asked. "Divorce, I assume?"

"No, no. Not at all. I guess... I felt... I mean... Lindy said I should meet you, but the truth is, this is far too—"

"In terms of your husband's financial assets, if you were to divorce, how would you like to leave this marriage?"

His question dumbfounded me. He was so direct. Brash. No small talk. No warm-up with a nice, civilized conversation. I sat there, my stomach fluttering with nerves.

"Hypothetically speaking," he clarified. "I don't want to push you in any particular direction, but it's always useful to know where you stand in a marriage, right?"

"I guess so."

"Do you have any questions?"

I fumbled with my hands.

"Anything you'd like to share?"

Silence. I filled the awkward gap with, "Well, I discovered Ashton has been hiding his assets from me. It's more a feeling of betrayal and him not trusting me that's been so... surprising. And, to be honest, hurtful too."

"Can you tell me about these assets?"

"Well, I don't know if I should."

"Money? Houses? Stocks?"

I looked around the room awkwardly; I felt pinned by his eyes. He wanted an answer. I finally said, "A house in Harbour Island, in the Bahamas."

"Do you know its net worth?"

"Well, on the deeds it said Ashton had paid 3.8 million. I have no idea what it might be worth now. I guess it's none of my business really."

"Is there money too, that you didn't know about? Savings? Offshore accounts? Shell companies?"

"Yes, that too. I don't have a well-paying job. I mean, I work for a charity, so I volunteer. I do it for the love of it, not for the money, but—"

"That's good. That looks very good." He nodded, his lips lifting a touch at what I'd said.

"Why?" I inquired, feeling betrayal etched on my face, my lips.

"Because it shows you're not after his money, that you married him because you loved him, right?" He drilled his gaze into me, and I felt extremely uncomfortable. I guessed this was what divorce attorneys were like. They got straight to the point and wanted to zero in on the truth.

"I've always been in love with Ashton."

"But you say he's violent with you?"

I lowered my eyes away from Silverman's intense gaze. "I didn't say that. I didn't say that at all."

He inhaled a sharp breath. "Mrs. Buc— Vivien. Did you go to a doctor and get that examined?"

I looked up at him and shook my head. "No, I didn't even consider doing that."

Mr. Silverman puckered his brow again. "Does your husband have any idea you're seeing me today?"

"No, none at all. I feel like I'm betraying him by seeing you. Going behind his back."

He gave me a sly smile. "Many women feel that way at first. I have a ninety percent success rate with my clients. Usually, we settle out of court, because the other party doesn't want to be exposed in any way."

"Exposed?"

"Usually somebody's hiding something, don't you think?"

I shrugged.

"Tell me what it is, Vivien, that you would like, that would make you feel comfortable and also vindicated. How would you like to leave this marriage, in practical terms?"

"I don't know. I hadn't thought that far ahead. I'm still not even sure I want to leave my husband."

"If you *were* to leave him, what would you consider fair in terms of his—*your*—assets as a married couple?"

"I feel that... well..." I couldn't finish my sentence.

"Hypothetically speaking, if you were to get a divorce."

"I don't know if taking anything would be fair? If I came away with a place to live... that is if... do you think that would be very greedy?"

"If I thought my clients were greedy, I wouldn't be a divorce lawyer. Most of my clients are women, and I have a great reputation for helping them get what they want. Okay? Please don't judge yourself or self-monitor your wishes and desires. I think I have an idea of what you want and what you need. Leave it with me. I'm sure we can come to a fair arrangement with your husband without having to go to court. Does that sound good?"

"But I don't feel it's right to ask for anything right now. I just thought I'd come and see you, but please don't put anything into motion."

"O-kaaay?" he said slowly, with an upward inflection.

"I just wanted to touch base, you know. But please don't do anything."

But Mr. Silverman steamed on ahead with his lawyer talk. "In South Carolina, there're five grounds for divorce, only one of them is no-fault... you know, irreconcilable differences? The other four grounds are adultery, desertion for one year, physical cruelty, and habitual drunkenness. Because you've been married for less than a year, and with a no-fault based divorce you need to be separated for at least a year before you file, well, that makes it complicated. Never mind, I'm sure we can get around that problem if divorce is what you're after."

A tear rolled down my cheek and I took off my shades to wipe it away.

He squinted at me as if assessing my face. "May I ask you a personal question?" he said.

"Sure." I moved my hand to my lips. It was trembling.

"Are you willing to try and work things out with your husband?"

"I've always wanted to work things out with Ashton. He's the only man I've ever loved."

He nodded. "Well, you've got my number so when you're ready, give me a call."

# CHAPTER TWENTY

The next day, something bad, as I had predicted to Lindy, did happen. Something very bad.

I had a charity benefit event to go to, and Ashton and Cady didn't get back from their boat ride until after sunset. I didn't have time for a huge great argument.

"Why didn't you let me know about the benefit sooner?" Ashton demanded, still in his shorts, his hair wet from a swim.

I stood there in a chic black dress and pearls, scowling at him. "I did. I told you about this event a couple of weeks ago. I can't believe you took Cady out on the boat like that when you *knew* we were going out!"

"Vivien, no, you did *not* tell me about this benefit, I would've remembered."

"Ashton, I did!" I wanted to add, *Are you gaslighting me?* But I thought that was pushing it. I simply added, "All the other Community Promise spouses are going. I can't believe you've let me down like this."

Ashton groaned. "Okay, have it your way, I give up."

"I have to get going. There's some leftover oyster casserole and peach cobbler in the fridge. All you have to do is heat them up. I'll be back around eleven."

But at ten-thirty p.m. I got a hysterical text from Cady. I rushed home from the benefit. When I got back, this is what I saw in our living room:

Ashton passed out on the sofa in his boxer briefs, two empty bottles of champagne in ice buckets sitting on one of the priceless mahogany side tables (no coasters, no mat!), an empty bottle of Highland Scotch. Ashton reeking of alcohol. Cady with mascara trails streaming down her cheeks, crying.

It was as if I were floating above a film set. It was surreal. Not happening. But it was happening, here, in the middle of my marriage. Everything had been fine until Cady arrived in Beaufort. I had been happy. Confused. Hurt. Feeling betrayed, but still. My marriage had been mine.

"He groped me!" she screamed. "Your husband, Ashton! You need to film this. Film the evidence!"

Ashton lay there, snoring. Oblivious. I sat beside him on the sofa, but it was hopeless. He was conked out. I was in a daze, wondering how all this had happened at breakneck speed.

"You need to film this," Cady said again. "Go on, what are you waiting for?"

I swiveled my gaze from Ashton to Cady. "What were you doing here, Cady? Ashton knew I didn't want you to come to the main house."

I took out my cell phone and filmed him, the surroundings, Cady in hysterics, almost as if another character had taken me over. I would confront him about this.

"Film me," Cady said. "And I'll tell you what happened."

"What?"

"Film me with your phone, duh!"

"Okay." My voice was a croaky whisper, reverberating in my throat. I reluctantly pointed my phone at her, my hands trembling. This was actually happening. I felt like I had driven into some cul-de-sac and was trapped.

Cady lifted her chin. "Around seven p.m. Mr. Buchanan, who'd told me to call him Ashton, called me on my phone."

"You'd given him your *number*?" I sounded accusatory. But with my job potentially on the line, the last thing I wanted was to be held responsible myself for this mess. I was the one who had organized for Cady to live in the guest cottage. I couldn't have people blaming me.

"No. I mean, I had texted him," she clarified. "There was a problem with the plumbing. A leak. I was worried about flooding. I was in the guest cottage, watching TV when he called back."

"A leak? Really? And what did he say?"

"He asked me what was wrong, but by that time, I'd already fixed the leak."

"How did you know how to fix a leak?"

"I found a spanner in the garage. Watched a YouTube tutorial."

*Really?* "So then what?" I asked. "How did it lead to this?" My phone was wobbling all over the place as I filmed. I steadied one hand with the other.

"He asked me if I'd eaten. I said I hadn't. He told me he had extra food he was heating up. I was hungry so I went over. He'd always seemed so nice, such a gentleman before."

"Did you know I was *out*?" Again, it sounded like I was blaming her. Maybe I was.

"No, I thought you'd be home too."

"And what happened?" I asked, my tone kinder, my phone still recording her.

"He offered me champagne."

"And why didn't you say no?"

Cady's face clouded. "He kind of insisted. Told me it was fine. I trusted him."

"You realize that even when an adult offers you alcohol in their own home, it's illegal if you're under the age of eighteen? For both parties? In the state of South Carolina, anyway."

Her mouth quivered and a fresh bout of tears gushed from her eyes. "I had no idea," she wept. "I thought if an adult in their own home…"

I stopped filming. What I was doing looked ruthless. I rushed over to her and gave her the biggest hug. "I'm so sorry."

She wriggled out from underneath my embrace and shook me free. "It's okay," she said, through sniffles, wiping her wet face with her sleeve, a little more composed. "You can film me again."

I fiddled with the phone, my fingers fumbling so much, it tumbled to the floor.

"I'll do it," Cady said, irritated, bending down to pick it up.

She did a panoramic scan of the living room, focusing on Ashton, still passed out on the dark green velvet couch, a mop of hair flopped over one eye, the opulent chandelier overhead highlighting the coppery tones that I hadn't even noticed before. Things that I did not know about Ashton, right here before me, lighted up in front of my eyes. It was incongruous: Ashton disheveled, in his fancy museum-like home. My normally handsome husband did not look like himself. I had never seen him passed out like this. Food stains were smeared all over his T-shirt. Cady turned the camera onto me.

"Speak," she said. "Speak to the camera."

I swallowed. My voice was shaky and thin. "I've just arrived home from a benefit for Community Promise—where I work—to find my husband passed out, inebriated, with empty bottles of champagne and an empty bottle of Scotch. For the record, I am not responsible for any of this. I do not want to be held accountable at a future date for what happened to a minor." I stared at Ashton and mumbled under my breath, "Ashton, how could you? How could you do this to an underage girl? To an innocent… child? To us? To our marriage?"

Cady stopped recording. I stood there, shaking.

What was I meant to do at this point? Call the police? My lips trembled as I tried to suppress my tears. Things were beyond my control.

"Am I meant to call the cops?" I said this almost to myself, dumbfounded.

"No! I don't want you calling the cops," Cady yelled, hugging my phone to her chest, terror alight in her eyes.

"Why not? I mean this was—"

"Because! Because it's too shameful for him. Nothing actually *happened*."

"But this picture paints a thousand words. I'm confused, I…"

"Exactly." Her tone was calmer now. "We have evidence if we need it. But if we call the cops? They'll put him in jail."

"But—"

"Leave the poor guy alone, all right? He didn't *do* anything! And if you call the cops?" Her stare was icy. "I'll deny everything."

I sat down quietly on the sofa, next to my snoring husband. Goosebumps on my neck, my heart racing, I didn't know what to do next. Cady's sudden change of heart was extraordinary. How could anyone flip on a decision so quickly? Was this normal behavior? Even as a teen my mind didn't work that way. Full speed ahead and then screeching to a skidding halt. One minute accusing Ashton of groping her, the next saying he hadn't done anything? She'd be capable, I thought, of changing her mind back again, surely? So mercurial. So unpredictable. *Unstable*. The idea that Cady was crazy flashed through my mind, but I pushed it away. I wished this whole scenario away.

My brain was sieving through all the possibilities. What would happen if Cady pressed charges? Even if this went to court and was thrown out the window by a judge for lack of evidence, with today's Me Too movement the papers wouldn't care. And if either of us called the police, the police themselves might press charges, whatever Cady decided to do. It would be out of our hands. This was a minor we were talking about. But in the end, it was Cady's call, not mine.

"Okay," I said, in a tiny voice. "I need to give this some serious thought. Mull this over."

Cady stood there, arms crossed defensively over her bony chest, my phone still clutched in one hand. "It's on film, on your phone. I need to think about this, need to think of the consequences. I really don't want to be a grope-victim poster child. Plus, Ashton's an important surgeon," she said. "If this gets out? He's screwed. For *life*. I'd be taking his career away from him. He wouldn't be able to work anymore. Did you think of that?"

I looked at my husband almost with pity. I expected him to stir, but he was still dead to the world, his muscular legs splayed open in a very unflattering and uncompromising pose. I shook him. Nothing, just grunts. I grabbed my phone out of Cady's hand and took a few snaps for good measure. Taking photos prompted a round of fresh wailing from Cady. Ashton didn't stir despite the commotion.

She dropped to her knees and clutched the hem of my silk dress like a child—more ragged sobs. "Please, *please* don't call the cops, *please*."

My heart went out to her. "Okay, I promise, I won't call the cops."

My gaze landed back on my husband. I took in the scene anew. Marrying this man had gotten me into a real mess. Whatever step I took next affected all three of us.

# CHAPTER TWENTY-ONE

"Today I'm going to tell you the truth," I told Dr. Becker.

I had her attention. She fixed her bewildered gaze on me.

I listened to my own voice as it rushed on in a waterfall of confession unable to stop itself. "I've been lying to you, Dr. Becker, and I'd finally like to set things straight."

"At what point have you been lying to me?" Her eyes were on me, clouded by betrayal.

"From the beginning. About who I am. About pretty much everything. I'm sorry."

"Oh,' she said. "I see."

"May I lie on the couch today?" The word "lie" grated in my ears. It was ironic, considering this time I would *not* be lying. For once.

"Sure. Sure, you can stretch out on the couch. Would you like some water?"

"Yeah, actually, that would be great."

She leaned down, and by the side of her desk seemed to be a mini fridge, which I had never noticed before, because she pulled out a drink from this secret place. She handed me a cold demi-bottle of mineral water. And a box of tissues. I gratefully took the bottle.

"Go and get comfortable on the couch, then," she said.

I did as she instructed, slipped off my shoes and lay down on the couch. There was a blanket on the arm and a large pillow, so I laid the blanket over my knees. She didn't have the air conditioner on, but something told me that the story I was about to tell her would send a chill through my body. Because, for once, I'd be telling it from the heart. For once, it would be real.

"One thing I need to clear up first. Do you take patient confidentiality seriously?"

"Of course I do," she replied, her tone offended.

"Even if what someone tells you is terrible?"

"Did you murder someone, Vivien?"

"No, the opposite. I saved a life."

"Did you hurt someone irrevocably?"

"Not in a physical way," I answered. It was true, I had not hurt anyone in a physical way, but I was aware of the damage I had done, and I knew I would never be forgiven. But I couldn't help but believe in an eye for an eye and a tooth for a tooth. Was that Shakespeare? Who had said that? I had no idea, but I'd heard that expression when I was a little girl and I liked it and had held it close. Gandhi had contradicted it, saying that *an eye for an eye makes the whole world blind.* I'd take my chances.

I cleared my throat. "When I tell you this, you're going to hate me and wish I'd never walked into this room."

She didn't respond and let silence stand between us for good couple of minutes. I knew she would be disgusted by me. I had let my lies trip off my tongue over the last six months, half believing the stories myself. But I couldn't bear it any longer. I needed to let the truth out. In some weird way I had grown to love her. She was the only person who seemed to care about me for the person I was inside. Would all that change now? Ashton didn't begin to know who I really was. He had come to love an image, a pretty shell, the way you pick up a beautiful shell on the beach and admire it and maybe even put it to your ear to hear it, to listen to the sound of the ocean rumbling back at you. An ocean that is only there in your imagination.

He didn't have a clue who I was.

"Take your time," Dr. Becker said. "Today a client canceled her appointment, so you're in luck. We can make this a double session if you choose to."

"Please don't hate me." I sounded like a needy child.

"If I hated my clients then I wouldn't be doing this job, would I?"

She was careful to always say the word "clients," not "patients." I appreciated that professional touch. It made me feel like a less sick human being.

"You're brave, Vivien, to be coming here every week, to bare your soul to me. Every story has its merit—its validity—even if it's a lie."

"Thank you," I said. "I appreciate your generosity. But I feel badly that I've wasted your time with my made-up stories."

"Sometimes it takes many months, even years to arrive at the truth. That's why I'm here. To help unpeel the layers. We all have our layers, Vivien. I often think of us like onions—excuse the rather odd analogy—with crispy, inedible outer skins that need to be peeled away, sometimes several layers deep, but what's inside is healthy and the main ingredient for some of the most creative and delicious cuisine in the world. Please don't judge yourself. What counts is that you're here and you're willing to share and willing to persevere. Take your time to get settled. I'm not going anywhere."

I stretched out my legs, contemplating her rather bizarre onion analogy, curling the blanket around my toes with my feet. I closed my eyes, inhaled and exhaled. There was no point prolonging this anymore. What I was about to do was risky, I knew. But I had to share. I took one more deep breath. Exhaled. Another breath, then let out a long groan. Finally, I was ready.

"Once upon a time," I began, "there was a little girl from Baltimore. She lived in a really poor neighborhood with her parents. Her dad was an alcoholic, and her mother a nervous wreck. But her mother refused to leave her husband and let him reign in their slummy, cramped apartment that was tumbling down around them. It was filthy. There was mold growing everywhere. Sticky oily grime from her mother's cooking, and from her father's cigarettes and her mother's cigarettes and everybody else's cigarettes when they paid a visit. The place smelled of boiled cabbage and ashtrays. They were Catholic, this family, and they didn't believe in contraception. So this washed-out, cigarette-coughing couple had kids, but the children kept dying. Dying in her womb. Or they were stillborn or something would go wrong. One of them made it, though: a girl. A girl called Maeve. Maeve O'Reilly. She was a bony, spindly little thing but she had a heart of gold and she wanted to please her parents. Her surroundings, she thought—as all children do until they see the light—were normal. She assumed it was normal that her father beat her mother pretty much every day. She thought it was normal that he wet the bed when he got too drunk, and her mother had to wash the sheets and hang them to dry in the kitchen, because the dryer in the apartment building was always broken, and the little girl thought it normal that her dad spent all his wages on horse bets or at the local bar, where he lorded it with his friends and told jokes and everybody thought he was a great guy. The men, at least. Few women went to that dirty bar.

"Maeve's mother didn't have any guts. She was a coward and cringed like an abused animal. She lowered her eyes and she didn't take care of herself. Stringy hair. Fluffy slippers, even when she went shopping. Maeve thought her mother was ugly, which is sad because actually, she wasn't ugly, but Maeve didn't realize this growing up as a child because her mom felt so bad about herself and passed this fear of herself and hatred of herself onto Maeve. But Maeve felt it too, felt it in her bones, in the very marrow of her, that her mother was a sad woman who had nothing to offer the world. Her mom worked at the local factory, took the bus there every day and when she came home, she made dinner, lugging the groceries up the stairs, the heavy plastic bags cutting into her pale bony wrists. She was always tired. She was gray in the face, and her eyes were hollow and lonely.

"The dad worked down at the docks. He was a big man and strong with a red face, because all the blood vessels in his cheeks had popped. Drink can do that to a man. The dad would complain about 'the bitch's' meals. That's what he called her. 'The bitch.' Sometimes he smashed the plate of food to the floor, once even stabbed his wife in the arm with a fork when he said the meat was overcooked. The little girl never said a word. She had tried on occasion to help her mom, but it never worked out well, and strangely enough it made her mother angry. Maeve spent more and more time in her bedroom.

"The local school she went to was not the greatest school in the world. It was dangerous; some of the kids had guns. Some of the girls would get pregnant when they were fifteen or even thirteen. But Maeve took an interest in her classes and worked hard, and there were a couple of teachers there who helped her. The kind of women who sacrifice their lives for others, who see good in the world even when there isn't any. Mrs. Lawson would give her books to read. Maeve devoured these books. Then she started getting books from the library and snuck them home. Once—and she never made the mistake of doing it again—her dad found these books in her bedroom. It made him livid. Blood vessels popped like popcorn on his face as he yelled, hurling half the things in her room, including ornaments and all her treasures, out the window onto the street, where they rotted in the rain, because he wouldn't let her outside to retrieve the only riches she had in the world.

"All Maeve could think about was leaving home. She tried to run away once, but because she was so small and skinny and obviously a child, a police officer found her and brought her back home to her parents. Her dad was so angry he beat her. But Maeve wasn't a fool, she knew what life on the streets was like. There were gangs and men who could hurt her. She'd seen prostitutes in tiny little skirts freezing in winter. She'd seen their arms and their pitiful begging, crack-hollow eyes. She did not want to be one of them, she did not want to be one of the statistics. So she stayed in her room and read after school, and studied, knowing that studying was her ticket out of the hellhole where was she was being raised."

I stopped talking and chugged down the rest of the mineral water, my throat parched and dry. Tears wanted to spill from my eyes but none came, because this story had made me rigid with strength. Tears would not save me, they never had, they never would. Life can do that to you sometimes. It can make you stop crying.

"Go on," Dr. Becker urged.

"Maeve studied hard in her room. Kept out of her father's way. All he cared about was watching sports on TV and drinking down at the bar and wolfing down his wife's food, or throwing it on the floor if it wasn't perfect, screaming at her, belittling her. It was as if he had forgotten he had a daughter at all. Everything was fine till Maeve turned sixteen. The skinny little girl began to blossom. She had breasts. She wasn't curvy, but enough to attract his attention. She wore a little makeup to school to make something of herself. She was okay looking, though Maeve hadn't really thought about her looks, one way or the other. It was *study* that concerned her and studying and reading that allowed her to escape into another world. But her father started pawing at her, his rancid breath, the rotten smell of his teeth, the filth of his greasy hair, which he combed over his bald patches. Maeve was disgusted by him. She didn't care that he was her dad, she wanted him dead. She wasn't like her mother; she wasn't a coward. She threatened her father with the same fork he stabbed her mother with. 'If you ever touch me, if you ever come near me, I will kill you. I will kill you in your sleep, I will kill you when you're sitting there dozed off and watching TV. I swear I'll do it. This is a promise, this is not a threat,' she told him. From then on, he left her alone.

"Maeve was still a virgin; he had not managed to sully her or take that away from her. But she was ashamed of him, and she was ashamed of her mother, and all she could think about was leaving home. She stayed out of the house as much as possible. She had a job delivering pizzas and promised herself she would save up as much money as possible and get the hell out of that cockroach-infested apartment. She vowed she would change her name legally, leave home and never ever come back. She had no love for her father, no respect for her mother and she knew the woman would never leave her husband. It made Maeve sad, but that was the way it was and she had given up a long time ago trying to understand her mom, trying to work out what made her mind tick. Maeve had to look out for herself. Maeve was an island. Sure, she had friends at school, but no one really understood her, and she was too proud to seek outside help.

"The first time Maeve saw him was when she delivered the pizza. She didn't know her way around the campus of this university, she had never been there before. She was pretty new to the job. She had a pile of four pizzas and tears in her eyes 'cause the pies were getting cold and it was winter and she was lost in the maze of the university campus. She finally found the right door and knocked. It sounded like there was a party going on inside: a bunch of guys watching TV, a football match, she thought—shouting and laughing. The door swung open and a guy in glasses opened the door. He was standing there, a furious scowl on his face and said, 'For fuck's sake, you call this delivery? You're twenty minutes late!'

"All I could hear was complaints, but I was shy and new to the job, so I said nothing. But then a boy came out and my heart beat as fast as it had ever beaten. But in a good way. He strode up to me and said, 'Just ignore this bunch of hooligans, it's not your fault.' Then I replied in a quiet voice, 'I'm sorry, I'm new, and this is the first time I've come to this campus.' He looked me in the eye, a kind smile, and said again, 'Hey, it's not your fault. How much do we owe you?' He paid for the pizzas and gave me a ten-dollar tip, which he surreptitiously tucked into my coat pocket. He said, 'Take this,' and I replied, 'It's too much, I don't have any change,' and he said, 'I'm not asking for change.' He smiled at me and I smiled back. I swear to God, it was like I fell in love with that man—that boy—in that very second. He was different from any boy I'd ever seen. His accent, the way he was dressed, everything about him seemed exotic to me.

"From then on, I delivered pizza a couple more times to the same dorm, but it was always one of his friends who answered, never him. I prayed *he* would answer the door, always prayed that *he* would be there. He never was. The boys began to ask my boss for me in particular to do the delivery, because by now I knew the dorm by rote and could get them the pizzas quicker. Then one day, the boy answered the door again. This time, the room was really rowdy, and I wasn't delivering just a few pies, but fifteen. He staggered to the door, drunk. I teetered with the weight of the pile in my arms, but still, I had arrived on time."

I stopped talking. And listened to see if Dr. Becker was reacting. The room was silent. I smuggled a glance from the corner of my eye, and she was sitting there patiently waiting for me to resume talking. I realized something: I had veered into the first-person narrative. I was no longer taking about Maeve, but "I," because that's how I felt, like I was reliving it, reliving this all over again, and the emotions inside me had begun to bubble to the surface.

"Carry on," Dr. Becker said. "I'm listening, I'm here."

Her gentle words prompted me to settle back and divulge the rest. "Well, there he was again, wearing a nicely tailored sports jacket, polite, even though tipsy. Something about him was just different from everybody I had seen before. Ever since that first time we'd met, I had made a huge effort with myself, always hoping he would answer the door. I wore makeup. A tight top that showed my cleavage, enhanced with a push-up bra. Lip gloss. I did everything to make myself attractive. He looked at me curiously, and he caught the plea in my eyes, I guess. My hope. My beg for recognition, for approval. One of his friends paid me, tipping me badly, and the boy said, 'Hey that's no way to tip a lady.' A lopsided, cute grin spread across his face and reached his dark brown eyes. His thick wavy hair flopped over half his face. He was so good looking.

"'I've got some money in my car,' he said, 'How about you come with me? I'll escort you down, and let me give you a better tip.'

"'Thanks,' I said, 'that would be great.' I told him about myself as we walked to his car. It all came blurting out about my family, how poor we were, how I was saving to get away, how I had my final exams that summer in high school. I thought he'd be impressed by my grades. He was. He showed an interest in my life, awestruck, almost, that I lived in such a poor, dangerous neighborhood. He told me he'd heard it was crazy rough there, and that what I was doing was very cool and that he too worked really hard to get good grades. Anyway, we got to his car. It was a Honda, I remember. Silver. With a dent on the back fender with a bumper sticker that read MAGIC HAPPENS. I loved that. And I imagined how I would have my own car too, one day, and how I'd buy one as soon as I'd saved the money and just drive away and have the same MAGIC HAPPENS bumper sticker. Go west, maybe. California. Somewhere far, far away. And I'd never look back.

"The boy opened the door and said, 'Hey, you wanna chat a while?' We talked for over an hour. About school. About where he was from. About my dreams for the future.

"A week later, this happened again. I delivered the pizzas, and he invited me to his car to talk. It felt like we had really connected. My heart was pattering a thousand miles an hour. He talked about stuff we'd do together. Go to the movies, for rides in his car. Eat at restaurants—he'd treat me, he said. He told me he'd help me apply to college. Even quiz me so I'd score high in my SATs. I imagined a real future with him. My first boyfriend! His accent was slow and dreamy, languid and lazy. Then, on this second time, we kissed. Not for long because of my braces—the elastic bands kind of got in the way. I felt ashamed so I kissed his cheek instead. It was smooth, not like the other guys with acne. The planes of his face made shadows. There was soft stubble on his chin. He smelled of soap. He smelled clean.

"Then he put the passenger seat down so it was almost horizontal, and I let him take off my top and allowed his smooth hand—he had clean nails—to feel my breasts and unbutton my jeans, and for some reason I linked all this with my ticket to freedom. It was his car. It was the fact that he went to this expensive school but he was choosing to hang out with me. It was because he was paying me so much attention, that I let him touch me anywhere he wanted.

"He fumbled in his jacket and took a condom foil from his wallet. It was dark. He handed it to me and said, 'Deal with this, will you?' His demand surprised me. I had never done this before. But then it all felt so special, and I decided in that moment that I would let him be my first. I told him as much, that I was a virgin. 'It's okay,' he encouraged, 'I'll be really gentle, I promise. Each time will get easier.' *Each time.* We'd do this again. Because we'd be dating.

"It took a while before I understood the only way to rip that silver packet open was to do it with my teeth. I was a real grownup for the first time in my life. 'Put it on me,' he instructed. I felt like I couldn't deny him, and because I'd assumed we'd start dating seriously, that we'd be a couple, I didn't see a problem.

"I battled with the condom, my long nails getting in the way of each other, in the way of the slithery, slippery rubber. My nails were false. My one extravagance. My acrylic lilac nails with diamanté tips combatted with this condom, determined not to let it escape to the floor of the car and prove how naïve I was. I unrolled it onto his enormous girth, the likes of which I had never seen before. It terrified me. It excited me. I felt emancipated but threatened too.

"I let him get on top of me. Opened my legs. All in silence. He pressed himself inside me and it hurt like crazy. It lasted less time than me drinking this half bottle of mineral water. It was over so fast it didn't seem like anything had happened at all, and I remember thinking it was like that song: *Is that all there is? Is that all there is?* It was so easy and it was so nothing, yet it was everything, also. I was concentrating on his hair, his beautiful thick hair, and his breath on my face even though he smelled of beer and Juicy Fruit. That's what I remember, that he tasted of Juicy Fruit. And then he laughed and he dug in his pocket and gave me money, saying it was a tip for the pizza—a twenty-dollar bill—but it felt like he was paying me for what had just happened, and it was so weird, and I was elated and disgusted and happy and sad and then that was that."

Dr. Becker cleared her throat. I had almost forgotten she was there. "And then what happened?"

"I gave him my phone number, but he didn't call. I was miserable, could think of nothing but him. All that stuff he'd promised about going to the movies and hanging out together? It began to dawn on me he had lied to get into my panties. There were no more pizza deliveries to that dorm. I never saw his car again even though I looked for it. Several months later, I realized I hadn't gotten my period in a while. I took a home pregnancy test. It was positive. I took two more. Both positive. I didn't go to the doctor because I didn't want the family doctor to know. Didn't want him telling my parents. I thought I'd have a miscarriage the way my mother had always had miscarriages. I didn't understand how I'd gotten pregnant in the first place, but then I looked it up and I read that fifteen women out of every hundred get pregnant with a condom. Then I wondered if my long fake nails had somehow nicked it and made a hole. I kept waiting for the miscarriage, but it didn't come. I got bigger and bigger, although I managed to hide my pregnancy with baggy sweaters. When it got closer to the time, I considered giving the baby up for adoption."

"Did you ever think of having an abortion at any point, Vivien?" Dr. Becker's voice surprised me, popping up from nowhere. "You were so young," she said, her voice sounding faraway.

My heart plummeted, remembering how emotional I had been at the time. The hormones. The tiny being inside me. Mini kicks. The vomiting. The aching love I had for the person within. "No," I told Dr. Becker. "Because by the time I realized I was pregnant, it was too late. I was four, maybe five months. I couldn't have brought myself to do it, anyway. It would've felt like murder. I mean, don't get me wrong, I was pro-choice and still am. I believe in a woman's right to do what she wants with her own body. It wasn't a religious thing, although, I guess, *Once a Catholic always a Catholic*, right? But I don't think it was that. I loved what was inside me. It was *his* child growing like a seed, and I felt all the possibilities created from this beautiful guy with beautiful eyes, who was clever because he was at this brilliant school and what was inside me was special and blessed and magical and I didn't want to break the spell. And I knew it was a girl already, even though I didn't do a gender test. The girl inside, the girl within, was more than just a living being, she was already a part of my soul."

I readjusted my position on the couch and threw a glance over my shoulder at Dr. Becker. Her expression was pained. She had taken off her glasses and was rubbing her eyes. Tiredness or tearful empathy, I couldn't make out. She was probably too professional to shed a tear.

"Please go on, Vivien."

I laid my head back down on the pillow and stretched my arms above my head. "I was still delivering pizzas. I needed the money. I guess it was stupid that I was fantasizing about this boy being my boyfriend. But I did dream about how we would live together and have this baby together. And then I guess I must've been, like, five and a half months pregnant, and I can't remember how I found his phone number, but I did, and I called him. No, I didn't call him, that's right, I sent him a text saying we needed to meet up. It felt crazy saying I was the 'pizza girl.' At first, he ignored me. Ignored the message, and then I sent him three more texts. Finally, he phoned and asked, 'Who the hell is this?' I told him, 'It's Maeve, the pizza delivery girl, remember we spent that night together?' 'The *night*?' he said. He couldn't remember. 'In the car?' I prompted. He laughed and said, 'If I had a dollar for every girl I fucked in my car, I'd be a rich man.'

"I felt like I'd fallen from a skyscraper and landed with a splat on the sidewalk. This wasn't the boy I had fantasized about. I had believed I was special. The only one. Even when he hadn't reached out in all that time. I had built up this big relationship in my mind. I persevered. I told him I needed to see him, that it was urgent. And then he said to me—when I prompted him more and told him about how I had delivered the pizza and we had gone down to the car to talk—he said, 'Oh yeah, I do remember you. You're the nose, right? The girl with the nose?'

"The *nose*? He could've remembered me as 'the virgin,' the girl who'd gotten straight As, but no, all I had been was a 'nose' to him. That was all he remembered about me. I could tell he'd been drinking. I was talking to a drunk man, but I told him anyway. I blurted out, 'I'm pregnant and I'm going to keep the baby.'

"He flipped out, of course, telling me that there was no way, that it was impossible, that it couldn't happen, that I couldn't fuck up his life, and he'd pay for an abortion, he'd give me all the money I wanted to have an abortion and we needed to meet and there was no way he could have that baby. He was *determined* I should not have my baby, yelling at me as if his life depended on it. 'I wouldn't even *date* poor white trash like you, let alone have her baby,' he said.

"His words were worse than any physical blow I'd ever had. I pretended I'd been kidding, that I'd made it all up. He was furious, said I was 'a sick human being' to make that kind of joke and to stay away from him, that he'd call the police and put a restraining order on me if I ever got close. I stopped working for the pizza company after that. It was safer to never see him again. I changed my phone. Changed the number. It was just an old flip phone anyway."

"And the baby now?" Dr. Becker asked.

"The baby is now seventeen years old. Her name is Cady."

# CHAPTER TWENTY-TWO

As I drove away from my therapy session with Dr. Becker, I felt a little lighter but asked myself why I had let so much flood out all at once. I rewound my life up until now. The decisions I'd made, the path I'd taken. Some people might have considered me crazy, but I felt justified. All my actions were the results of someone else's cruel behavior. All I wanted to do was even the score.

Originally, I had planned to have Dr. Becker as one of my witnesses. For her to see me with the black eye, to testify against Ashton on my behalf if I needed to go to court. But now she knew too much. And maybe even deduced who the father was too. She was my genuine confidant. My friend, in a way. I had to share my pain with somebody about my past. Not that I'd told her everything. Lord, no. She was too good a person to be privy to all the nitty-gritty—all my plots and schemes. She'd be horrified by my deeds.

I thought about the options I'd had back then. Not so many. Nowadays they have special support programs to help pregnant students. On-campus childcare, scholarships and child-friendly resources. There are grants. Back then it was a lot harder. Fine if you had wealthy parents who could help out, or if you had guaranteed means to pay back a big loan in the future. I had the grades, I even had a place at college, but I was a poor, ignorant seventeen-year-old, pregnant and scared as hell. I was forced to make a choice. I ended up forgoing my place at university, getting out of my parents' house before I gave birth—they never even knew—and I found a job to support my child. I put "father unknown" on my baby's birth certificate, changed my name legally the second I was an adult, and started afresh.

But one thing was certain:

Ashton Buchanan had ruined my life.

And all I had thought about was getting even. Make him pay for his sins.

So here I was now. Married to Ashton Buchanan. It had taken me a long time to get here. Thousands of hours of strategizing my sweet revenge.

Ashton had never hit me. Never pinched me. Nor belittled me during our marriage. Nor whispered mean things in my ear. What he had actually said at that dinner table—after that flippant comment June had made about my dead parents (faux parents, but still) was, "Ignore her, honey. I love you." My tears were real because all he'd been was kind to me, and I was still as attached to my revenge as a soldier is to her parachute. Ashton had not done the things that I was now accusing him of doing. The black eye? Sweat- and water-resistant face paint. I'd searched online for tips from movie makeup artists and photos of battered women. Watched a ton of tutorials on YouTube. The mauve-magenta color, the gradually turning sallow yellow as the bruising healed? All makeup. I had wanted everyone to see my black eye. Linda. Susan, the attorney, and everybody at work. Belle. All my "witnesses." That's why I couldn't go to a doctor to be examined. I was frightened my doctor might touch it or try to dress it and the makeup might come off. I was careful. I changed our sheets from white to a purple tulip print, just in case any rubbed off—I didn't want Ashton catching me out. He thought I'd hurt myself down by the dock, bumped into a post. I never did smash a plate—all those scenarios were made up. Strange, though, because Ashton started acting a bit cool with me around that time. I had assumed word had got out, or he suspected something.

Ashton groping Cady? All planned in advance. He hadn't touched her. Cady hanging out with him? All her instigation… although I had to admit, I was surprised at how malleable he was.

Quite simply, we, mother and daughter, had set him up.

It was Cady's idea to drug him, slip a Rohypnol in his Scotch. After a few hours, the substance is untraceable if, that was, she had chosen to call the cops. That side of things—calling the police—didn't go according to her/our original plan, because she changed her freaking mind at the last hour. That wasn't part of the script, her doing a one-eighty. Ashton always poured himself a Scotch on the rocks when he got home from a long day. And no, I had not told him about the Community Promise benefit. It was the perfect excuse to get out of the house and leave him alone with Cady. After he'd passed out, she "dressed the set," before I "unexpectedly" arrived home from the Community Promise benefit early.

Cady had known pretty much all her life whom her father was, and she too itched to get even, wanted to get back what was taken away from her as a baby and growing up: a chance for a better life. Money, the inheritance that was her birthright that she would never have. All she was doing was claiming it ahead of time. That's why I moved her into the guest house. She was meant to finish her year at boarding school, complete all her exams. Then start university the following fall. That way, she would be entering university without any baggage if anyone happened to hear about the "assault." Operation-get-even was meant to happen during next year's summer vacation, not at the beginning of this year—I had already paid for the semester upfront! Well, not all of it, because Cady had received a scholarship, but the school fees were outrageously expensive at Wonderwood School, so even paying for a small percentage was still a chunk of change. Her turning up out of the blue was a surprise. She was doing so well there academically—the teachers loved her—until she fell out with her roommate, Amy. Hence Cady's arrival in Beaufort. It was Cady who precipitated everything, egging me on to follow through with our plan so much earlier than we agreed. I went with the flow; I didn't have much choice.

That evening when Cady gatecrashed our dinner à deux? And I was so furious with her for using the upstairs bathroom, et cetera et cetera? All planned. The reason why I made such a fuss was so Ashton could hear. Admittedly, she had pushed things ahead of schedule (again) by showing up unexpectedly for dinner, and it did make me feel a little miffed, and a wave of jealousy did whoosh over me seeing her be all friendly with her father, despite myself. I'd worked my whole life to be her mom, so how come Ashton got to breeze in at the last minute and be the charming, fabulous daddy? It veered us off course, his rapport with Cady, and it grated on me. She and I had been working as a tight team. The "sexual assault" evening, though, had steered our plans into unexpected waters because of her sudden saintly attitude. What we'd do next, I was still trying to work out. She had stymied our plans. She was adamant she didn't want to press charges.

After all, Ashton *was* her biological dad, so I kind of understood.

The truth was, there was a time when I too had wavered. I had settled so beautifully into our marriage and had genuinely fallen in love with Ashton. Almost forgiven him. If Ashton and I had had a child, I would have called the whole thing off. But when Cady turned up at Community Promise, out of the blue, I got shaken out of my fantasy.

"Mom, what the hell are you doing?" she'd said. "Let's get a move on with this thing."

That time at Community Promise when she was railing against her mother, saying how her mom didn't care? It was the truth. For a while there, I had forgotten about my oath to Cady; I had become so involved in my marriage and my new life with

Ashton and had pretty much left Cady in the lurch. She had felt abandoned at boarding school since everything had blown up with her roommate. Unloved. Suddenly, she needed me.

Cady had snapped my attention back to the job in hand. Reminded me that Ashton had trashed my dreams of university, my future. Knowing he wanted her aborted, Cady had an axe to grind with her biological father. She was bitter. And I didn't blame her.

The first time I saw Georgia-May, all I could see was an elderly Cady. Like when they do makeup in movies and age the actor into dotage? Cady's delicate wrists and ankles, her birdlike neck, her frail shoulder blades, and the nose—which thank the Lord, Cady had not inherited from me—was just like her grandmother's. But with Cady's punky dyed hair, luckily it wasn't obvious to anyone but me. Cady's big brown eyes? With all that eyeshadow and eyeliner she slathered on, flicking up the corners with thick black wings, that too went unnoticed. Of course, *I* could see Ashton in Cady's eyes. Always had and always would. But I was confident nobody else would notice what was buried in her DNA.

Did I feel guilty about my clandestine methods? Sure. Don't most of us feel guilty about something? And we Catholics feel guilty all the time anyway, even when we've done nothing wrong. But sometimes you don't have a choice, do you? Sometimes karma needs a little helping hand. Ashton had gotten off scot-free with too much already, had escaped without punishment. He deserved his comeuppance. Naturally, I hadn't imagined I'd become so enamored with him along the way. That was a tricky pill to swallow. He turned out not to be that eighteen-year-old in the Honda, after all. Transfigured into a pretty amazing man, in fact, and genuinely in love with me. We all do dumb things when we're young. But still, I had already put my plan into motion, and when Cady showed up as that runaway (even had a fake ID with a different last name) saying she had nowhere to go, it was as if I just couldn't stop... I had to see it through. I needed to get even, make him suffer the way I had suffered all those years as a single parent, forgoing my place at college, never getting the education I deserved after all I'd worked so hard for. Meanwhile, Ashton had just swanned through life, not giving a damn about anyone else, least of all me. The "poor white trash." The "nose." To him I wasn't even a human being when he'd tricked me that night into having sex with him in his car. All those promises he'd made me—the gullible, trusting girl—I was nothing to him. Those kinds of scars never heal.

MAGIC HAPPENS? For people like him, yeah, magic happens. His life had turned out frickin' perfect. But what about the rest of us? What about me and Cady? We had to manufacture our own magic. Cast our spells.

It wasn't as if I had liked my nose before my encounter with Ashton, but after that, after his rejection of me and my baby—of Cady—I became obsessed with changing my nose. Transforming my whole persona. I wanted nothing to do with sad, pathetic, trusting little Maeve O'Reilly. Vivien was the name I picked out, inspired by *Gone with the Wind*, starring Vivien Leigh. I'd never seen such a beautiful woman. The film itself? Pretty racist by today's standards—it sugar-coated the horrors of slavery, for sure. But Vivien Leigh herself? Well, she was superb.

*Vivien*, I thought. *What an exquisite name. How elegant.*

I promised myself I would be an *elegant* woman. My last name was lifted from *A Streetcar Named Desire*. DuBois. Vivien Leigh had won Oscars for her performances in both films.

Vivien DuBois.

It sounded beautiful. Just the sort of classy person I longed to be. I even enrolled in acting classes. Learned to fill the shoes of the characters I portrayed. With my new Academy Award name embedded into me, what could go wrong?

I kept tabs on Ashton Buchanan. After Facebook was launched, I started silently stalking him. I knew exactly what he was doing in life, whom he was seeing: Belle. I became obsessed with her, too. I dyed my mousy hair a rich dark brown like hers, and like Vivien Leigh's. I still go to the hairdresser's every thirteen days to have my roots touched up.

When I had enough money saved, I printed up Belle's Facebook profile picture—along with a photo of Vivien as backup—took the photocopies to the plastic surgeon and asked him to make my nose just like either Belle's or Vivien's, whichever would turn out best. He did a remarkable job. My nose is somewhere between the two. When I saw Belle at that café in Beaufort, it was almost like looking into a mirror.

I studied everything during my self-induced makeover. Etiquette books, how to cook, how to set a table properly, how to speak. I practiced getting rid of my Baltimore accent. Walked with a book on my head. Studied fashion magazines and learned how to dress.

No, I never did get that double degree in English Literature and Psychology, but I could have. I'd read enough books. I self-educated myself to the point of perfection. I read Dickens, Jane Austen, Thomas Hardy—even *War and Peace* and James Joyce, for heaven's sake. All the classics. I still subscribe to *The New York Times Book Review*, *The New Yorker*, you name it; if I haven't read it, I'll still know all about it. Strangely enough, Ashton is the one who seems uneducated these days, next to me. Clever he may be, a brilliant surgeon, but he's not well-read the way I am.

The chic, bohemian Paris-loving parents I cooked up? Who died in that nasty car crash? It was true in a sense. I *was* left to defend myself after my parents had "died." Because they were dead to *me*. I never saw them again after I left home, gave birth to Cady, and changed my name. I supposed that if they had ever given a damn, they could've tracked me down, made some effort, but of course they never did. They were not the types to hire a private detective and find out where I was, because they had never cared in the first place. I don't even know if they're alive now, and I don't care. That's my past and something I never want to think about again. I kept them a secret from Cady, too. I couldn't have that trashy pair asking me for money—which no doubt they would have. Cady didn't know, either, about me changing my name. I just told her that her grandparents were dead.

A hard nut? Too right I'm a hard nut. I've had to be.

It was tempting to give in, to enjoy my new married life with Ashton, to carry on being his beautiful, sporty, "perfect" wife after our dream wedding. But I knew that wasn't fair on Cady. For some unknown reason he didn't want children, even with me, "Vivien," so why would he suddenly embrace the child he'd spawned unknowingly from the "poor white trash pizza delivery girl"? He'd find out I was "the nose." I couldn't allow that to happen. How humiliating!

All I had ever wanted was justice. Nothing more, nothing less. *Justice.*

Ashton ruined my life when I was only seventeen years old, without any thought, without any guilt, without any feelings whatsoever. Just stomped all over me and everything I stood for. Trampled all over that innocent girl inside me too, by insisting I abort her. How is that fair? For his life to work out so nicely and mine and Cady's to be annihilated? No. Not fair at all. "Revenge is a dish best served cold." No, that's not Shakespeare, funnily enough, although it sounds like it could be. It's an old saying that may, or may not, originate from France.

And that's what I was doing. Serving Ashton up a nice, chilled, haute cuisine meal.

And if he didn't like my gastronomical delight? Tough shit.

# CHAPTER TWENTY-THREE

I thought back to the sequence of our courtship, just one month after we had first "met" at the Citrus Club roof terrace bar in downtown Charleston. It was the golden hour, when the light glows in the most flattering way. He spotted me sipping a cocktail at the bar. But I wasn't there by coincidence. Of course not.

I was waiting for an invisible "friend," who of course never showed. Ashton had popped by after a long day's shift. I knew his schedule, surprise, surprise. We got talking and, after a good hour or so of conversation, he shyly asked me on a date to meet for lunch the following day. I told him I couldn't. I had to be careful, despite my inward excitement. I played very hard to get. I knew that was my only chance with a man like Ashton Buchanan—to play the cool game. I had finally worked out the secret recipe. *Never give them what they want until they've committed.* Anne Boleyn knew that. Timing always plays an important part too. The moment comes when a man is ready to settle down. Get there too soon and you're screwed in more ways than one. Get there too late and you might be left with bitter or jilted warmed-over love. I knew exactly what I was doing. How to play him.

Date three. Dinner at Maison.

I was wearing a chic black dress and beige heels, which matched my lightly sun-kissed limbs. A tip I learned long ago: shoe color to approximate your natural skin tone—to make the legs look longer. My hair was very Kate Middleton. I wore a fake diamond solitaire ring on my right hand. It had cost me fifteen bucks but looked so real. "Diamond" stud earrings to match. I had once read that Natalie Portman (another of my idols) avoids real diamonds in case they come from conflict mines. She prefers knock-offs from Claire's because faux jewelry glitters just as well at the Oscars and nobody can tell the difference anyway. (Unless you're a jeweler, gemologist—or Liz Taylor.)

*Yes, Ashton, my admirers do buy me expensive jewelry*, I said wordlessly, as I rested my chin on my manicured hand and smiled at everything he was telling me. *And if you don't snap me up soon, someone else will*, I intoned, when I declined that third call on my cell phone that I had scheduled myself to ring during this dinner. *Oh, the beauty of modern technology!*

"You're a popular lady," he noted when I glanced at my phone in my classic Dior bag, shrugging off the call. (The Dior purse—real, not fake, as you *can* tell the difference—I'd found secondhand at a consignment store.)

I gave him a little shrug-with-a-smile as if to say, *Yep, you'd better make your move, buster. Time's running out.*

Ashton shuffled uncomfortably in his chair, his gaze skimming over me, before he said, "Vivien, may I ask you a personal question?"

*Uh-oh*, I thought. I smiled an adorable smile. "Of course."

"How come a beautiful lady like you isn't already married?" I suspected he wanted to add, *at your age*, but of course didn't, being so well brought up. But I had prepared that answer well in advance knowing the question might arise. After all, I was thirty-four. And "childless."

"I was engaged to be married. To Tom. He had Hodgkin's disease," I said dramatically. "Sadly, he didn't make it. After that... I... I just never met the right person." I cut my gaze away from Ashton's concerned face and bowed my head.

He cleared his throat. "I'm so sorry for your loss."

I looked up at him. Blinked. Squeezed out a teensy-weensy tear. "It was a long, *long* time ago. Time does heal. But… thank you, anyway."

There was an appropriate, respectful silence, while Ashton's brain-cogs revolved in his male-centric mind. I suspected my answer had pleased him. I wasn't secondhand goods rebounding from a divorce, and enough time had passed since Tom's "death" for Ashton not to feel like he would be competing. Naturally, Tom was make-believe. The truth was, being a single parent hadn't given me much chance to date at all. Besides, I had always had my sights homed in on Ashton Buchanan, and that was that.

"Have you ever been to Beaufort, just over an hour's drive south of here?" he asked, all of a sudden, staring into my eyes, his mouth tipped into a seductive, crooked smile.

I gave him a confused look as if I'd never heard of the place.

"The Beau is not pronounced like the bow of a bow tie, like Beaufort, North Carolina. Our South Carolina Beaufort is like the beau in *beau*tiful. The *beau* part rhyming with *you*."

I laughed at his veiled flattery.

Of *course* I'd heard of Beaufort! I'd been there. Done a tour. I knew that Ashton had always lived on Distant Island. I'd even read in an architectural magazine about the amazing restoration job he'd done on Distant Sands. I was shocked because I had always taken him to be a spoiled, privileged, entitled prep-school trust-fund brat, born with oodles of wealth. It turned out, as I'd unearthed his past with my "research" on him, that, to my surprise, he had earned a scholarship to Johns Hopkins. That his father had been an honest, blue-collar worker. A shrimper. Not quite the spoiled brat I had supposed. This did tinge my plans with a little self-guilt. I had Google Earthed Beaufort and its surroundings a thousand times. Watched *Forrest Gump. G.I. Jane. The Big Chill. The Great Santini.* Beaufort had quite a claim to fame.

"Actually, come to think of it," I deliberated, "it does ring a bell." To sound clever, and knowing from a magazine article what a history buff he was, I added, "I think I read something about Beaufort being colonized by the English hundreds of years ago?"

Ashton's face lit up. He gave me that tilted smile again. His brown eyes glinted with warmth. "I love a woman who knows her history. The English arrived in 1711. But long before that the Spanish had beaten them to it, founded the area in 1520, only thirty years after Columbus arrived. Named the region Santa Helena. Then the French came forty-odd years later with a bunch of Protestants to settle this part of the Lowcountry, then the Spaniards returned and claimed it back, and by 1580 the Spanish settlement was the largest outside Mexico. But then England's Sir Francis Drake sailed into the sea islands looking for a place to build a colony and..." His words faded in my ears as I faux-listened.

I gazed into Ashton's eyes, feigning interest, as he prattled on about the history of Beaufort, adding the odd, "Wow, that's absolutely fascinating, I didn't know that," or "Really? That actually *happened*?" I held my neck high, my back rod-straight. The elegant Vivien DuBois in her diamonds, as she nodded sagely at everything Ashton said, her lips curved with such a pretty little smile, her legs crossed daintily.

They say when you spend ten thousand hours doing something, you'll be a pro. I had spent at least that amount of time studying royalty. Particularly Kate Middleton. Noted the way she always held her hands gently clasped in front of her. I had perfected her hairstyle, too. Long, sexy hair tipped into waves at the ends. Just like Kate, Vivien DuBois would never be caught blowing her nose or picking spinach from her teeth or, God forbid, let out an unexpected burp or fart. Vivien DuBois was perfect. Laughed at Ashton's jokes, gave coy smiles, lowering her head like Princess Diana, looking up at him at opportune moments from beneath her dark lashes. And, like

Princess Diana, she showed a little leg—never too much—and on occasion a touch of see-through with her dress. Just like *that photo*, the one that the press took of Diana at the kindergarten school where she worked. The photo that launched her.

Vivien spoke about books and plays and travel. Especially Paris and her artistic parents and her happy childhood. She was so well adjusted. From such a healthy, happy home! Until her parents' tragic death. Poor Vivien. Just enough sadness in her life (but not too much) that Ashton couldn't wait to look after her.

But most of all, Vivien DuBois listened attentively to everything Ashton said. Because men always love talking about themselves, and no other conversation would ever be as fascinating to a man as his own discourse.

"It must be so fulfilling being a neurosurgeon," I gushed, as I spooned just a tiny mouthful of key lime pie into my rosebud mouth. I let my tongue dance a little on the spoon. Subtly, just enough so that Ashton could imagine the kinds of things I could do to him in bed. Even though this was our third date, I hadn't even let him kiss me. Ooh, nooo. Vivien DuBois was a *lady* and Ashton Buchanan was lucky to be dining with her. Vivien played the book of rules to a T. Sometimes she wouldn't answer her phone. She would never return his call, but wait for him to call back. She wouldn't dream of accepting a date at the last minute or be "spontaneous." She had things to do, places to go, and a string of beaux demanding her attention. I could feel the heat coming from Ashton each time I was "finally" available. He had no idea I was sitting in sweatpants in front of the TV with greasy hair, counting my last pennies, cutting out food coupons. I was renting the cheapest Airbnb rental I could find in Charleston, in a less than desirable neighborhood. I never let Ashton approach the place. I pretended I was staying with a friend and that this friend had a young child in school. The last thing I wanted was Ashton coming over. Meanwhile, Cady was in her lovely boarding school in upstate New York. I had saved every cent I had. My job in insurance had been dull as ditchwater, but it did pay well. My savings were running low, though.

I stared dreamily into Ashton's eyes.

"It *is* very rewarding being in the medical field," he droned on. "I had always wanted to be a doctor, ever since I could talk. I played doctors and nurses with my s—" He broke off. "It's wonderful knowing you can make a difference in the world."

"That's why I love my work, too," I agreed. "I *love* giving back. Love helping people."

The truth was I didn't have a job at all at that point. I'd heard about Community Promise and the timing would be perfect—someone was leaving, taking maternity leave. Assuming Ashton was on track and he was getting serious with me. My job would be voluntary, no pay. I had whipped up a fancy resumé of all the voluntary work I'd done in New York. If they checked out the websites, fine. Anyone can make a website. If they hit the "Contact Us" button. No problem. The "Us" on these make-believe websites was me, myself and I.

My real job was Ashton Buchanan. But I needed Ashton to make a move soon, because I had not been working for two whole months.

So far so good.

"When lives are on the line, nothing else matters," he continued. "My patients come first. I guess I'd make a pretty second-rate husband." He shot me a tiny smile as if to test me. My heart leapt. Bingo! I was making real progress. If ever I got tempted by him—and I did, the man was gorgeous—I thought of Anne Boleyn again, another of my royal heroines.

"No, that shows you're compassionate," I said, remembering that Cady's life—inside my womb—had been "on the line" and Ashton hadn't given a damn. "I'm sure those close to you understand completely and love you all the more for it."

He nodded. "The stakes are so high in my profession. The complexity and risk of each individual patient is humbling. We have to be meticulous and pay attention to every detail. And you'd be surprised how a simple task of simply washing one's hands can be a matter of life or death. But it's not just about a surgeon's diligence or performance: there can be obstacles. Sometimes shortages of nurses or operating rooms come up, an unseen problem with the patient herself. Or himself." He furrowed his brows. "Unexpected pitfalls. Humans can fail in any profession through misunderstanding, weakness, or arrogance, but we in medicine… when a life is on the line, there are no rehearsals, we have to get it right first time."

"I'm in awe," I cooed, wondering if "getting it right first time" applied to me—if he was entertaining the idea of marrying me, and if there was some double entendre, or if reading into this was my imagination. I thought of us in his Honda, all those years ago. *You got it* wrong *the first time, buddy*, I thought. I blinked at him and smiled sweetly. "I have so much respect for what you do, Ashton. I really am in awe."

"Betterment is my mantra," he went on. "Human caring is my job." He topped up my wine and suddenly said, "Vivien, I'd love you to come for lunch this weekend to my house on Distant Island. Are you free?"

I pretended to look surprised at his invitation and made a little O shape with my mouth. "Why thank you, Ashton, I'd absolutely love to." Very Scarlett O'Hara. Then I added, "I'll have to look at my agenda as I know I'm pretty booked up. I'll let you know tomorrow." I fiddled with the little gold crucifix on my neck. One thing I had made absolutely clear to him—silently of course—was if he wanted me? If he wanted *it*. He'd have to marry me first.

# CHAPTER TWENTY-FOUR

Every time I thought about Clark Gable earning $120,000 for his role as Rhett Butler, and Vivien Leigh earning only $25,000 as Scarlett O'Hara—when to my mind *she* was what made *Gone with the Wind* a success—it made my blood and all the proverbial slugs and snails and puppy dogs' tails simmer in my witch's cauldron. Vivien Leigh had worked almost double the amount of days as Clark Gable on set. Apparently, she had worked sixteen hours a day for a full one hundred and twenty-five days, one day a week off. Clark Gable had worked only seventy-one days, *yet* had earned five times more—if my math is correct. It caused all the injustices of inequality to pop into the forefront of my mind. (And don't get me started on the super-talented, Oscar-winning Hattie McDaniel.) In all this time, nothing had changed regarding the supposed worth between men and women.

It was not fair.

I had worked 365 days a year for seventeen whole years raising my child. Totaling: 6,205 days, not even counting my pregnancy.

Ashton: zero days.

Not fair.

Cady and I had set out to make things right. She wanted money—for him to feel a tight squeeze on his wallet—and I wanted Ashton to feel, to *experience*, that basement-level humiliation that I had suffered during all those years as a single, low-income parent, because I didn't have the chance to earn a college degree and had had to take lesser-than jobs. I'd had my dream snatched away from me by Ashton and his lies.

But now with the cops out of the picture, and Cady refusing to press charges (although Ashton didn't know that), it looked like the only thing left for me to do was reap financial rewards and divorce him. I did have those photos of him passed out to wield as evidence to keep him in line, and the stuff we'd filmed. Not quite the full humiliation operation-get-even (which was Cady's name for it) we'd both had in mind. Still, it would have to suffice.

I'd take my half. A nice big chunk of severance pay might, just might, set things on an even keel. Cady, too. She needed to claim back pay.

I owed it to her to make things right.

# CHAPTER TWENTY-FIVE

With a big grin on my face, I remembered how things had played out the night before with Ashton.

When he finally awoke from his drugged stupor, groggy and woozy, he rubbed his eyes and surveyed his surroundings, baffled. Empty bottles of champagne were strewn around the living room. I stood over him glowering. Cady was back in the guest cottage—sent there by me after she had screwed up everything at the last minute. She might have ruined our opportunity to call the cops, but I wasn't about to let this man—who had trashed my life—escape some kind of poetic justice. It pleased me to see him looking so pathetically shameful, diminished. I noted Cady's fine touches: the tomato ketchup she had poured on his T-shirt, now dried.

I smiled to myself as I observed him, his bewildered gaze drifting around the room then to himself. He croaked, "What the hell…" His mouth was dry; he could hardly get the words out. "Damn, I need some water." He tried to get up but stumbled and tumbled back on the couch.

I appraised his slovenliness with glee. I almost wanted to laugh, call the whole thing a truce. Ashton looked comical. *This* was comical, in a way. Mother and daughter plotting and scheming—oh, we'd had such fun doing it! This "pillar-of-society" man completely oblivious, having no idea at all who Cady and I really were. Dishing up our tasty revenge. He was clueless about what had happened to him and why.

"What the hell…" his voice chafed again, his throat sounding like it had been rubbed with sandpaper.

"Exactly," I said, arms folded over my chest. "What the *hell*, Ashton? What the hell? What did you do to Cady? She was hysterical."

His split-dry lips were stuck together. He managed to peel them open, flicking them apart with his tongue like a sunbaked lizard. He rasped, "To Cady? Nothing, I swear. My mind's a blank, I—"

"I have evidence," I taunted, waving my phone at him. "Photos. Cady explaining what happened. And a video of you passed out."

He looked down at his ketchup T-shirt—it looked like dried blood—and gasped in horror. "I can't remember anything," he murmured. Then a flash of lightning threaded through his eyes. "Someone set me up."

"You set *yourself* up," I countered. "You'll be hearing from my attorney. I want a divorce. Plus, all the trimmings that go with it. And you can bet your bottom dollar that poor, compromised, abused teenager also wants plenty of compensation. Unless you want her to sue your ass to kingdom come. I need you out of the house by the end of the day. Go to your apartment in Charleston and *stay* there. I have a video. I have photos. Say what you like, think what you like, deny it all if you will, but I'm sure you can work out what's best for you. I advise you not to put up a fight if you don't want your reputation trashed in the gutter. A respected surgeon accused of groping a teenager? Plying a minor with alcohol on a school night? Not good, Ashton. Not good at all. Just one whiff of this getting out will destroy you, your reputation, and your career. And even if you did get off in court—if she pressed charges—imagine what the papers would say? The public lap up these kinds of stories these days. Cady is underage! Nobody listens to dirty old men anymore, and at thirty-nine, you're more than twice her age. The Me Too movement has put a stop—thank

God—to men's patriarchal *bullshit*. You'll be hearing from my lawyer. Remember: OUT by the end of the day!"

Leaving him there in a pathetic heap, I sashayed out of the room.

# CHAPTER TWENTY-SIX

"What the hell were you thinking?" I said to Cady, after I'd arrived home from my session with Dr. Becker, the "morning-after-the-night-before." We were in the guest cottage. Ashton had loped off, tail between his legs, to Charleston, as instructed by me.

Now I was trying to make sense of the mess she and I had created as a team. Yet I, as usual, was picking up after my mercurial, inconstant teenager. We'd had such fun together, bonding over this, and now? The whole thing was up in flames.

"I thought that was what you wanted?" I snapped. "To pin your baby-killing father into a corner. Ruin his life. This whole operation-get-even has turned out to be a frickin' fiasco!"

"If you didn't notice, Mom… hello?… I'm still *here*! Alive! He never killed me!"

"Correction. *I* didn't kill you. Me, your loving mother, who has sacrificed her life to give you yours."

"Oh, please, I've heard this self-righteous bullshit a hundred times already."

I clamped my hand over my mouth. Why had I said that? What horror had just spilled out? Sometimes I wished I could shut myself up. Why I had ever told Cady about her biological father in the first place, I had no idea. It had been a weak moment, after she was desperate to know her family history. I should have lied. Should've told her he was dead. But I wanted her to feel proud of who she was, where she came from. That her dad was a surgeon. Smart. Respected. *What a dumb move!*

I was a crap parent. Started so young at this game I'd gotten off on the wrong foot too long ago. It was almost as if Cady and I were sisters. I was the worst example of motherhood ever. Still, I loved that girl. Watching her sleep made my stomach fold with butterflies. She was my everything, my world. At least she was until I had foolishly decided to go ahead with my marriage.

I stepped closer to her, gingerly tried to touch her hand. She backed away, giving me a glowering, withering look.

"Cady, hon, I'm sorry. I didn't *mean* it! You've been my light, my joy, my everything. But you know how it hasn't been easy for us?"

"Mom, I'm not the one at fault here! I didn't ask to be born."

Her recriminatory words spiked my guilty heart. "Don't you say that, don't you ever say that!" Sickened by the sewage that had poured from my mouth that I could never take back, I folded her in my arms to squeeze some loving out of her but, as usual, she wriggled away. Another stab to my heart. I couldn't win, no matter what I did. I knew not to take it personally. It was her age, just a phase, I told myself.

She sat on the sofa, chin on her knees, knees to her chest. She stared out into middle space, not blinking. "I was happy the way things were with just you and me. Now everything's all messed up because of your stupid scheming."

"Don't say that, honey."

Finally, after staring like an automaton, she turned her head and shot a glance at me. "Why not? It's true, isn't it? I wish you hadn't come here. I wish *I* hadn't come here."

"Cady, hon, you've got to think positively. We can't change the past. We have to turn things around, make the negative stuff *work* for us."

"You know what my gut's telling me?" She mumbled something inaudible.

"What's it telling you... *what?*" —my voice a frantic squeal— "What's it telling you?"

"Never mind."

"No, honey, please tell me what's going on in your head."

"Never mind."

I pushed an angry strand of Cady's hair out of her eyes and stroked her brow. "Cady, hon, have you been eating properly?" I had noticed this with her since she was a little girl; she could get "hangry" if she didn't eat right. Angry because she was so hungry. Low blood sugar. "Have you been getting enough protein?" I asked.

She gave me a withering glare and pushed me away. "By 'protein' you mean meat, fish, and eggs, right? Not my deal, you know that. Has it occurred to you this has nothing to do with me eating or not eating right and everything to do with *you* and what you've done?"

"I'm going to make you something really special." I went to the kitchen and pulled out her favorite vegan cookbook, *THUG KITCHEN*, *Eat Like You Give a F*ck*, and thumbed through the pages. Cady was lazy about feeding herself properly if I wasn't around. I had spoken to the teachers at her school to make sure she was getting enough lentils and pulses in her diet. I had forgotten to stock up on trail-mix ingredients. Usually I kept a jar of nuts and raisins for her to snack on. I browsed the recipes but decided that first I'd whip her up some guacamole; fast, easy, nutritious. I started amassing the ingredients from the fridge.

"Why did you do it, Mom? Why did you drag me into your shit?" She unfurled her body and sat up straight on the sofa, holding me with a withering gaze. Her eyes were usually two pools of liquid chocolate, but now they were two hard stones. I couldn't understand Cady. Here was a young woman who had been raped in an alley, yet she never spoke of this horrific act of violence, refused to discuss it. She focused everything on me. Blamed me for all that went wrong. Her hurt was gnawing at my insides. I'd let her down. I'd screwed up.

I stared out the window, just to calm myself, blanking my mind for a second, blanking out her cruel words that hit me with the truth. I mashed the avocados, squeezing in some lemon, chopping tomatoes and onions. Outside, the breeze murmured and leaves were tumbling like confetti in shades of red and gold. I needed to get some food inside Cady, fast. Cheer her up. Take the focus away from me and what a terrible mother she thought I was. I poured in a dollop of olive oil, sea salt, and pepper, mixed it all up and set it on the coffee table in front of her with a big bowl of organic corn chips. She launched into the snack and I felt temporarily triumphant. I knew better than to contradict Cady, or try to mollify or humor her when she was in this kind of mood. "Mm-hmm," I agreed as she seethed on, not sure what it was I was agreeing with. I looked in the fridge again and decided on a pasta dish with vegetables and pine nuts.

She said with her mouth full, "You totally let me down."

I started chopping vegetables for the pasta, forcing myself to be cheerful, while my recriminating daughter talked about how wrong I was about everything. I couldn't deny it, she was right. This was tearing me up inside out, knowing this baby I had given birth to, now nearly a grownup, thought I had failed her as a mother.

"Do you remember Mandy from Community Promise?" I said jollily. "She has the most adorable little girl, cute as a button. Mandy has a fabulous job now, I'm so happy I got to—"

"Mom, why can't we have a conversation about *this*? About how screwed up things are. About what you've done."

I fried the onions, garlic, and celery. I listened to her tirade with half an ear, panicking about how she might react, how she might do something unexpected. We'd had such fun planning operation-get-even, but now it seemed like it had been the worst idea ever.

Cady suddenly sprang up from the sofa, her arms crossed accusingly over her THERE IS NO PLANET B tee. She regarded me while I cooked, her mistrust and disgust hanging in the space between us. I had let her down, and I wasn't sure how to pick up the pieces. Damn! Things had been going so well. We had discussed how she wanted to work in the Bahamas with Alex Leader, this marine biologist Ashton had told her about, saving sharks and dolphins, living with me in my new place in Harbour Island—assuming I got what I wanted from Ashton. We'd also played cards and watched movies, cooked together. I'd shown her how to bake Georgia-May's biscuits, swapping over some of the ingredients for vegan. We'd laughed. We'd bonded. We'd grown so close again!

Except now—everything had gone pear-shaped. Since she'd gatecrashed that dinner with Ashton, she'd become distant once more, treating me with disdain, with a haughty look or a toss of her cold shoulder. I'd noticed her eyeing up the beautiful furniture in the main house—the chandelier, the Persian rugs—and then shifting her condescending gaze to me as if to say, *You don't belong here, Mom.*

And now this. What a hot mess. The irony was, I'd embroiled myself in all this operation-get-even madness for *her* sake!

"Cady," I said. "This is what you wanted! This is what we planned together. And now you pretend like you're a bystander in this? You know that's not fair!"

"Oh, please. What? You're gonna blame *me*, like this was *my* idea?" Her raccoon eyes shifted uneasily in my direction. She had not taken off her makeup properly last night, mixed with her tears—black eyeliner was smeared all over her face. Her mouth was turned down in a sullen, defiant pout.

I could feel myself about to give out and snap like an old elastic band that had no more stretch in it. "Don't you dare play the innocent with me!" I yelled. "You were all *for* it! Wanted to get your hands on your father's money. *You* were the one who kept sending me texts, telling me to get a move on with operation-get-even. You were the one who left Wonderwood early and showed up all of a sudden at Community Promise. You think that made me happy, you leaving your expensive boarding school early, missing a whole semester? Going to the local school here instead? I did this for *you*."

She leapt up from the sofa, pointed a finger at me and screamed, "Bullshit, Mom! You did this for *yourself*. Couldn't wait to humiliate him."

Her defense of Ashton cut me to the bone. "Oh, so who do you think felt humiliated for *your* entire life, missy? Working crappy, uninspiring jobs for *years* to pay the bills? To give you a fancy education like I never had? To give you opportunities—"

"Bla, bla, bla!" She put her hands over her ears and started humming, tuning out my lecture, yelling over her own sing-song noise. "I've heard this broken record before. I'm not liiiisten… ing. I'm not heaaar…ing you!"

"Ungrateful, that's what you are," I yelled back. "*Entitled*. At your age I was delivering frickin' pizzas."

"Yeah, and look where it got you!"

"Okay, fine," I shot back, draining the pasta, then frantically mixing it up with the vegetables with a big wooden spoon. "You back out of operation-get-even. But *me*? I'm going to live in Harbour Island and start my life again. In a beautiful big house down by the ocean. Or maybe I'll stay here in South Carolina. I like it here. Force Ashton to sell this place and take half, and you can take your cut and do whatever you want with it. Come and study sharks in the Bahamas and live with me like you said you wanted to do—work for that marine biologist you told me about. Or not, if you're so holier-than-thou and find operation-get-even so distasteful. You choose. I'm *done!*" I got out a plate, a fork, and put them on the coffee table. Back to the fridge and poured Cady out a glass of almond milk.

She was still humming over my words, dancing around the room barefoot, covering her ears like her hands were headphones. "I'm not listening, Mom!"

Things were really screwed up now. Cady was a wild card and she made the hair on the nape of my neck stand up. I had to think on my toes. Think fast. That "mother" of hers who was waiting for things to "settle" until Cady could come and live with her? The one I'd written emails to? That very same mother, yours truly, needed to get Cady the hell away from South Carolina. I slapped the bowl of pasta and milk down in front of her.

Cady stopped humming, took her hands away from her ears, snapped her eyes at me and said with a sneer, "I'm getting out of this sick environment and away from you. You disgust me. I don't even want to eat your food. You know why? You make me puke!"

"Eat this pasta!" I yelled. "Eat!"

"No, Mom, I'm leaving." She turned her attention to her phone.

"Where are you going, might I ask?"

She didn't look at me, just carried on texting. "Back to school."

I heaved a sigh of relief, but quietly. "The school here? Or Wonderwood?" Because she had cut the semester after it started, I never got the fees back. But it was all paid up. Her stuff was still in her dorm. Her books, bedding, posters, the electric kettle. A packed-to-the-gills car's worth of paraphernalia. At least I wouldn't have to worry about picking it all up again.

"Yeah, I'm going back to Wonderwood."

"When?"

"Like, now. I'm gonna take the Greyhound."

"Today? Isn't that a little—"

"I need to get away from you and your sick head games."

I ignored her remark. "Should I call the headmaster?"

"No, I'll do it. I don't trust what you might say." She went back to texting. I wondered whom she was communicating with.

"You need money?" I asked. "Let me pay you back for the bus ticket. Wouldn't you rather fly? The bus'll take forever."

She rolled her eyes. "*You* offering me money? Ha! I make more than you, if you hadn't noticed. I don't want your dirty money that isn't yours anyway but your husband's."

I bit my lip to stop myself from saying anything. Her words cut deep, mostly because they were true.

"Let me drive you to the bus station."

"An Uber's coming"—she looked at her phone—"in twenty minutes."

"But that's crazy! Let me drive you, let me—"

"You need a therapist, Mom, you know that, right?"

I was tempted to tell Cady I already had a therapist, but that would only make her gloat. "Hon, please don't reject me, please let—"

"Spare me your Baltimore 'hon,' you Balti*moron*."

"Don't you speak to me that way, young madam, don't you—"

"BaltiMORON," she yelled. "Just leave me alone! I don't need you." The cottage walls practically shook. Thank God nobody was around to hear. She pounded upstairs and slammed the door to her room. I could hear her flinging things about. I guessed she was packing her suitcase. I made a quick sign of the cross in thanks. My prayers had been answered, she was going back to school!

Her "Baltimoron" insult rang in my ear. She knew how this hurt. We were Baltimoreans, those of us who hailed from the city of Baltimore, with an acute accent on the e, not "Baltimorons." Just like people from Maine were Mainers, not Maniacs. Is that how she saw me? As a moron? She despised me so much she didn't even want me to drive her to the bus station.

The food sat there untouched. For some crazy reason this was more painful than even her attacking words. A symbol that she was rejecting me in every way. I was a total failure—I couldn't even feed my child.

It occurred to me in that moment that Cady might actually hate me.

# CHAPTER TWENTY-SEVEN

I slunk back to the main house, giving Cady space. I knew how her mind worked: if I crowded her or made her feel hemmed in, she'd only resent me all the more. The last thing I needed was her changing her mind about going back to Wonderwood. She'd come around in the end. She was sophisticated for her age, in some ways. Knew what she wanted. Only one more year and she'd be an adult. Going back to school was a smart move. Thank God she was choosing to do it of her own accord.

I didn't want to risk saying goodbye or for her to make a scene in front of the taxi driver. I had no desire, either, to watch my daughter be driven away by a stranger because being with me was so detestable to her. I couldn't bear the agony.

I slunk down to the dock, deep in thoughts of self-recrimination. It seemed nobody, not even animals, wanted me near them. A cormorant, balancing on one of the dock posts, was drying its dark wings in the sun and took flight as I approached, soaring high in the sky. As it flew, I thought of Cady, also taking flight, wishing herself away… far away from her mother.

Being a parent sucked.

I'd been a fool; I hadn't thought all of this through thoroughly enough. The ramifications, especially for Cady. I'd been selfish. And too "buddy-buddy" with my daughter, acting like her sister or best friend, not a proper mother. I hadn't imagined the possibility of Cady feeling sympathy for her biological father when he hadn't wanted her in the first place, or how she might feel guilty about operation-get-even. Neither had I weighed up Ashton's charm against a virtual child's impressionistic vulnerability. One thing I was grateful for: however furious she was at me, at least she hadn't blown our cover.

I was sick of the whole thing. Sick of Ashton dominating my life. He had been at the helm of it without even realizing. Like a tiny pebble in your shoe niggling you or worse, one of those invisible thorns you can't find but hurts like crazy—Ashton was impossible to dislodge. When you have a child with someone, that child's parent never leaves you. You can't put them behind you and pretend they never existed like you can with ex-boyfriends. No, when you share a child, this other half lives with you *forever*, whether you like it or not. Resides within the child, too. Every time you look at your daughter, you see that man in her eyes, in the lift of her smile, the gait of her walk.

DNA is a powerful thing.

Ashton was embedded in Cady like grain in wood. Even Georgia-May had staked her claim on my daughter.

I had gotten this far; I couldn't have any regrets now. I needed to think about the future, *my* future. Start fresh. All my life—or at least half of it—I'd been living for other people, never myself. I hoped Cady would start college next year. Together we had applied to a whole host of universities and would probably hear back by April. Maybe sooner if they were eager to have her. We were banking on her getting a scholarship. Luckily, she was earning great money with her drop shipping business, which didn't seem to interfere with her studies. More than I was—she'd made that clear. One thing I'd done well, whatever my failings: I had raised my daughter to be strong and self-reliant. Savvy too. Nobody could outsmart her.

What did I want? I wanted my independence. My autonomy. On my terms. I'd take an online masters' degree, do something that fascinated me, find a job I really loved. The irony of everything was that I did actually love working for Community Promise. Something that had started out as a ruse, as a means of retribution and redress, had morphed into an almost spiritual vocation. I discovered I *did* love helping people, after all. And I wanted to continue. The feeling of taking someone vulnerable under my wing and me personally being able to make positive changes was so rewarding. I could continue to do that. I had genuine experience now. *Real* things I could put on my resumé, real skillsets.

I made my way back to the house, balancing my options. There'd be some alimony from Ashton, too. Enough to set me on my feet until I figured things out. And no, I didn't feel bad about that. Ashton had glided through life burden-free. Nine months I had carried Cady, protecting and nourishing her in my womb, and then once born, seventeen years of hard slog. Worry. Nursing her through illnesses, feeding and clothing her with only the best. Sacrificing everything to give her a classy education. And Ashton, with his crooked grin, his easy-boy relationship with Belle, as he drank and partied, had swanned into the right school and college, and sorority, and aced all his exams with his photographic memory, while I couldn't squeeze a sandwich into my lunch break, let alone squeeze a decent relationship into my life. No, I refused to feel bad about giving karma a helping hand.

The main house felt nearly empty without Ashton. I'd been used to his absences when he'd been at the apartment in Charleston, but this time was different knowing I had kicked him out of the house. *His* house. The place felt like a mausoleum ringing in its own silence. I walked through the elegant rooms, my fingers skating over the dark heirloom furniture that Olive Oyl, the cleaning lady, had polished to a shine. I browsed the leather-bound books in the library, with onionskin-thin pages and miniscule fine print—books I knew I'd never read. I was a stranger. Everything seemed to be judging me cruelly. The house, the walls, even the furniture warning me I didn't belong here. The silence was deafening, save for some kind of scuffling around on the roof or in the attic. Possums? Raccoons? I wouldn't tell Ashton or out would come the shotgun. One thing Cady had rubbed off on me was her love of nature and the environment. "This isn't a dress rehearsal, Mom," she'd often say. "There is no Planet B."

She was right. However militant she was, I admired her for her ethics.

And my Plan B? I was all alone again. Worse, because now I didn't even have Cady.

My eyes brimming with tears, I texted her:

*I'm sorry honey please let's be friends.*

She answered after only five minutes:

*I forgive U mom this has been very difficult for both of us need some time alone love you.*

My heart lifted, I replied eagerly:

*Love you more.*

Ashton seeped back into my thoughts. Didn't he always? I tried to second-guess what his next step would be. I supposed he'd be off to see his lawyer, pronto. Maybe even right this minute. Ashton would know he hadn't done anything, know for sure he'd been set up. Would he blame Cady? Me? Work out there was a connection between us? No, impossible. But he would be angry as hell. There was no turning back now, no retrieving what we'd had as a couple. That part of my life was over. A short, sweet interlude, based on lies.

I'd played a role. Acting is fun for a while, but when it becomes your life it's exhausting. Not that I wasn't Vivien, because by now I pretty much was. But it's a huge weight to carry, being married to someone and not sharing your past with them, pretending to

be so frickin' perfect all the time. Ashton was disgusted by Maeve
O'Reilly. He'd told me right then and there that he would never
date "poor white trash," and poor white trash was who I still was
inside. I didn't have any money of my own. No savings. It had all
gone on Cady's education. Rent. Our clothing. Food. I was white
trash in my heart, too. No "lady" would've pulled off this kind of
stunt. Not one single person of Ashton's class would've done what I'd
done. They didn't need to. They were born with it all anyway. Even
Ashton. Financially, maybe his parents had hit low moments with
their house crumbling down around them, but Ashton would never
understand what it was like to have parents like mine or live in the
hellhole where I was raised. Nor Belle, nor any of these highfalutin
people. They would never "get" what it was to be born into grimy
poverty and have to claw your way out, simply for survival.

I *was* a survivor and I refused to be ashamed of that. It was
who I was. It was me.

Skewed thoughts rambled through my mind, contradicting
each other. Cady. My marriage. Ashton. My new life ahead of
me in the Bahamas. I congratulated myself and, seconds later,
I disgusted myself. Cady was right, I needed therapy like a
plant needed rain. This life I had been leading... of Ashton's
wife, with him as my breadwinning husband, as my benefactor,
and my job helping people at Community Promise with no
pay, playing tennis at the country club, sipping cocktails with
friends... wasn't so terrible, was it? I'd carved out a nice niche
for myself, and it had worked. I'd moved from being white trash
to white privilege.

And now look what I'd gone and done.

I had set it all alight. It had streamed down on me like a trail of
fireworks ending with a bang... then disappearing into nothing.

I had created my own void.

*

When I came back to the cottage, Cady was gone. She had packed everything, even taken the toilet roll and some of the food. The only thing she'd forgotten was her toothbrush and toothpaste. I sat down on the sofa and slurped up some of the pasta I'd made for her, cold and congealed, into my mouth, washing it down with the almond milk.

Car wheels scrunched on the driveway. For a moment my heart leapt, thinking it was her coming back to kiss me goodbye, but it was only Olive. I went out to meet her.

"Hi, Olive," I said, mustering up a big smile, despite the gamut of unhappy emotions baying in my mind, tugging me this way and that. I was a failure, I was a winner, I was one screwed-up human being.

Olive's gangly legs emerged from the car, one by one like they belonged to a spider. Then her black bun popped out, and her bright red sweater—just like her cartoon character. Her spindly arms followed holding a box with a bunch of cleaning products sticking out of it. I rushed to the car to help.

"All natural, ecological products," she announced. "On Miss Cady's orders."

"Olive, you're an angel. How much do I owe you for all that?" I took the box from her.

"I'll work it out later."

"Well, add extra shopping time on top. That was very kind of you to go to all that trouble."

I helped Olive clean the cottage. I decided that instead of staying on in the main house, I'd move in here. I'd feel more comfortable, especially at night. I cleaned with gusto, expending pent-up energy, unleashing some of my self-recrimination, which kept trying to sneak into my conscience. I scrubbed the toilet, cleaned the bathtub. Olive was impressed, said she had never expected a doctor's wife to get "so down and dirty." As she mouthed those words—*down and dirty*—I thought, *If only you knew* how *down and how dirty*.

# CHAPTER TWENTY-EIGHT

I told Silverman the whole story. Well, not the whole story, the whole fake story. That poor Cady had gone to find her mother, and I'd spoken to her mom and they were figuring out what to do about the assault. But that Cady, for now, did not want to talk to the police or press charges, pending, of course, that Ashton would settle with her out of court. A big lump sum. As for myself, I let Silverman know that I definitely wanted to go ahead with the divorce. I wondered how I would wing all this: the problem about Cady's settlement. As she was still a minor, I supposed her mother—me—would have to sign something. And then he'd find out who I really was. I'd worry about that later. First the divorce—get that done and dusted.

"You've made the right choice," Silverman said. He got up and paced around the room, hands clasped behind his back in thought. "Since you were last here, I did some digging into Ashton's assets."

"Oh yes?" Silverman would, of course, be getting a healthy cut. No wonder he was so swift to move and on the ball.

"This is what I'm thinking: Distant Sands is—"

"I don't want to live in Distant Sands," I interrupted.

"Well, that's a good thing because it's all wrapped up in easements and trusts. Dr. Buchanan is leaving it in his will to Beaufort County, to be run as a museum after his death. It would be over my head to even try and—"

"Like I said, I don't care about Distant Sands."

He paused a second before saying, "The house in the Bahamas, in Harbour Island? Is that what interests you?"

"Well," I said carefully. "If you don't think that's too grabby of me?"

"Not at all. I'll also be asking for either a lump sum settlement or alimony. Have you discussed the divorce with Ashton?"

"No. This has all come as such a shock. I'm worried about angering him... arousing his dark side. I mean, I'm fearful of him." I touched my eye, even though I wasn't wearing any stage makeup this time around. "And with everything that's happened with that young girl, Cady, well—"

"Absolutely," Silverman said. "It's best if you don't discuss things. Emotions are high. Let *me* deal with this."

"Well, that's a big relief. And about the money? I think the lump sum would be better, then I can get my husband out of my hair. I don't want to feel beholden to him in any way or feel he has the upper hand or is in control. Considering the circumstances."

"I agree," Silverman said, settling back in his stately leather chair. He held my eyes and gave me a knowing smile. "I happen to know Dr. Buchanan never uses the Bahamas house anyway. He won't even miss it."

"You do? How?"

"This is a small town, Vivien. People talk. I'll be in touch with your husband's attorney today and see what's what. Relax. I'm ninety-nine percent certain Dr. Buchanan will go for the deal. His reputation means everything to him. If word gets out about the thing with Cady, it won't be good for him. But at the same time, South Carolina's pretty conservative, with a "boys will be boys" attitude in some circles, so we need to watch ourselves. Have you told anyone else? We don't want your husband on the defensive. If he feels accused, penned into a corner, he may fight back. I know Ashton Buchanan. He might get tough."

I shook my head. "I haven't said a thing, but some people can read between the lines."

"Like who?"

"Lindy Williams. You know Richard Williams. The Sea Oats Country Club owner? Lindy's his wife."

"Yes, I know Lindy. Well, let's keep all this hush-hush, get the money without too much of a fight as quickly as we can. Strike while the iron's hot. We don't want to waste time. Then we can all move on, don't you think?"

I sighed with relief. "Absolutely. I agree. I just want this over with."

"I'll get back to you soon. You have someone to serve the divorce papers? A disinterested party?"

"Lindy, I guess? I'll ask her."

"Fine. If not, and your husband's in agreement, all he has to do is complete an acceptance of service form for me to file with the court. Normally, for a no-fault divorce, you need to be officially separated for one year in the state of South Carolina—I think I told you that already—but there are ways around that. I'm thinking we could go for an annulment, stating that the marriage was never consummated. You don't have kids so it's easy enough to do. Leave it all with me. Several of the judges here are old friends of my dad's."

I nodded. So grateful this was all in his capable hands. I'd had friends who had downloaded forms online and done their divorces that way. It was great having someone who could do all the legwork for me. "Your father's an attorney too?" I asked him.

"He's a judge. Attorneys, judges… my family's trade for generations. Oh, and I have some photos of the Harbour Island house," he said. "I did a little poking around. Would you like to see?" A satisfied smile edged the corners of his lips.

"Yes," I said. "I'd love to see. I did Google Earth the house, but I didn't get to see the interior."

Silverman swiveled his laptop around so I could see the photos of the house. I spent the next twenty minutes drooling over the pictures, while he regaled me with his shotgun annulment plan: something about filing a Summons and Complaint and how, with his clout and contacts, he could "get this baby wrapped right up in no time" as long as Ashton didn't contest, which he doubted he would, given the circumstance. He went on again about the "acceptance of service" or whatever and other technical terms, assuring me how quickly it could all go through. *Phew!* I was so wrapped up with the house, I was only half listening.

The canary-yellow clapboard house—that looked like it was made of wood but wasn't and was hurricane-proof—was adorable, with a view to the ocean, the sea so turquoise it was almost blinding, the sand a shimmering pink. The house was not millionaire-swanky, despite its location. No bigger than the cottage here and crawling with purple bougainvillea and pink hibiscus. French doors leading to small yards in front and back, with a hammock swinging between two trees. In one of the photos there was a stand-up paddleboard leaning against the side of the house. Perfect. Just what I had in mind. Two bedrooms, two bathrooms, wooden floors, ceiling fans, a little kitchen and a living room, all painted in pretty pastel colors. Very simple, shabby-chic. A veranda. But the position? Unbeatable. The place was absolutely perfect for me. Cady could come and live with me and study her beloved tiger sharks. The idea of not owning this house made my heart actually ache—it had my name all over it. I was so close to calling it mine. All this had been worth it. All these years of plotting and planning would finally pay off.

Freedom at last.

# CHAPTER TWENTY-NINE

Hardly had I got out of my car, back at Distant Sands, when a deep voice boomed out from behind the privet hedge, pumping me with a shot of adrenaline.

"Why, hello, Mrs. Buchanan." It was John, the gardener.

"John, hello. You took me by surprise!"

John, hardly able to hold the gardening shears for his arthritis, was snipping the hedge, his dark arms shaking in the process. "Did you know that wild turkeys have between five and six thousand feathers apiece?" He was often coming up with tidbits of information like this about nature—he was a very intelligent, informed man. Today I wasn't in the right frame of mind for chit-chat, though.

"No, I didn't," I answered.

"And did you know," he continued, seemingly oblivious to my nerviness, "that Benjamin Franklin felt that it was *wrong* that the bald eagle was chosen as the emblem for our nation. He said the bald eagle had *bad moral character* because he did not get his living honestly... too lazy to fish for himself... Benjamin Franklin said this, that the bald eagle stole from the fish hawk and that the turkey was a more respectable bird and a true native of America."

My mouth fell open. *Too lazy to fish for himself. Bad moral character.* Was that a hidden message? Was I reading too much into this? No doubt John saw me as a usurper. A woman who had married Ashton for his money and position. Did he know I was now planning to divorce my husband?

"That's fascinating, John." I smiled weakly and told him I needed to make an urgent call. Then, just as I reached the side door, fumbling with my key, Ashton's car rolled up. The last thing I needed. I scurried inside, up to the bedroom and hit the shower, locking the bathroom door. I was not in the mood for a big discussion. I had somehow fantasized about getting away with this unscathed. Like they do in the movies: lawyers fighting it out with each other while their clients go shopping or drink wine and sob on their friends' shoulders, without having to talk to their spouses at all.

I had the longest shower in history, my fingertips ending up shriveled like dried figs, even my toes, the soles of my feet. When I finally emerged from the bathroom, hair in a turban, hoping Ashton would have gotten bored waiting, he was there, sitting on the edge of the bed.

"Hi," I said, not looking him in the eye. "I'm afraid I can't talk, I'm on my way out."

"On your way out."

"Yeah."

"On your way *out*?"

"Look, I know what you must be thinking—"

"What must I be thinking?" Ashton's stare was sharp. A thousand little knives darting around in his pupils. Like wormholes, wanting to suck me in and spit me out.

This was the first time we had seen each other face to face since my lies about him hitting me had been exposed to third parties. My twisted truth glowered at me now. I had nowhere to seek refuge except my own soul. I wondered what he thought of me, if he asked himself how I justified myself for doing what I did. Telling people he'd hit me when he hadn't. What did he think? That I had done it for attention? That I had married him for his money? Probably the latter. I reminded myself that he had no idea at all who I was—the pizza delivery girl awash with feelings of betrayal and revenge—so for him, my actions must have seemed crazy. I was pretty sure he had forgotten that miniscule period of his life that had meant nothing to him, but everything to me. And even if he had remembered that girl, no way in a million years would he connect her to me. How strange that Ashton had haunted me all these years like a living, eating, breathing ghost. Yet I had been nothing more to him than a dust mote caught in the wind.

Until our marriage.

"You think I'm ruthless," I said.

"Please continue," he said. "Tell me what else I think."

"You think that… I don't know, Ashton. The truth is I have no idea what's going through your mind."

"What is it you want from me?"

"My attorney told me that he'd deal with things, that it was better not to talk to you directly. Emotions are high."

"Interesting. What else did he say?"

"That you wouldn't want this to be a scandal, that your reputation is important to you and—"

"A secret I'd like to let you in on, Vivien: your attorney Noah Silverman does not care one whit about you." His words sounded spiteful. It was true, Mr. Silverman was in it for the money. Of course he was. But I didn't care. I needed a shark on my side.

"You say you have 'evidence' then? You and this young girl?" Ashton asked, his foot tapping, yet his voice cool, controlled.

"Look, as far as I know you tried to molest Cady! I was shocked. Destroyed. My marriage meant everything to me and you simply threw it all away!"

"Your marriage meant everything? But it doesn't now? Is that what you mean? We *are* still married, Vivien, you're *still* my wife. And by the way, despite what you've done, I don't want a divorce. Buchanans don't divorce. You *know* the Cady thing is a lie."

"I can't be married to a man who's so untrustworthy, Ashton. Look, I really don't want to discuss this with you. I'm the injured party here!" I towel-dried my hair and padded to the closet to pick out a dress. I no longer wanted my husband to see me naked; it felt wrong somehow. I grabbed the first thing I saw and made to go back to the bathroom. He held me by the arm.

"Ouch, you're hurting me."

"I could hurt you, for real this time. Why did you lie, Vivien? My attorney tells me you're citing physical cruelty as a reason for divorce. You know I can't agree to that! You know that's a bald-faced lie."

I couldn't deny this or twist the lie around on him.

His grip tightened. "You really, really want a divorce?"

"Yes," I said. "I do. Our marriage is... a sham."

"You can say that again."

"If I'm such a despicable person, why do you want to stay married to me then?"

"Because in my family, we don't do divorce."

"It's an annulment, not a divorce."

"Same difference."

"It's not. Annulment means it was never right in the first place. That it should have never happened. Look, we've only been married six months. What's the big deal? You'll have a ton of pretty women waiting in line for you who'll make fabulous wives. Better than me. Smarter, more beautiful. You could pick anyone. With your profession, your looks... you're a catch. Forget about me."

"Like I said, in my family, we don't do divorce."

"But I'm not your family anymore. Families tell each other the truth. You've been hiding stuff from me. About your sister, for instance. I don't trust you. I don't know who you are. You're dangerous."

"Oh, man, that's rich, coming from you."

I looked him in the eye—he was still holding onto my arm. "Don't you get it? I don't love you anymore, Ashton. Marriage is a two-way thing. Why would you want to be married to a wife who doesn't want to be with you, a person who wants her freedom?" I wriggled from Ashton's clutch and marched back to the bathroom, where I slipped the dress over my head. I didn't bother with makeup. Silverman was so right. I now understood the coward's way of doing divorce… to not speak to each other, to let the lawyers fight it out. Was Ashton going to go to battle with me on this annulment? I could feel a headache bloom. I just wanted this to be over, take my money and go live in Harbour Island. But I couldn't look him in the face and tell him I wanted the house. Let Silverman do that. Let him deal with the details.

"I've moved into the guest house," I shouted from the bathroom. "Meanwhile, I would really appreciate it if you left me in peace." I would have liked to move into a hotel, but I didn't have any money. The guest house would have to do. I'd change the locks. I came out of the bathroom. Ashton blocked me by the door.

"You broke my heart," Ashton said. "You've broken my fucking heart, Vivien."

His expression said it all. I looked away. For a second I felt a pang of guilt, of remorse, but then I remembered the seventeen years of being a single parent, the sneaky lies he showered on me in his Honda. No, he didn't get to be the victim. Ashton Buchanan would be just fine. No way would I feel sorry for this man who had the world at his feet.

"I'd appreciate it if you left me alone," I said again. "It's in your interest to do this annulment. If you want a big fight, I'm sure the attorneys will be delighted to take a huge chunk of the pie. Your choice. Think about it. Mull it over. But I don't want to discuss this face to face again, got it?"

I shoved him out of my way and walked out the bedroom.

I was done with this man.

# CHAPTER THIRTY

Over the next two months, I kept tabs on Ashton, following his movements with the odd call to the hospital. I guessed his colleagues had no idea of what was going on in his personal life, judging by their friendly tone when they spoke to me on the phone. He hadn't returned to Distant Sands, luckily. He'd kept to himself at his apartment in Charleston. The lawyers were dealing with everything. Nice and discreet. No drama. What a relief.

My independence was on the horizon, and little by little all the relevant papers got signed, the annulment finally going through. Ashton had reluctantly agreed. The Harbour Island house and a lump sum of one million dollars, in cash. In exchange, I signed an affidavit stating that he had never physically abused me and that no third parties were involved in our break-up.

The Harbour Island waves were waiting for me. I imagined the soft pink sand between my toes, the sun in my hair; pictured myself reading novels in my front yard, looking out to sea, munching on local conch salad, sipping a cool cocktail, watching the sunrise, curled up in sweatpants, my hair a mess, no makeup. Just being me.

Finally… just being the real me.

I decided to wait for the one million until I got to the Bahamas and then open a new bank account—the Bahamas being an offshore tax haven. I'd be a wealthy woman. I couldn't wait for my independence, to start my life anew.

Next week would be the last I would ever see of Ashton. He'd been traveling a lot lately, doing conferences abroad and around the US. Talking about his upcoming publication, *The Fundamental Brain*. He was revered and deferred to by doctors all over the world. Secretly, I felt proud, which was ridiculous, but I couldn't help it. I thought a lot about Cady, how she had inherited his intelligence, and I stalked her too, on Facebook. We weren't friends, because that was a bit of a weird thing to be friends with your own daughter on Facebook, wasn't it? But she had no filters on her page and I'd get a thrill following her, seeing her photos and what she was up to. She also had an Instagram page. So many lovely photos of the Wonderwood campus in Upstate New York, the foliage, all her friends. Sometimes she would post what book she was reading. Lately she was into Sylvia Plath and Virginia Woolf. That made me a little less delighted.

My last few months seemed like some sort of surreal dream, with Cady here at Distant Sands and operation-get-even. It was as if it hadn't happened. My flight to the Bahamas was in ten days' time. Ashton had sent me an email, rather formal, in fact, letting me know he would be back next week, and he wanted to come over and talk. Nothing heavy, it said, just say goodbye properly in person. An era of my life would be over. Cady would be going to university next fall, and I would be alone to start afresh. I had sent out my resumé to various different places in Harbour Island. If all else failed, there were plenty of jobs in swanky hotels working as a manager or receptionist. Something to get me on my feet anyway. My life would finally be my own.

I had gotten in touch with Georgia-May's care center to arrange a visit. I'd miss that funny old lady. We'd bonded in a way. It was a shame I couldn't come clean, let her know she had a granddaughter, bring Cady to come and visit her. Of course, that was impossible. My last visit had been such a disaster and I so wanted to leave on a good note. Would she recognize me this time around? I sincerely hoped so.

I pulled into Heritage Park. They had told me on the phone that Georgia-May had had a relapse. What kind of relapse? I parked and entered. This time, the new nurse, the skinny one with translucent arms, came down to meet me and took me straight up to Georgia-May's room. What was her name? That's right, Lucy. This was a first, going to Georgia-May's private room. It struck me that she was no longer my mother-in-law.

"Where's Mariama?" I asked Lucy. We were standing in the hallway. I had never ventured this far into the inner sanctum. I was usually always met by someone in reception, and Georgia-May and I would go for a stroll around the grounds.

"Mariama's not working here anymore," Lucy said. "Well, she is, but she's taking maternity leave. Well, not exactly maternity leave, but her daughter had a baby, and she's helping out."

"How nice," I said, thinking how wonderful it would have been if I'd a half normal mother and could've had her helping out with Cady all those years ago. "Lucky daughter."

"Yeah," said Lucy. "Lucky for the daughter, not so lucky for Mrs. Buchanan."

"What do you mean?" I asked. "Is this something to do with her relapse?"

"Come in and see her for yourself, then we can talk. Boy, trying to step into Mariama's shoes has been a tall order. Mariama this, and Mariama that. 'Mama Mariama,' Mrs. Buchanan sometimes calls her. She cries for Mariama in her sleep. Sometimes during the day, too. Mariama was her world, her sanctuary. She was like a therapist, psychiatrist, doctor, mama, sister, friend, all rolled into one. Mrs. Buchanan's suffering without her. It's because of Mariama's absence that Mrs. Buchanan had an episode. She's become as frightened as a little girl."

"Poor thing."

"Speak quietly and don't bring up anything upsetting, okay? Lately Mrs. Buchanan's been as nervous as a long-tailed cat in a room full of rocking chairs. This relapse has set her back several years. But it's not surprising considering her condition. Schizophrenia is a *very* nasty disease."

"But she has Alzheimer's," I corrected, then suddenly wished I'd kept my mouth shut. Ashton had told me very specifically that his mother had Alzheimer's. This whole time I had assumed that was what was wrong with Georgia-May, and now Lucy was talking about *schizophrenia?* Was it because this nurse was new and had no idea what she was talking about? I knew that Heritage Park was an assisted living home for residents with mental health problems. But light mental health, like dementia. I'd assumed schizophrenic patients would be in a psychiatric ward, not in a care home. I obviously hadn't done my research.

Lucy shot me a confused glance. We were still in the corridor. With her hand pausing on the door, without opening it, she went on, "Where did you get that idea about Alzheimer's? True, there *can* sometimes be an overlap in terms of symptoms. Disruptions in thought processes is typical of schizophrenia—motor impairment and cognitive impairment—so in that respect schizophrenia can mimic Alzheimer's and dementia."

"I see."

"I mean, with dementia you can have paranoia and even delu-sions," Lucy continued. "But short-term memory loss is the primary symptom. But Georgia-May doesn't have any kind of dementia, as far as I know. Her medical chart says nothing about Alzheimer's or dementia. Many people with schizophrenia have cognitive deficits: memory problems and slower processing speeds, so maybe that's where the confusion arose? Of course, Heritage Park is pretty unique. That's what's so special about this place. It isn't a hospital but we provide all the same individually tailored psychiatric care. Maybe better."

I said nothing. The fact Ashton had kept me in the dark about my mother-in-law's real condition—I was his wife!—was embarrassing.

Lucy opened the door and we entered the room.

I found Georgia-May in her bed, something that I had not been privy to before. She looked pale, her white hair brushed so nicely—fluffy like a chick's. She wore no makeup, no pearls, no pink. Just her snowy nightie as she sat up in bed with a bunch of pillows propped up behind her. I sat down beside her. She lifted her eyes to me and gave me a quivering little smile. She looked so delicate and vulnerable. Like a breakable, porcelain doll.

"Georgia-May, hi, how *are* you?" I hadn't forgotten our last meeting, how she had warned me to keep away.

"Hello, my dear, how nice of you to come by and visit." She didn't seem to recognize me, but at the same time she didn't *not* recognize me. Her eyelids—the skin as thin as rice paper—fluttered a little.

"How are you feeling, Georgia-May?"

Her eyes appraised me. "Better, thank you. I had some difficulties."

I held her tiny, veiny hand. "What kind of difficulties?"

"Well, I got all wrapped up with the duet again."

"The duet?"

"They were rattling me, hounding me, wouldn't leave me alone. Things got a little bit out of hand."

"Classical music?" I asked.

"Some people are more powerful than others. Just when I try to forget, it all comes rushing back. I didn't do it. It was the duet. I'm exhausted even thinking about it."

"It? What happened?"

Lucy was eyeballing me, standing at a safe distance listening to everything I was saying.

Georgia-May let out a little yawn, covering her mouth with her shaky hand. I noticed great white moons on her nails. "Well, my dear," she quavered, "I do declare I'm feeling a little sleepy. I'm as slow as molasses these days, not much energy, so if you don't mind, I reckon I'll take a nap."

"Ashton sends his love," I lied, testing the waters.

She looked up at me and blinked. "Well, how ironic is that."

Lucy came over and took away one of Georgia-May's pillows and settled her comfortably in her bed. Georgia-May slithered under the sheets and her eyes flickered and closed. Lucy turned out the light and drew the blinds. It was only three o'clock. She whispered, "She's been taking a nap lately in the afternoons, after lunch. They need to fix these blinds—I can never get them to close all the way!"

I kissed Georgia-May on the forehead. Her complexion translucent like Italian marble, the pale blue veins spidering her delicate skin. She smelled of powder and old lady. It made my eyes smart. A far cry from the woman I'd gone for a walk with just a couple of months ago. I noticed her medical chart lying on the table next to her bed. While Lucy was fiddling with the blinds, I snatched it up to sneak a peek. But Georgia-May's white arm, like a ghost's limb, shot out from the bedclothes and clutched me by the wrist. Her hold was surprisingly strong for one so frail. "You won't find it written there, my dear. Oh, no, they never arrested me for murder, but the duet cast a deep enough shadow on me to lock me up here, in this home. Oh, but I'm so lucky, they'll tell you, to not be in a state hospital. But it was the duet, not me. It was the duet."

Georgia-May's fingers released themselves and she fluttered into a sudden sleep.

I jogged her arm. "Georgia-May, what are you talking about?" She said no more, and I might have thought her dead but for the gentle heaving of her chest, the tiny puffs of her breath.

*Murder?* Was she talking about her husband, Buck? Here I'd been all along, jovially thinking Georgia-May had Alzheimer's. What a dunce! How had I missed that? The other nurses must have been sworn to secrecy. And all that security? The fences around the care center? I'd put that down to being cautious because of the aged people here with dementia and Alzheimer's. They needed to have tabs kept on them, I'd reasoned; it wasn't safe for them to go wandering.

Ashton's story popped into my mind. How he had supposedly been with his father when he'd drowned. In the boat during that storm. All a lie? And how come none of this about Georgia-May had made it into the papers? I thought about how she had been accompanied by her "nurses" to come to our wedding. I had noticed how burly they were—the two men who'd escorted her.

Lucy finally managed to close the blinds properly. "There, done. Mrs. Buchanan needs her rest. Time for us to leave."

As we tiptoed out of the room, Lucy grabbed the medical file I'd had my eyes glued on. She started nattering away again, oblivious to what Georgia-May had just revealed to me. "The relapse happened after Mariama left," Lucy let me know, in a hushed voice, after closing the door behind her. "Mariama was basically the only person Mrs. Buchanan trusted. Mariama could calm her down and made her feel whole. She was able to banish the demons from her mind. I know this because everyone told me what big shoes I had to fill. Mariama, apparently, had everything completely under control. The duet, the delusions. The bright lights, when Mrs. Buchanan felt separate from everything and when she heard the voices telling her what to do. Only Mariama can dispel those voices, chase away those demons. Mariama was able to give her back the contact with reality that Mrs. Buchanan so needed."

"Let's hope Mariama comes back," I said, hoping I hadn't insulted Lucy by saying that.

"You know Mrs. Buchanan really loves Mariama?" Lucy went on. "She was her world. Even still, in her sleep. She pines for her. And when things went pear-shaped, Mariama would speak in the third person. Say things like, 'Don't worry, honey, Mama Mariama's got you covered.' Mrs. Buchanan—just last week—was convinced the duet was out to trick her again. Inanimate objects came alive in her mind. Even chairs and tables can feel threatening to her. She thought they were mocking her, out to get her. You have no idea how tough this has been for me."

I grimaced. "Nobody said it had gotten that bad."

"We called your husband and explained everything to him. I'm assuming he told you and that's why you came?"

I smiled. "Thank you for caring so much."

"It's my job. Poor Mrs. Buchanan. Her psychiatrist is on it with a new course of treatment. The latest antipsychotic medications are working, so Mrs. Buchanan's calmed down *a lot*, but she still gets the auditory hallucinations. The other day she was listening to music on the radio. She heard a voice, somewhere *inside* the music—she said it was crystal clear—telling her to remove her clothing. I assumed it was the duet, as always. But things are so much better since the doctor upped her dosage. But the only thing that will really make a difference to her recovery? Is to get Mariama back. That woman is worth her weight in gold."

We spoke some more, and when I turned to leave, Ashton was standing at the end of the corridor like a specter. Tall and looming, anxiety flitting in his dark eyes. My heart missed a beat to see him there so unexpectedly. Had he heard that entire conversation?

# CHAPTER THIRTY-ONE

"Mr. Buchanan! What a nice surprise. I've just been having a long talk with your wife. Mrs. Buchanan's sleeping, I'm afraid. Give her an hour? Meanwhile, I'll leave y'all alone." Lucy gave us a friendly nod and shuffled off toward another patient's room.

"Vivien, hi," he said, standing there, not making any gesture to greet me.

"Hi," I replied, my voice weaker than I wished. "What a novelty to see you here."

His eyes were sad, his face drained. Our marriage was over. I'd be getting on a plane soon. I stood there, planted to the spot, feeling equal parts shameful and defiant. I took a deep breath and told myself that Ashton had gotten his just deserts. I refused to feel remorseful. Refused to feel like a bad person. We locked eyes.

"I had no idea that Mama had a new nurse," Ashton said, breaking the ice. "If I'd known I would have—"

"Lied better?" My accusation came out as a bark.

His mouth tipped into a kind of sardonic, almost-smile. "I can't deny it. I would've briefed that nurse to keep her mouth closed. I guess it's all out in the open now."

"Why did you lie to me?"

"Oh, we're going to pull out the lying card, are we? You want to talk to me about *lies*, Vivien? That's rich, coming from you."

I had no rebuttal to that. He was right.

He shook his head. Deep creases furrowed his brow. "I'm not sure why you wanted to turn me into this great big ogre. Very strange behavior."

"I'm sorry." But I wasn't sorry. Yes, I'd lied. But… so had he. My lie was black and white, his gray. *It's those gray lies that cut the most because they blur the truth.* Those "innocent" paper cuts so much more painful than a real nick deep in the flesh. As I recollected the injustice, I put myself back in his Honda, ripe for the picking, eager for attention, love, an escape from my parents and the chaos around me. There, Ashton was all charm and Southern drawl, telling me how he'd help me with my college entrance essay, how cool I was to want to rise above my poverty by working hard and going to university. When his hand strayed to the fabric of my panties, he was working me, a pre-meditated rape, really, but dressed up as "consent" because poor teenage Maeve O'Reilly didn't know any better, with her tacky acrylic nails and cheap tight top. He had already branded me as "trash." Even before he kissed me, even before he pushed himself inside me. He had cajoled me. Groomed me with promises of a future with him. He was twenty-two. Too old for excuses. Five years age gap was a lot for a seventeen-year-old back then.

No, Ashton Buchanan did *not* get to be the good guy, the victim. He'd lost a house, so frickin' what? I'd lost nearly *two decades*. Yes, I adored my daughter and I wouldn't swap her for the world, but that wasn't the point. I'd had my choices ripped away from me with lies.

Ashton regarded me now, as if reaching into my thoughts. "Hey, it's over now," he said. "You got one tough-cookie attorney, that's that truth. That Silverman? He had me over a barrel." He gave me a crooked smile. A real smile this time.

"You find this funny?"

"You're really something, you know that? The *lengths* you went to, Vivien! Un-fucking-believable. Really crazy. But kind of commendable, in a way. Got your ticket to the Bahamas?"

"Yeah," I said. "Leaving next week. You told me you wanted to say goodbye. I was expecting you to come to the house next week. I thought you were in Chicago doing that conference?"

"I was, but I canceled. I reckoned seeing Mama was more important than work. They told me she was in a bad way. I wanted to see for myself."

"Why did you lie to me, Ashton? Can you just answer that question? Why did you lie about your mom's condition?"

"Because gentlemen never tell. I had my story and stuck to it. You think I was gonna let my mama go to jail? For"—he lowered his voice to barely a whisper—"first, or even second-degree murder? No, no, that's not how things work with family."

"So you made up the storm? That boat trip with your dad, how he'd forgotten his cell phone and yours went overboard, the two-hundred-mile-an-hour wind, how his feet got tangled in weeds and he got hit by a piece of flying driftwood and drowned. You invented all that?"

He smiled again. Pleased that he'd fooled me with his tale. "I'm impressed with your memory. There *was* a storm. Just happened on a different day is all."

Ashton scanned our surroundings, his eyes traveling around the clinical hallway with apprehension. "Look, can we talk about this outside? Let's go for a walk."

Outside, in the grounds, we sat on a bench underneath a magnolia tree. The leaves had started to drop and a cool breeze caressed my hair.

"So you took the rap for what your mom did? What about forensics? What about police reports?"

"It's a small town. Nobody wanted a sweet old lady to go to jail. And, no, I did not 'take the rap.' We all figured out a solution. Mama saw a psychiatrist and it was confirmed that she had schizophrenia. There was no way she could testify or be held accountable for her actions. But when anyone asks me what happened to Pa? That's the story I stick to. And so should you, if anyone ever asks."

The way he'd said "we" made me wonder who "we" was. Influential people in high places who were friends of the family, who could make problems disappear?

I buttoned up my raincoat and adjusted the silk scarf I was wearing around my neck. Ashton had on a camel cashmere overcoat, his shoes spit-polished to a gleaming shine, as usual. He looked dapper, elegant. A far cry from that character Cady and I had created in his ketchup-stained T-shirt. A wave of shame washed over me. I hated these see-saw feelings I had. Self-reprisal followed instantly by self-congratulation, and justification. Guilt paired with glee.

As we sat side by side on the bench, I didn't want to give Ashton even a sideways glance. Didn't want to see the self-pity etched on his face or let him make me feel like I was the Wicked Witch of the West.

"You said 'confirmed that she had schizophrenia,'" I asked. "What do you mean by 'confirmed'?"

"Things had never been quite right with Mama," he said. "Not since as long as I can remember. She was always unstable. Unpredictable. Mood swings high and low. One minute the sun, the next a hurricane. Decisions flipping on a dime. We didn't analyze it—it was who she was. Never knew if we had to prepare for war or a cuddle. We were on constant alert, especially Lily. Between the two of them… my parents? Boy, there'd be some fights. Crockery flying. Screaming matches. Once Mama stabbed Papa in the leg while he slept."

This was the first time Ashton had talked about Lily.

"They didn't do couples therapy?" I asked.

"Did you and I do couples therapy?"

*Good point.* I cast my eyes down. He was right. I'd beelined us straight into the annulment.

"Ha! 'Therapy's for wimps,'" Ashton said, imitating an exaggerated, gruff Southern twang. "That's what Pa always said. Mama agreed. They thrived on their battles, like fire thrives on wind. They took gleeful pleasure out of hurting one another and even more pleasure in making up."

"What happened… finally?" I asked. "What was the tipping point?"

"She told Papa she wanted to go fishing. Oh, my word, that was music to his ears. He was a very proud man, proud of his job as a shrimper. She hadn't been out in the boat with him for years, not since they were courting. Felt it was beneath her somewhat. He used to invite her out all the time, but she never went. Told him she didn't want to mess up her hair. Anyway, they set out on the boat together one summer's day—not his fishing boat, but the FlatsMaster—one Sunday. I wasn't even home. Seven-some years ago. She made a picnic, fixed it all beautifully. Wore a pretty dress, all gussied up. Hair nice. Makeup. Papa was in his element, thought the marriage was back to where it had been once. Romantic, special. After lunch, after he'd done drinking a whole lot, when he was peacefully fishing, sitting at the edge of the boat, she whacked him over the head with the oar. He'd been drinking enough and he was surprised enough that he toppled into the water. As he was trying to scramble back in the boat, she smashed him over and over and over again with a butt end of the oar till his head split open. Left him bleeding in the ocean. Then she started the engine and motored away, cool as icebox pie."

"Wow. Really pre-meditated." He nodded at my choice of word, *pre-meditated*. "So Georgia-May was admitted here, to this private clinic?"

"Took some managing to get her here to this nice place. I pulled a lot of strings."

"Lucky she didn't go to jail."

He nodded. "Jail was never on the cards. I held tight to my story, even if people did guess the truth. You know how many mentally ill patients are locked up right now? The jails are chockablock full of people with mental health issues. Vulnerable people who are in places they shouldn't be."

I wondered if it really had been "the duet" who had told Georgia-May to smash Buck over the head with an oar, or her own free will. A "vulnerable" murderess. Now I knew why Ashton hadn't wanted her to live in the guest house.

He angled his body toward me with an urgent jerk of his neck. "By the way, everything I've shared with you, Vivien, is in the strictest confidence. I never want to speak of it again, and if you, or anyone else brings it up, ever, I will refute what I've said, is that clear?"

Georgia-May's denial popped into my mind: *I'm telling you that Buck and I had the perfect marriage, and if anyone—I mean anyone—tells you different, they are quite simply… lying.*

"Course," I agreed. "I won't say a word."

I half expected Ashton's confidence to be somewhat hammered because of everything that had happened lately—the annulment, losing the Harbour Island home to me—but he was still the smooth-talking, high-walking Ashton I had always known. Nothing I had done seemed to ruffle his feathers. I guessed he was thrilled to be getting rid of me. Probably thought our marriage had been a close shave and money didn't mean that much to him. He'd paid me off, no big deal. *What's a house when you're earning a couple million a year?* He could buy another vacation home if he so chose. For me, it was everything. My lifeblood. A chance to start afresh, to not be haunted by anyone, controlled by anyone. A man like Ashton was in control of everything. Even his patients' brains. *It must make him feel like God,* I thought. *A kind of arrogance that we mere mortals never experience.* I had read in the papers recently how he had saved a famous senator's life. It was everywhere: Twitter, Facebook, the news. Ashton had become a bit of a star.

We both remained on the bench, not speaking, each to our own musings.

*Do we live inside our memories? Or do memories live inside us?* I wondered this. One thing was clear to me: I would no longer be held emotionally hostage by this man.

A crispy leaf fluttered down, landing on my head. I was surprised when Ashton picked it out of my hair—a tender gesture. Almost as if to say, *I don't hate you.* I was curious what he'd do for Christmas. I would be in Harbour Island, far away from gift shopping and malls playing "Jingle Bells," and laced with the aroma of hot apple cider and holiday decorations. I'd be on the beach, kicking up pink sand, reading novels, sunbathing, swimming in the ocean. Cady would come and stay for the vacation. Maybe Ashton would start hanging out at the Citrus Club again and meet another woman? He probably had females already lining up for him in droves. Maybe he'd have a baby with his next wife? He certainly hadn't wanted one with me.

Neither of us spoke for several minutes. I filled the silence with an out-of-the-blue question.

I dropped my voice to a whisper. "What about your sister, Lily? Did Georgia-May kill her too?"

Surprisingly, Ashton didn't flinch. "Lily's life was made a nightmare by Mama. I never understood why. Sometimes I wondered if she was jealous of her. It was okay when Lily was younger but later, when she approached her teens, Mama just wouldn't leave her alone, picked on her constantly, broke her spirit. Even tanned her hide whenever she could. Lily spent every moment possible out of the house. Swimming, boating, fishing with Papa. Anything to stay away from Mama. I should've intervened a lot earlier than I did. Lily never fought back. Sometimes silent voices speak the loudest."

I wasn't sure what Ashton was trying to tell me. *Silent voices speak the loudest?* "So Georgia-May killed her? It wasn't suicide?"

Ashton smiled at me. A fatherly, vaguely exasperated, you-really-wanna-know smile, as if I were a bothersome child. "I think that's enough for today. One confession's quite enough, don't you agree?"

I banished my suspicions away. Whether Lily killed herself or one of them did it, it was no longer my concern. I'd be out of their lives forever. I needed to let all this go. It wasn't any of my business anymore.

I got up abruptly. Brushed the wrinkles from my raincoat. "Well," I said efficiently, annoyed by his condescending attitude. "I guess this is goodbye."

Ashton sprang up too. Pushed a swathe of hair, flopping over one eye, out of his face. "Guess you're right. I've got conferences in New York all week. I won't be able to make it over to Distant Sands. This is goodbye then."

Hearing those words made my stomach roil. It was the finality of them. I had lived with Ashton Buchanan—in my heart, mind, and then in the flesh—for over seventeen years. Would this really be goodbye? I wished it so with all my might. I wished him away, out of my life, out of my thoughts.

"Do you hate me?" I said, catching myself off guard, my resolve veering into dangerous waters. What had just spilled, unbidden, from my lips? He probably thought I was like a petulant little girl wanting to have her cake and eat it too. Retaining both my pay-off and the best parts of our marriage—the happy memories intact. The love we'd shared unmarred even if the foundation of that love was sand. But I had asked my question out of curiosity, more than anything. *What is he thinking? What's going through his mind?*

Ashton cocked his head, the way a painter might do with his subject to measure tone, shadows or perspective, as if boxing me into a frame. "I don't know yet. I'm still trying to work that one out. If I hate you or not."

I lifted my gaze to his six-foot-three frame, always a head taller than me. Was he sad? Amused? Furious? What was going on behind the gateway of his soul?

He narrowed his eyes. A poker face, still studying me. "One thing's for sure. You've been one helluva pain in the ass."

"We're both free now, what a relief," I retorted, hoping I'd spike him with a little taste of hurt. "Short but sweet. No harm done. No kids, nothing to bind us."

He clucked his tongue. "You understand now, of course, why I never wanted children with you?" he said.

I looked at him, nonplussed.

"Schizophrenia can be hereditary," he explained. "It runs in my family. Has for generations. Especially with the womenfolk. I didn't want to take the risk of having a schizophrenic kid."

My blood ran cold.

# CHAPTER THIRTY-TWO

Sitting in the safety of my car, I thumbed through Cady's Facebook and Instagram pages, and text messages we'd sent back and forth to each other, frantically searching for signs of schizophrenic tendencies or symptoms. Or any indication of mental health problems. Nothing jumped out at me. Typical teenage behavior, I decided. Teenage likes and dislikes, taking into account her place in the modern world: Generation Z. These kids had been raised with floods, fires, lying politicians, climate change disasters, online stalking pedophiles, and burgeoning unemployment. Her generation was angry and wanted answers. They were doing great considering the trials they faced and the mess they'd need to clean up after the "baby boomers" and generations before, and after. Cady was an outraged teenager, *not* a schizophrenic. She was a normal, mouthy, opinionated young woman, finding her voice.

I punched in various keywords into the Google search bar: adolescents, mental health, schizophrenic. Reams of results flooded the page. I deleted "mental health" to narrow it down. It talked of the possible signs of early schizophrenic behavior. "Shy, withdrawn. Fears. Clinging more to parents." Nope, that sure as hell wasn't Cady. "Feelings and perceptions grossly distorted from reality." Again, no. That described Georgia-May but not Cady. Cady's militant stance on climate change et cetera was definitely based on scientific evidence. So, no, Cady's fears about the planet in peril were not exaggerated. Some kids her age were drowning their fears with alcohol and drugs and were in total denial.

I scanned more results: "Suspiciousness. Paranoia. Hallucinations. Difficulty in performing schoolwork."

None of this applied to Cady. She was a straight-A student. She was superstitious, yes—obsessed with omens and numbers, endlessly throwing salt over her shoulder, but not *suspicious*. She was just fine. My daughter's mental health was in great shape! A lot of things I read about schizophrenia did, however, apply to Georgia-May. "The duet" and voices telling her what to do. That was a typical sign of schizophrenia.

I sucked in a long breath and exhaled with gratification, started the car, relieved to know there was absolutely nothing wrong with my child whatsoever.

No, I had absolutely nothing to worry about with Cady. My daughter was just fine. If there really were mental health issues in Ashton's bloodline, it had skipped over Cady.

I called her. She picked up on the third ring. "Hi, Mom."

"Honey, hi, how are you?" I was careful now not to use the word "hon."

"Just hanging out with friends. Made a ton of new ones. Catching up with work. I missed a lot when I was away. Still, I got A's in AP World History and Honors Biology. My faculty advisor's super happy. I'll send you my essays by email. I'm going to join the creative writing club next semester."

"Great, honey. I'd love to read your essays. Happy to be back at Wonderwood?"

"So happy. I made the swim team. So cool having the new indoor pool."

"Great. Good on you."

We chatted on for a while, my bones feeling more weightless with each minute that passed. Everything was hunky dory. Being at Distant Sands had been the worst thing for Cady, ever.

Thank God she was back where she was meant to be. A renewed current of guilt passed through me, thinking about what I'd put her through with my own selfish behavior.

"Love you so much, honey, take care." But even as I said those words, a niggling voice inside me told me that things with Cady were not quite right.

# CHAPTER THIRTY-THREE

It was a strange thing that I had done, moving into the guest cottage from the main house. The cottage suited me so much better. I peered through the window at the garden. Eve, the great oak, a barrier between me and that perfect specimen of antebellum architecture that felt too grand to be my home, too imposing. The backyard was so lush and green—it had been raining a lot the last week. I was glad I'd be leaving Distant Sands behind, especially as winter was on the horizon.

The wind had picked up, the sound a little eerie, although it was beautiful here, I couldn't deny that. As my eyes drifted over the view, I made myself a cup of coffee. Then curled my knees up under me on the sofa and, on my laptop, changed my ticket to the Bahamas for the day after tomorrow. No point staying here any longer. I browsed through my e-reader for a book. I'd uploaded hundreds, one-clicking on all sorts of different genres, sometimes regretting the purchase afterward. Flicking through, I decided to go back to an old favorite: *Jane Eyre*. I hadn't read it for so many years. The last time, on my second read, I remembered how disillusioned I had been with Mr. Rochester: not the romantic hero I'd discovered on my first read of the masterpiece. I wondered how I'd see him now. Funny how men can seem like heroes and then years later be jerks. The same book, the same story, but you perceive them in a different light, from a different, perhaps more mature perspective. Suddenly Mr. Rochester wasn't the brooding alpha male, after all, but an undeserving cad. Jane should've left him. But women do strange things in love, don't they?

I spent the day holed up on the sofa, a hot drink here, a snack there, listening to the patter of rain, the breeze rustling through the trees, ensconced in Jane Eyre's head. I'd gotten to the part in the book where we find out Rochester's courtship with Blanche Ingram is a ruse to make Jane jealous. Meanwhile, his wife is locked up in the attic. How had I found this man so romantic in the past? On this third reading, I demoted him from three stars to two. The attic… that reminded me. Earlier this morning I had noticed the attic window—the big window in the pediment—had blown open. I wasn't sure how long it had been unlatched. Had owls or possums or some kind of creatures gotten through the window and set up home? Maybe that's what those scuffling noises were that I'd heard last time I was in the house. A storm was predicted this evening. I needed to go and deal with it, pronto.

My attention got sucked back into *Jane Eyre*. A quote reared out at me: *I desired liberty; for liberty I gasped; for liberty I uttered a prayer; it seemed scattered on the wind then faintly blowing.* So apt for how I was feeling now.

As I was pontificating, celebrating my upcoming liberty, I heard a car roll into the driveway, headlights on. Not surprising they needed lights on this gray, cloud-filled day. Footsteps crunching on the gravel, but uneasy ones. I rushed to the window and observed a figure approach the front door, hesitate, peer through the window then walk away. I couldn't see if it was a man or a woman. Who could it be? My first thought was that it was a cop. Word was out that Cady was my daughter and that we'd set Ashton up! *Oh, God.* A sense of doom burned deep in my belly. Had Cady called them, after all, and reported the "assault"? Had Ashton tattletaled on me? I wanted to hide. Panic pattered—along with the gentle rain—in my head. It brought me back to when I was a child and the cops would haul my dad home, plastered, staggering, his breath rancid with beer or rum or whatever he could lay his hands on. Sometimes they'd fish him out of the gutter. Other times it might be a breakup from a punch-up, my dad usually the loser. Cut lip, blood on his clothing. My mother hysterical when he lurched through the doorway, me cowering in my bedroom, pretending to be asleep, dreading what would happen next. Hoping he was too drunk to whip off his belt and strike Mom. He'd crash around, usually, until he collapsed on the couch asleep, snoring the world away.

I braced myself, raised my chin and walked out of the cottage, head held high. Whatever they wanted would catch up with me at some point; better to face it now. But the car's engine started, and the car, a silver one, and too fast for me to catch the number plate, headed in a dash out the driveway.

The big house loomed over me with its grandeur. As I looked up, remembering the attic window, I noticed the French doors by the upper back porch on the second floor were also wide open. How had that happened? The wind wasn't *that* strong. The phantom iced tea drinker popped into my mind. The *LEAVE ASHTON WHILE THE GOING'S GOOD* note. The idea of going into the main house alone on this gray day spooked me. The light was fading. The house would be getting gloomy, ominous. All that dark furniture… all those portraits…

But I couldn't leave the windows open. I headed back to the cottage, grabbed the house keys and unlocked the door to the main house.

I entered the hallway, switched on the lights. The elegant, curved marble staircase always took my breath away. The baby grand piano, the paintings, the chandelier. The first time I saw Distant Sands, my mouth had dropped in awe and I still felt that goosebumpy "wow" shiver run along my arms.

I slowly climbed the stairs, taking in with appreciation the corniced ceiling, the ornate wrought-iron bannisters and the opulent surroundings. This would no longer be my house. *This could be my last moment in this place.* I stopped at the landing and went into the upstairs drawing room to close the offending French doors. Rainwater had gushed in and there was water pooled on the herringbone parquet floor. Whoops, there'd be a water stain; I'd have to ask Olive to work her magic with whatever oils or polish she used. I closed the doors tight and wandered around the room to check the windows. My gaze rested on the mahogany legs of an exquisitely carved ball-and-claw-foot Chippendale card table: something about those grasping talons made me feel uneasy.

A spooky feeling ran through me—left over from childhood, no doubt, watching movies that were too grown-up for me, holed in my bedroom while my parents fought. I had their old portable TV—they had a shiny new one. My dad would sit glued to the sports channel, while I'd watch *Friday the 13th* films, and slasher movies. Knowing that people had it worse than me back then was comforting.

Outside, the night had stolen the dusk away. It was almost dark. The sky moody, swathes of purple rain clouds rolling in from beyond the woods. I locked the front door and went to the kitchen, checked the doors and windows were also locked, and grabbed a mop and pail, went back upstairs and cleaned the rainwater from the floor. The house was so eerily silent—*thank God for the cottage.* I braced myself to do the rounds of each and every room to make sure there were no other windows or doors open for more water to get in. The silk curtains could be irreparably damaged, not to mention the floors. It took me a good twenty-five minutes to go around the house, checking all the doors and windows were locked tight—ears perked up for any tiny noise. I heard some bangs. The wind. Probably the window in the attic, the last place I had to deal with, which I was dreading.

Just for good measure, I first grabbed an old baseball bat from the closet where we kept the tennis and badminton rackets. The old wooden bat looked like something left over from Ashton's childhood. It gave me courage. I fished my phone out of my jacket pocket, double-checked it was charged. Eyes wide, I carried on with my ascent. Up, up, up. Past the landing, where my bedroom was. Heart racing, I thought I heard something banging again and couldn't make out if it was from below or if it was just the wind rustling through the windows or the slamming rain, which had suddenly started lashing from the deep dark clouds. I started to take off my sneakers (it's always faster to run barefoot), but then I decided, no, I shouldn't take my shoes off, because I needed to protect my feet. Just in case there were splinters in the attic floorboards. Or if I needed to kick someone. Although my sneakers wouldn't do much damage.

At the top of the marble staircase, on the third floor, the stairs changed to wooden ones leading up to the attic.

I heard an almighty bang.

# CHAPTER THIRTY-FOUR

I tightened my grip around the baseball bat, my hands clammy and sticky holding onto it for dear life, feeling like I had eyes in the back of my head as I kept my body at an angle, looking ahead and side to side, turning around every so often with rolling furtive eyes, to make sure nobody was behind me. The bogeyman. The man in the mask. The axe-man. I put one foot in front of the other as I slowly mounted the wooden steps.

I got to the top of the staircase and gingerly slid open the bolt on the door, my heart thumping so loud, me still clutching the bat. My pounding blood almost hurt my ears. I was close to turning around, going back downstairs and calling it a day, but I went in. I needed to close that window. I stood at the entrance of the attic. Clenched the baseball bat between my knees as I turned on my cell phone's flashlight, because I couldn't remember where the light switch in the room was and didn't want to fumble about in the dark while some nutjob chopped me up with an axe. I hardly ever came up here so I didn't know my way around. It was too freaky. I found the light switch to my right, but the bulb in the light exploded the second I flipped the switch. Gripping the bat in one hand and holding the phone in the other, I pointed the flashlight around the room.

The attic was bigger than I remembered from last time. My eyes darted around the space. Bookshelves with piles of dusty books. An old bird's nest that nobody had taken away. A stack of paintings. A massive oval mirror, the frame cracked. A dusty old camelback sofa, the upholstery torn. Some stacked Queen Anne dining chairs with holes in the rattan. A ripped-up love seat. It smelled of dust and the sweet smell of rain, which pattered on the roof and in great dollops against the window, which was swinging back and forth on its hinges. Beneath the window was an old fire escape rope ladder, fixed to the wall. A dusty fire hydrant too, probably well out of date. Other than the open window, nothing out of the ordinary. Outside it was now dark, the sky a smear of blue and purple… the opaque gaze of the moon peeping through scudding thunder clouds dipping low and threatening menace. Everything quiet save the relentless rain slashing the side of the house, the roar of the wind.

I looked around cautiously. I couldn't see any traces of animal droppings. No possums or birds. No rats or mice. I stepped in, leaving the door ajar, holding the baseball bat in one hand, ready to swing, turning my body around in circles as I walked to make sure nobody could sneak up behind me. The roof pitched in the middle at the highest point. Below it, an aluminum stepladder, which drew my focus up to the top wooden beam. Sweat started to trickle down my forehead of its own accord. My scalp tingled; blood crawled through my veins… my eyes focused on something so sinister my throat closed up: a hangman's noose. Right there, dangling from the main support beam. The hessian rope, new. I had never seen it before.

I counted the turns in the rope. Seven turns wrapping around the base of the loop forming the noose. And I wondered… was I going crazy? Had this been there all along? Was it left over from Lily's time? But they told me she had drowned. And then there was the possibility that Georgia-May had killed her. Was this a dress rehearsal, before Lily switched her medium of suicide from hanging to drowning? No, this rope was brand new, and her death had happened ages ago.

Then it clicked. Cady had made that knot. Had contemplated suicide (her interest in Sylvia Plath and Virginia Woolf made sense). Thank God she'd changed her mind and decided to go back to school. A whoosh of panic. Would she try this at Wonderwood? No, I'd seen all those happy photos of her on Facebook, she was doing so well with her studies. I had even had a couple of emails from her teachers praising her work. This noose gave me the shivers. Blood pounding behind my eyes with fear and nausea, I quickly raced back to the door, closed it behind me and locked it from the outside again. I hadn't shut the window. Too bad, I'd do it in the light of the day. I tore downstairs, jumping two steps at a time, still holding the bat, shoving my phone into my jacket pocket.

Being in this house alone was crazy. No wonder I'd moved into the cottage. I couldn't wait to get out of Distant Sands altogether. Only two more days to go until the Bahamas.

An ominous voice snapped in my head, warning me, *Dumbass, don't you GET it?*

Get what?

*Ashton!*

I felt a dip in my solar plexus. Had *Ashton* made that hangman's noose? He was great with knots. Was that possible? *One confession's enough, don't you agree?* he had said. It wasn't Georgia-May who had killed Lily. Maybe *Ashton* had given Lily a helping hand—was that why he was so cagey? I'd lapped up his whole story, and who was to say his story was true? Was I next? With a nice, new, fresh noose waiting for me? Was that why he seemed so laissez-faire about the Harbour Island house? But then… that didn't make sense either because it was part of the annulment deal. My mind was doing acrobatics, trying to make sense of everything.

My phone buzzed and my heart exploded out of my chest with the shock, as if someone had leapt out from behind a curtain and said *Boo!* I was halfway down the stairs, looking onto the baby grand in the hallway, the room bathed in chiaroscuro shadows from the chandelier. Someone had left the lid on the piano keys open. That wasn't like Olive. I fished my cell out of my pocket, the flashlight still on. I turned it off. Thank God, it was just a text from Cady.

*Hi Mom, making biscuits with Jenny. Can we use rice flour instead of regular flour? Love you miss you.*

As I was about to reply, thinking how late in the day it was to be cooking, another thing dawned on me: one of the hallway lights I'd definitely left on was off. I'd locked every door in the house. The only people who had the keys beside me were Ashton and Olive. Yet… I'd pulled the bolts across too. In which case, having keys would do no good. How had anyone broken in? Unless they were *already in the house!* I stood stock-still, cocked my ears for any tiny sound. My pulse thumped wildly, my temples beaded with sweat.

It was then I heard her laugh, high-pitched and raucous.

Cady shot out from behind the marble staircase and positioned herself on the bottom step. I was about to rush toward her with an embrace. But froze. She was pointing Ashton's shotgun at me. At my racing heart.

"Fuck, I hate this thing," she said. "What a jerk Ashton is to be into hunting." She looked at the gun like it was a toy.

I clung onto the bannister, adrenaline surging through me in great waves. I knew, from all my arguments with Ashton, that thing was loaded. I wanted to run, but my body wouldn't obey. I felt as heavy and immobile as rock. *Is this a practical joke?* "Cady, my God, you terrified me. I thought you were at—"

"School?"

"Yes, you just texted, you—"

"Joke!" she said, then burst out laughing. "Jeez, you should have seen the look on your face when I pointed this at you!" She put the gun into a vertical position, nose down, like a child soldier from some war zone. "In all these years you haven't changed, Mom. Still so naïve. Believing whatever bullshit you wanna believe. You are *so* gullible." She laughed again.

I was shaking from the shock. "Did you make that noose in the attic?"

"What the hell are you talking about?"

"How long have you been in the house?"

"Got here today."

"I wish you hadn't left the French doors open."

"Wasn't me. But I *did* snoop around the house some. That's when I found this shotgun. What a great guy to go around killing animals for"—she made air quotes—"'sport.' You know what I say? It's only sport when two parties are playing."

"What are you thinking, Cady?" My voice rose several octaves. "Messing with that gun? Prank *over!* Set that thing down properly on the floor, and *gently…* it's loaded!"

She did as I said. I closed my eyes, half expecting it to go off.

"I'm, like, so disappointed with that man," she groaned. "Can't decide who's more selfish, you or him. The world's fucked up enough without you guys making it worse. Great biological parents I got dealt—because neither of you can even begin to know what parenting means."

"Please, honey. Come on. Give me a hug and say hello properly. That was crazy what you just did pointing that thing at me." But I still stood there on the steps, not moving, wary of my daughter, remembering what Ashton had said about schizophrenia running in his bloodline, *especially with the womenfolk*. I was scared of that rifle. Cady was behaving very strangely. My heart was pattering behind my ribcage.

She didn't move from her spot. "Oh yeah? *You're* the crazy one. You lie, you cheat, you've stolen from your husband. You think I'm proud of being your daughter? A person always out for revenge? Bitter, vengeful? Full of spite?"

I held my own. I would not go down the accusation rabbit hole. "Why aren't you in school?"

"I'm done with that place."

"But, honey, I saw your pictures on social media, it looked like everything was going so well!"

"People will believe whatever they wanna believe. That's what social media is: a big fat fake platform for people to post their bullshit."

My gaze strayed from her face—her mouth taut, her eyes on fire—to her translucent hands. Her knuckles were white.

"This whole situation's fucked up. I wanted to get to know my dad. Went on a bike ride, out in the boat. He showed me how to drive it. He's kind of nice, but like... he hunts, for fuck's sake. And you? You *used* me. Used me to get to him. Used your own daughter for your fucked-up revenge plan. I was totally manipulated by you."

"No! That's not true, that's—"

"I mean, imagine. Let's just imagine for a minute. If I was a bad person? I could kill you right now, Mom." She nudged the rifle with her foot. "Dr. Ashton Buchanan's fingerprints are all over this thing. He 'accosted' me, remember? Dirty old man falls in love with nymphet less than half her age, becomes obsessed and kills wife. Perfect."

"Stop it, Cady! Please, baby." Tears sprang to my eyes. I wanted to rush toward her, embrace her, or the opposite: charge at her with the bat and smash the shotgun away like it was a baseball, but I continued to stand on the stairs, rigid with fear. *What if she's serious? What if she picks up that gun again?* I needed to stay calm.

She laughed. "Imagine the scenario, Mom. I'd clean the mess up so badly so there'd be traces of blood under ultraviolet light—you know, like the light they use in *CSI*? But it wouldn't look obvious. Sloppy. Then Ashton would look even guiltier." She laughed. "I'd dig a shallow grave for you because it wouldn't be easy for me, just a girl—it must be a shitload of work—and they'd accuse Ashton of first-degree murder."

My blood slowed to a cold crawl. "You're crazy." My voice quivered, hardly getting the words out. I knew if I made a dash for the gun to get it away from her, things could turn ugly. *That's how people get killed. Stay calm.*

"A nice shallow grave just behind the backyard in the woods. The first place those dumb detectives look is on social media. I'd have an alibi. It wouldn't even occur to them that I wasn't at school. My friends would lie for me… for cash. Or drugs. I'd have tight alibis. I've been handing in all my work at school, sending it in by email to my teachers, which is how they ask us to deliver homework anyway. A friend's been signing me in to classes, so I can graduate, you know? Don't want to miss out on any credits. The teachers are so up their own asses there, they won't even notice I'm not there."

What she said was likely. Cady's school was one of those cool, hippy places, where they called their laidback teachers by their first names. It was a very casual institution. They were encouraged to be independent and "freethinking." I should've sent her to a normal school, not a school for trust-fund kids. This scenario she was describing of killing me was terrifying. Not my idea of a joke, even though she was half smiling as she said it all. It was sick what she was playing at. I drew in a breath. *Stay calm.*

"At first, I wanted my daddy back," she went on. "Didn't think you deserved him and we really bonded—at least when I got to know him over dinner. Thought he was a very cool person. But when that shit hit the news about him saving that fuck's life. Oh, man, what a disappointment! So not cool. And when I found this hunting rifle? Even worse. The guy's got his priorities all screwed up."

"What do you mean?" I said. All I could think about was getting her away from that shotgun. *Keep her talking. Keep her talking.* "Ashton saving lives is the most admirable thing about him."

"He shoulda been a vet or something honorable."

"Even vets have to make hard choices sometimes. You know what, honey, why don't we get out of the hallway, sit down somewhere and talk this through?"

She ignored my suggestion. "You know *who* the asshole was he saved, right?"

"Does it matter? A life is a life."

"Not when it's some white supremacist scumbag fucker who's just signed a bill to end the endangered species act. But oh! Logging and drilling are so much more important than grizzly bears and bald eagles. *Not!* My 'genius' father went and resurrected that monster's gaga brain. That racist, trophy-hunting, oil-drilling, gas-lobbyist fuck senator!"

Cady sat down in a cross-legged position. Right next to the freaking gun. I had to play this right. How she was behaving was nuts.

"Cady, doctors don't sit around discussing whose lives they save or who they'll let die. They make an oath. Creed, color, religion, even politics or ecology cannot, and does not, come into it. It can't. He did what he had to do." I couldn't believe I was defending Ashton, the man who'd gotten me into this mess in the first place.

"Oh, you're protecting him now? You know, up till he saved that douchebag's life I thought maybe I could love him a little, as a father. But when Ashton—sorry, 'Dad'—plucked that tumor from that asshole's brain, I changed my mind. Then I found this gun behind a bookshelf. And it got my imagination going. All I could think about was, 'What if?' I remembered you'd bitched about that—Ashton keeping a loaded shotgun in the house. Poetic justice, right, Mom? You know all about that one. Wouldn't that be kind of cool?"

Suddenly everything went into slow motion, as if I were hovering above the scene and was airborne, watching myself on the staircase below, a woman who had nothing to do with me. *Cady, this isn't you! This isn't the person you are.* My floating body sank back into itself with a jolt, my arms and legs were mine again, re-joining in a heart-skipping shudder. I was back in my petrified self, sweat pouring down my face, my underarms, the small of my back. Terrified that Cady might do something crazy, terrified that that noose in the attic was made by her. She'd been in the house. The noose was new. For a flash I wondered if she really did want to kill me, but I knew there was no way. That wasn't who she was. There was a whole lot of love inside of her for me, there had to be. I was her flesh and blood. I was her mom!

"Honey, I love you so much, you're my everything, you're my light, *please*, please stop talking this way."

"Oh, shut the fuck up. You think I'm gonna fall for that bullshit talk again? You've never given a damn about me... all I've ever been is a burden to you. All my life. You sent me to boarding school to see the back of me then all summer at camp while you loved it up with Ashton, trying to get back what you lost when you were seventeen, like jumping into some pathetic Clearasil commercial. Desperate to go back in time, weren't you, Mom? You told me enough times how having a kid stopped you from going to college and when I was born your chances were screwed of having a good life. You don't think that rubbed off on me? You don't think that destroyed me inside a little bit more every time?"

We held each other's gaze. Her beautiful brown eyes belied this dark character trying to possess my daughter. I blamed this house. Some negative spirit had got to her.

"It's not true, Cady, honey. When you were born, you were the best thing in my life. I counted your itty-bitty fingers and toes—so tiny! The mini nails, like they belonged to a little doll. I'd inhale your soft scalp that smelled of baby and soap and all things wonderful. You were the most beautiful thing I'd ever seen, you were like—"

"*Were?*"

"Still. *Still*, baby. You're my *life*, you're everything. Forgive me, honey. We can start afresh. Forgive me."

"Please spare me your Catholic bullshit about forgiveness."

"Yes, I have my failings, and I failed you and I'm sorry, honey, I love you so much. You're right. I was eighteen when I had you. Can you imagine? Could you imagine having a baby now? I was a child, practically almost the same age as you. Please, honey, please don't say those cruel things. I love you more than life itself."

A door slammed… was it the wind? Cady and I both turned simultaneously. It creaked eerily, then silence. I couldn't make out which door. Hadn't I bolted the kitchen door from inside?

Cady picked up the gun and aimed it at the hallway.

"That must be the wind," I croaked, half hoping it was Ashton. But I knew it wasn't possible. Ashton had gone to that conference in New York. Who, I wondered, could it be? Olive? No, she never came in the evenings. John the gardener? Ditto, he never came later than three o'clock. Lindy? Possibly. Possibly Lindy.

"Cady, please, put that thing down. It might be someone we know." There was another creak… on the floorboards this time. Cady's eyes snapped to the door.

"What was that?" she said. In an instant, I took my chances and charged upstairs. She bolted after me, the shotgun swinging from side to side in her grip, her thin pale arms flailing wildly as she careened up the stairs, only a few feet behind me. I kept speeding up, leaping three steps at a time, adrenaline coming from some place deep within me, giving me superhuman impetus to gain ground. I whirled around the stairs, Cady's footsteps flying after me. I wasn't running from an intruder, but Cady herself. What if that thing went off by mistake? I wanted to separate myself from her, get the hell away until she calmed down. As long as I could get into the attic and lock the door behind me, I'd have enough time to make it to the window, throw the rope ladder out and scramble down. Get away from her. Call the police. Tell them there was an intruder. *What if she turns the gun on herself?* I just didn't trust my daughter in the state she was in. The police would calm the situation down. I was torn in two; half of me wanted to stay with her, the other half flee. My car keys were in the cottage—damn! I wouldn't be able to drive away until I knew help was on its way. I felt like a bad mother. My instincts were telling me one thing, my mother-brain another. *I shouldn't abandon her, we need to talk this through.*

But adrenaline pumped through my body as fear propelled me up the steps. I barreled into the attic door, but the brusque movement made my cell phone slip out of my pocket and go tumbling down the stairs. *Noooo!* That had been my only hope. To call the police. Get them to get that freaking gun out of the house or at least get the thing unloaded. I hurriedly slid open the attic door bolt, hurled myself into the room, my eyesight blacked out by the lack of light. Slamming the door behind me, I grappled for the bolt the other side, wandering my fingers around the door. A slash of white lightning crashed outside the window, enough seconds for me to see that the bolt was broken. Swaying back and forth on its rusty old screws. I couldn't lock the door from the inside! I flew over to the window, the rain dashing in in great sheets. I threw the baseball bat down first, straddled the ledge while I pulled the rope ladder over the edge.

Cady stormed into the room. "What the fuck are you running away from me for, Mom? Don't you dare bail on me!"

I turned my head. Cady was just ten feet behind me, holding up that horrible rifle that Ashton had insisted on keeping loaded 24/7. I hated him so much in that moment. What had he been thinking, keeping a loaded shotgun in the house? I froze, not knowing what to do. It's amazing how the brain goes into lockdown when you're scared.

Cady's voice tremored. "If there's an intruder in this house I'm holding onto this gun. And you're staying by my side."

It was dark but my eyes adjusted slowly. I could just make out Cady's expression, fueled with murderous intent—her lips drawn into a thin line as she continued to point the gun around the room, her eyes peeled for an intruder. If she pulled that trigger at the wrong moment, not being able to see properly in the dark, I could get blown to pieces. She had no idea how to use a gun.

"Cady, put that thing down." I eyed up the stepladder, the aluminum glinting in the semi-darkness. The noose above it, dangling from the beam. Dread roiled in my stomach.

The window was swinging back and forth on its hinges. Flashes of cracked lightning lit Cady up like a specter, her mouth twisted in a cruel pout. An expression I'd never ever seen before. A bloodthirsty look, too, shining in her eyes. *What if she turns on me for real?* I weighed up my options. The rope ladder was dangling out the window, swaying in the wind. I could use it to scramble down, or grab the stepladder, and swing it so it would knock the shotgun out of her hands. I didn't trust her not to point it at me again and maybe even pull the trigger, especially after all that "what if" talk.

I eased myself away from the ledge, tiptoed toward the aluminum stepladder, grabbed it, and swung at the gun. She leaped sideways. I rammed it at the gun again, but this time the stepladder hit the mirror. The glass came crashing down to the floor, shards flying into every crevice, every corner of the attic.

"You fucking idiot, Mom, like you need more bad luck!" She doubled over, manically laughing. Amazingly, the gun hadn't gone off. It was still in Cady's hands. I wished now I had scrambled out the window when I'd had the chance.

I took another swipe at the gun.

"What the hell, Mom!" The force of the smash sent the gun flying out of her hands, and I pinned her against the wall with my body, edging my foot toward the rifle. By this time, my eyes were well adjusted to the dark. She thrust her head at me in a furious charge. I kicked the gun with all my might and it went sliding across the floor toward the doorway, too far for her to nab it now. Good! I was now by the bookcase. I threw a massive dictionary at the rifle to skid it further away, but I missed. It grazed Cady on the cheek as it went flying. Uh-oh.

"What the fuck? You wanna fight?" She bent down, seized a piece of broken mirror and came lunging after me.

"No! Cady, I didn't mean to hurt you," I yelled, ducking out the way. I pushed the bookcase over and it went crashing to the floor. I grappled for the stepladder again lying tumbled on its side, but this time I swung so hard it went careening across the room, knocking the gun in its wake, skidding it out of the attic door as the ladder itself wedged the door open. I heard the clunk, clunk, clunk of the gun tumble down the stairs. Relief fizzled through me. Grateful the weapon was far enough now out of Cady's reach.

She was armed with that shard of mirror, her temper roused after having been hit by the dictionary. Nothing I said would placate her. I tried, but she was in a rage. We were playing cat and mouse, and the crazy glint in her eye told me not to trust her. I swung my leg at her hand to knock away the spiky shard. Cady tripped me up, and I went skating across the floor, landing on my face. I rolled over in agony, my knee smashed, my head bleeding. She bent down, a sidelong smirk matching the menace in her eyes, lit up momentarily by another flash of lightning. Thunder rolled outside. Still horizontal on the dusty floor, Cady dragged me by the feet across the room as I kicked and splattered curses at her, waving my arms wildly. Somewhere between the kicking and the scuffling and the dragging, I realized I was bleeding from my midsection, too. I doubled up in pain. I felt the blood ooze from my stomach like water from a tap. She still hadn't let me go. Had she stabbed me on purpose? Was it an accident? I had no way to tell. With all my will and might, I swiped back at her with my corner of mirror and caught her on the hand. She let go of me. I managed to roll myself back up into a standing position.

"Fuck, bitch, that fuckin' hurt." Blood poured from her thumb. She swung her leg at me high, and I regretted the day I had enrolled her in taekwondo classes. Luckily, she'd only taken a few months' worth but still, her swing hit me on the chin, and I went flying backwards. My head knocked the wall, but I was still standing. Wind howled through the window; the storm had taken hold. Black thunder rumbled outside and another flash of lightning lit up the room again. Cady was making her way toward the gun. I didn't have time to think. I charged after her with a voltage of adrenaline that took even me by surprise.

"No, you don't!" I hurled myself at her. At that moment, the stepladder budged sideways and the door swung open. Footsteps on the stairs… men's footsteps, heavy and strong. The door flew open. A pair of hands held the gun. Cady wheeled around in shock.

Ashton.

"Enough!" he screamed. "Enough!" He pointed the gun at me.

For a second I thought he was going to kill me. His eyes glared enraged, pupils black and terrifying. *Oh my God, these two have trapped me in this attic and are in it together… they want me dead, both of them want me dead! Cady got her wish… Daddy's little girl…*

"Enough! It's over," he shouted again, this time veering the gun in Cady's direction.

Her eyes seemed to pop out of her head, and she turned and flew toward the window. Ashton steadied the barrel at her, and I waited for him—as if in slow motion once again—to pull the trigger. Instead of my life flooding before me, Cady's life began to uncoil inside me. It felt like minutes, not seconds. Floating in the endless sea of my womb, a heart forming, little blind eyes, scrunched and tight, led only by her miniscule limbs kicking and reaching for life. A mini brain nourished by the only thing in her embryotic world: me. Ashton had seeded her soul. I had embodied it. How could we destroy that?

"Don't!" I yelled. "Don't shoot our daughter! Don't you dare, don't you dare kill my daughter!" My instincts were like any mother's, even after everything Cady had said and done to me. "My baby! Our baby girl, leave her *alone*!"

Ashton kept the gun pointed at Cady, but he hesitated because of my screaming, giving her enough time to plunge her body out of the window, grip the rope ladder and scramble down. I raced to the ledge and watched as she and the rope ladder swung wildly in the thunder, sheets of rain whipping at the side of the house, swaying the flimsy ladder from side to side. I leaned out, hopelessly staring after her, watching as she made her frantic escape, blood soaking my shirt, my jacket, my jeans. But the rope ladder was dangling by a thread, shredded with age. One side had snapped. Cady grappled with it, her foot lost its hold with the jolt and, as the other old part of hessian rope gave way, she fell. I heard her screams as she plummeted to the ground. She had tumbled sideways, her head smashing on an iron urn at the bottom of the house. I couldn't see the full damage through the lashing rain. There was silence below, just the noise of the hissing wind, the rain, the bouts of thunder. Lightning lit Cady up in an eerie silhouette, and she lay quite still. I couldn't see if that was blood pooling out of her head forming a crown of red, or if it was rainwater. My mind went monochrome, trapped in a Hitchcockian nightmare. I stood there, dazed, blank… numb. I felt breath on my ear, whipped around to find Ashton right there. He blinked at me, pain in his eyes, then put his arms around me. I was too dumbstruck to move. For a second I feared he might strangle me. He had heard my scream: *Don't shoot our daughter*.

My charade was over.

"I thought you were going to kill me," I murmured, my body trembling, blood still pouring from the gash in my belly.

"Even if I had pulled the trigger, it wouldn't've done any good."

"What do you mean?"

A ghost of a smile. "The gun wasn't loaded."

I gawped at him.

"After the fuss you made," he explained, "I decided you were right. Not living alone anymore, I got your point. Keeping a loaded shotgun in the house was a dumb idea."

I leaned out the window. Cady's body was motionless.

Dead.

Our daughter was dead.

# CHAPTER THIRTY-FIVE

I snapped myself out of my reverie, jiggled away from Ashton's grasp and started to scramble from the attic. I didn't hear what he said calling after me in a plea. My one hope was that somehow a miracle had happened and Cady was still breathing. That's what it's like having a child—your love never runs dry, no matter what they do to you, no matter what they say.

Oh, the irony of that shotgun! The damage was done, loaded or not.

After my initial rush from the attic, I found myself doubling over, the blood still seeping from my wound. Not in great torrents like before, but I was weak, depleted. I hobbled down the stairs, balancing myself against the bannister. By the time I reached the landing where the marble stairs began, Ashton had caught up with me.

"Vivien, wait! Let me bind that wound." He tore off his shirt and stopped me from running further, trying to wrap it around my waist.

"We don't have time to mess around. Cady might still be alive!" I shook myself from him and loped down the stairs. My head was spinning; stars sprinkled themselves behind my vision then turned to blotches of color... red and green, then glaring white. It took all my effort to make my legs carry me down, one foot in front of the other, as carefully as I could in my panicked, weakened state. In a frantic bid to save every second on the clock, I tried to steam ahead. My head pounded as I wobbled on my jelly legs, which finally buckled with fatigue. Ashton caught me.

"You think Cady's my priority right now?" Before I could answer he had swooped me into his arms and was carrying me downstairs, his hand pressed on my wound like a plug.

"Damn, that's a nasty gash," he said. "So lucky I came home."

"We need to call the ambulance," I rasped, my mouth and throat feeling like cotton wool. I was thinking of Cady, not myself. Then I blacked out.

When I came to, which felt like only seconds later, my stomach was bound up. Ashton had stretched me out on a sofa in the hallway, hydrogen peroxide bottles scattered next to me, and first aid paraphernalia—scissors, bandages, gauze, ointments—Ashton acting as nurse.

"Cady!" I said.

"She's—"

"Dead?"

"No," Ashton replied. He shook his head. "She's gone."

"But that's impossible! She was lying there! Smashed on the ground!"

"The police are on their way. We'll find her, she can't be far."

I staggered to my feet. "I need to see with my own eyes."

I leaned on Ashton as he led me outside to beneath the pediment, beneath the window at the front of the house where Cady had fallen. What was left of the old rope ladder swayed back and forth in the wind, dangling and broken. The wildness of the weather had calmed down; the thunder had rolled off several miles away, distant and faint. The rain had slowed to a drizzle. My eyes scanned the spot where Cady had fallen. What I had taken to be blood was rainwater. What I had thought was an iron plant urn had been a trick of the eye. It was the baseball bat I had thrown down.

No sign of Cady. No trail of blood.

Cady had vanished.

# CHAPTER THIRTY-SIX

I spent two days in the hospital. I had lost a lot of blood and needed stitches in my stomach. Luckily, Cady had missed piercing my spleen and vital organs. More than anything I felt mentally exhausted and, as the date for my Bahamas departure slipped away from me, sadness swooped in. Ashton may have saved my life, but I had lost my daughter. The daughter who had attacked me. Or was it self-defense? It was all a blur. I had also lost my faith. I felt empty, my emotions splayed out on a chopping board. Meanwhile Ashton came and went, checking in on me. I was at his hospital and was treated like a queen. All the while, my words rang in my ears: *Don't you dare shoot my daughter.* So far, he hadn't mentioned what I'd said.

But he knew. The setup. Our scam. Every time he came in for a visit and I opened my mouth to explain, he'd tell me to "Just get some rest, we'll talk about it later. You need to heal."

Guilt rattled my brain. I felt like a prisoner of my own wicked deeds. Caught red-handed, still waiting for some kind of punishment.

Three days passed. Then four.

He'd found my phone smashed on the stairs but still working. I called Cady over and over. Voicemail every time, until a message came on saying her voicemail was full. I'd reported her missing to the police. She was only seventeen. Still a minor. I gave her real name, not the fake ID one that she'd turned up to Community Promise with.

All incoming calls I avoided. I felt too ashamed to speak to anyone. Waiting, waiting… waiting. Waiting for Ashton to confront me, but he said nothing. It was slow torture.

Finally, he told me it was time for us to go home.

"Home?" I echoed. The word felt so strange. I didn't feel like I had a home anymore.

"Yeah, home."

"Which is?"

"Why, Distant Sands of course."

I wanted to ask about my Harbour Island house but now wasn't the moment.

Ashton bundled me into his car, wrapped a blanket around me, put the seat back, and started for the highway. I closed my eyes and pretended to be sleeping to ward off the imminent conversation. I had no excuse, no comeback.

He knew Cady was my daughter. His daughter too. He knew we must have teamed up, had done everything to sully his reputation, to blackmail him. Blackmail him with lies.

He started to speak. "All right there, Vivien? Comfortable, honey?"

"Yes," I mumbled.

"Guess we need to talk."

I stayed silent, not knowing what to say.

Ashton continued driving. I felt safe with his driving, felt safe with him. How ironic was that, after everything? But he had saved my life, bound my wound, acted like some gallant hero. No recriminations. No accusations. He'd been a fucking saint. I closed my eyes again, wishing the inevitable away.

"Your black eye," he began.

My heart thrummed, not wanting to hear, yet curious. His voice was calm, not reproachful, in his trust-me-I'm-a-doctor tone.

"I realized it was fake," he went on, "when those frozen peas I put back into the freezer had purple makeup smeared on the packet. That was the first alarm bell. I just couldn't work out why. *What the hell's she doing?* I thought. *What does she want?* At first, I suspected you were a drama queen and wanted attention because I was working too hard, away at the hospital so much. But then I got wind you were spreading rumors about me in your oh-so-subtle way. My friends gave me the heads-up. Yet, I still couldn't work out what your angle was. I waited a while to see what would happen next, but the rumors got worse, your lies deepened."

I opened my mouth to speak, but I had no words. I remembered now. That was when Ashton had become cool toward me: after he took the frozen peas away. Duh! I had missed that. I'd double-checked the makeup was waterproof, had tested it. It was bad enough to be caught out, but to be caught out for being a fool…

He carried on talking. "So, then I came up with an idea. Lindy was fabulous, very inventive. We came up with a scenario—"

"*We?*"

Ashton laughed softly. "You forget that Richard's one of my closest friends. And Lindy's his loving, loyal wife. You think Lindy would put you before her own husband?"

"No, I—"

"We were all curious as hell to find out what you wanted. Was it money? A divorce? So Lindy lured you into my office to do some snooping around. Tempted you with the Harbour Island home."

It came back to me. How Lindy had that odd, knowing look on her face. And the too-cool tone of her voice when she told me Ashton didn't trust me. And the flash in her eyes of excitement when I let her in on how much the Harbour Island house was worth, when I had unearthed it from the drawer. Why hadn't I put two and two together when she'd found the key so quickly? "Secreted" in the model ship above the mantlepiece, as if she knew where it was hidden all along. Thinking about it now, yeah, a setup seemed so obvious.

"And," Ashton continued, in his Southern drawl, "you fell for Lindy's bait."

"Bait?"

"Your attorney, Silverman? Lindy's idea, if you recall. That you just *must* call a lawyer because of your terrible abusive husband! And she happened to know just the right person, didn't she? Even had his card at hand. Noah Silverman and I go back a long way, Vivien. Friends since we were six."

"But he's real! I checked him out! I checked out his website—he's one of the best attorneys in—"

"Oh, yeah, he's real all right. One of the best lawyers in the state. He's also one of my best friends."

"Lindy told me you hated him. That the only reason he was at our wedding was family obligation."

"Lindy's a pretty good actress, huh?" He laughed again. "Oh, Vivien. We had such *fun* fooling you, we really did. You were so gullible."

I sank into my seat, mortification flaring on my face, humiliation netting my body from scalp to toe. I didn't want to mention Cady or ask Ashton how much he knew. Didn't want to add salt to my festering wound.

He chatted on, one hand on the wheel—a casual glance at me, here and there. Suave talker. "The divorce? Or rather, the 'annulment'? It's not real, sweetie. It never got filed. There is no Harbour Island house waiting for you. No million bucks. Nothing, in fact, except what I can offer you on a day-to-day basis. We're still as married as we ever were. I still hold the reins in this marriage. You, my dear wife, belong to me. I told you, Buchanans don't do divorce. I have a pretty wife and I'm going to keep that pretty wife. Granted she's a bit crazy, but that's okay. I'm used to crazy. Crazy runs in my family. I refuse to be seen as a divorcee, a failure, a man who can't keep his woman under control or keep her happy. If there's one thing I pride myself on, it's my successes. And you are one of my successes, Vivien. At least that's the way I want the world to see me. Simple as that. Come along now, sweetheart, stop your silly games—we were doing so nicely as the perfect couple, the happy newlyweds, let's keep it that way."

"That's fraud, what that lawyer did!" I heard myself say indignantly. "I could sue Silverman for... for..." I couldn't even finish my sentence.

A honk of laughter. "I love it! *Love* the fight in you still when all's so horribly lost. Fraud, you say? It takes one to know one, honey." He put on some music. A beautiful clarinet concerto by Mozart. We glided along the highway in his navy-blue Porsche. Lights flickering past. Every time my face was lit up, I screwed my eyes shut. *See no evil, hear no evil.*

He smoothly changed gear. "The whole Cady thing really got me thinking. When you shouted out the other night in the attic about her being our daughter, you thought you'd let the cat out of the bag, didn't you? But I already knew. Boy, you made quite a mother-and-daughter team!" His laugh simmered away in his throat—he was so freaking amused.

My voice quavered. "How? How did you find out Cady was your daughter?"

"I decided to run her DNA. When I invited her in for a beer and then dinner? I kept the bottle and her glass. An old friend of mine's a detective; he did me the favor. Ran your DNA too. I assumed you both had some kind of criminal record. Because who in the world would scheme and plot like you two? I figured you were a pair of con artists, drifters."

I stared out of the window, not wanting to look him in the eye.

"Imagine my surprise, when not *only* were you two mother and daughter, but Cady was my frickin' daughter too!"

"You have your *own* DNA on a database?"

"I think I told you about that time when someone broke into the house and threatened Mama at gunpoint. Detectives took fingerprints and DNA samples from us all, to rule us out. I'd forgotten all about that, though… the DNA samples they had of me, so when my friend got in touch with me with the results… well, as you can imagine, it blew my mind. Then the puzzle pieces began to slot into place. You know why?"

Silence hovered in the shaming space between us. I wasn't going to satisfy him with a guess.

"Your Baltimore accent," he said. "The way you said 'bureau' like 'beer-o.' 'Bawl-mer' instead of 'Baltimore.' 'Merlin' instead of 'Maryland.' Only occasionally would your cute, funny accent slip out. If you were happy or tired. And that 'hon' you say so often? A dead giveaway. I knew all along you didn't hail from New York like you said, but from Baltimore. Hell, I spent enough time there at Johns Hopkins, at college, and all those years during my internship at the hospital. Lived in Baltimore half my life… I know a Baltimore accent when I hear it."

I cringed in the car seat.

Ashton went on, "There was something in particular you said that jogged my memory… I can't remember now what it was. A hazy memory of a really young girl telling me she was pregnant one time then promising me it was a bluff. It popped out of my subconscious and into my mind, because all those years ago it had freaked me out. Then it came to me. The pizza girl! You were the pizza girl whom I liaised with in my car! It occurred to me it must've been you! When we had sex in that old Honda I had when I was at college? You were the pizza girl, right? Tell me I'm right, Vivien."

My lashes wet, I nodded a yes.

"The frickin' pizza girl who decided to come back and give me a piece of her mind! I do declare, I probably did wrong by you. I was a young hotheaded student drinking way too much, giving very little damn about anyone but myself. Thought I'd used protection, but hey, my memory's not that sharp. Sex in a car sure as hell isn't the most romantic thing. Mother and baby came back to haunt me eighteen years later, pissed as hell!" He slapped his hand on the steering wheel gleefully. "And I said to myself, *what balls these women have!* I had to take my hat off to you both, but especially you, my dark angel, because I had fucking fallen in love with you—of course I had, that's why I married you. You know that, right? That you held my heart like glass in your hands?"

I couldn't reply. My humiliation was too great. Anger mixed in there, too, at having to relive the shame of being the wronged pizza girl with the big nose, all over again.

Ashton shot me a wry glance, then his eyes focused back on the road. "And I wondered to myself, *how did they do it?* When I found your phone on the stairs after Cady attacked you, half smashed but still working—I finally guessed your password—there were all sorts of texts between you and Cady filling in the blanks to my questions. I rubbed off the incriminating video of me, by the way… your 'evidence,' crossing fingers you hadn't already sent it halfway round the States. But kept the evidence of your scheming… for proof, just in case I needed it."

He shook his head and chuckled.

"Oh, the madness of it all! The sheer genius of it all! *This is a woman*, I thought, *who was—and still is—obsessed with me.* Has been plotting and scheming for nearly eighteen years and is obsessed. And you know what, my dear wife? It turned me on to think about you thinking about me *that fucking much! Well that just dills my pickle*, I thought. Hate. Love, it's all the same in the end. You 'hated' me so much I was all you thought about night and day."

"You're so arrogant," I mumbled, almost inaudibly. I wiped my tears with the back of my hand.

"You bet I'm arrogant. But I'm not dumb. I was born at night, but not *last* night. I had your number, Maeve O'Reilly. You got your

Blanche DuBois-slash-Vivien Leigh hand caught in the cookie jar."
He was grinning now, as if this whole thing was a fabulous joke.

"You seem to know everything," I said to the window face-
tiously.

"Yep, I know everything. I have a file as big as a phone book
on you. The private detective I hired did a great job. Very detailed,
down to your old address, your parents, et cetera, et cetera. Of
course, your medical chart was easy for a person like me to get
my hands on. I found all your medical interventions and elective
cosmetic surgery. I know everything about you. Even things you've
probably forgotten about yourself. The time you had chicken pox,
and measles, even the time your dad ripped out your earring and
you needed stitches in your ear, and when you won a prize for
an essay with that local magazine."

My whole life flooded behind and ahead of me. The Harbour
Island dream… dead like a poisoned fish floating in the ocean.
My past exposed, out in the open to be pecked and feasted on
by scavengers. I was a joke to Ashton. I was a joke to his friends.
All of them in on it together. My operation-get-even paled in
comparison with his operation-humiliation. Everyone would
know who I was now. What I'd been. What I'd done.

Ashton held his smile and then laughed again. "Pretty nuts, to
say the least. But then all the women in my life are crazy. Mom.
Lily. It makes sense my wife should be crazy, too. I can deal with
crazy. I'm a doctor."

I didn't share his sense of humor. "I'm not crazy!" I mumbled,
under my breath.

"Tell that to a judge or your friends at the country club."

I sat there glum and silent, fury emanating from every cell
in my body.

A cascade of merriment. "Why so sad, Vivien? Did Chevrolet
stop makin' trucks? Lighten up. Celebrate the fact you're still alive,
that you're still married to me!"

*Lighten up?* Was he crazy? Why wasn't he livid? Livid I could deal with. But being laughed at? The humiliation was sinking me. He'd *won*. He'd beaten me at my own game.

We rode along in silence, only the classical music, the breeze whistling through a small crack in the car window.

Finally, I said quietly, "So what now?"

"Till death do us part, baby."

"Are you *serious?*"

"Never more."

"And the Harbour Island house? It isn't yours, then?"

"Technically, kind of."

"What does 'technically kind of' mean?"

"I bought it for my sister, Lily. She's not called Lily anymore, of course. Like you, she changed her name. Many years ago. Needed to get away from the family, start a new life. I helped her on her way financially. Mama disowned her when Lily left home. Pretended to herself that she never had a daughter. Refused to ever speak of Lily again."

"Lily lives in that house in Harbour Island?"

"She lives in that house. She's a marine biologist. Pretty notorious for her work with tiger sharks. In fact, she's the one who got me into sharks in the first place. Her name now is Alex Leader."

Alex Leader, the same one Ashton had told Cady about? But there was something in the way Ashton said her name that made me suspect he was lying. Right there, in the car, I googled on my phone, *Alex Leader marine biologist Bahamas.*

The only photos that came up were longshots of someone diving with sharks.

It could have been anyone.

# CHAPTER THIRTY-SEVEN

It's an odd feeling when you've created your own prison, designed your own gilded cage. You want to fly, but you can't. The gold is too shiny, the cage too comfortable. I was an ornate bird with clipped wings. A beloved pet. But that didn't stop me from plotting and scheming my escape.

To the outside world, my life carried on as before with Ashton, yet the lies that hung between us were more intricate than Chantilly lace and thicker than Louisiana mud.

Nobody called me out on my fraudulent behavior. All his friends continued to smile and say things like "bless your pea-pickin' little heart," while secretly being disgusted by me, although they never let on, so I couldn't be sure what thoughts ticked over in their minds. To my face everyone was perfectly charming.

*If you don't have anything nice to say, then keep your pretty little mouth shut.*

Even *I* began to live by that mantra.

For now.

I thought of another one of their expressions: "Too poor to paint, too proud to whitewash." That was me.

I understood who I had been all along: the kid looking through the window of the candy store. Now I was inside the candy store and could have anything I wanted. But there was a catch: Daddy was paying. I had lied to Daddy, kicked up a fuss, stolen the candy and got caught red-handed. The shopkeeper was eyeing me warily. The customers, too. I had to prove to them that I was no longer a shoplifter and could be trusted. After all, why steal when something's being given to you anyway? If I wanted the candy, I could have it. Daddy would buy me whatever I liked. But I had to be a good girl.

My future plans for my life and interior dialogue would change from day to day. Sometimes I gobbled up the candy. Other times I was disgusted by its sweetness; *I will bide my time and get a real divorce. With an attorney whom Ashton doesn't know, this time around.*

Other days I admired my husband. It was extraordinary how he didn't hold a grudge. Maybe there was a lesson to be learned there. He had let go of the past. I should too. Those were the candy-gobbling days when I was high on sugar. When I convinced myself how good I had it and that I was a fool to throw it all away. Yes, I could leave with nothing, start a new life. But then what? I'd gotten accustomed to beautiful clothing, a nice car, bills paid like clockwork, help around the house, a gorgeous home, gifts from my husband, and, let's face it… great sex.

Although, something inside me doubted Ashton's benevolence. I was sure that someday, when I was least expecting it, he'd get his revenge. Send me to bed with no supper and lock me in the basement, chained up. That's why I needed to leave him first. Get out of this marriage when the time was right. Separate officially, then file a "no fault." Take my fair share. Ashton Buchanan still owed me, big time. But I had to be savvy. Had to play the game. Strike at the appropriate time. He was watching my every move. He had proof of what Cady and I had done. Taking anything more from this marriage than my birthday suit was unlikely, given the circumstances.

As for Cady? She simply disappeared. The police had tried to find her and failed. We found out that she had taken Ashton's boat for her getaway, down by the dock. She'd had enough time to run that night, and with the noise of the storm nobody heard the motor. The boat was found several miles away in Tybee Island. She must have found the keys in the kitchen. The police came across her phone, on the boat. Smart girl… she didn't want to be traced. But she'd wiped all incriminating messages off. No clues to where she was heading.

I imagined Cady making millions somewhere, branching out her drop shipping business—that girl didn't need a high school diploma or college degree to get ahead. Or maybe she'd hooked up with Greta Thunberg and her team and was fighting for ecology? I missed her, despite what she'd done. I hoped she would reach out, apologize. Was she aware she could have killed me with that slash to my stomach? What if Ashton hadn't saved the day? I often wondered about that. She is forgiven for what she did, but not forgotten. Ashton and I contracted his private detective, the one who found out pretty much everything about my past, but had no luck with tracking her down.

I carried on with my job at Community Promise, just part-time. Because Ashton was lavishing more attention on me than before and wanted to keep me close. Luckily, they hadn't found anyone to replace me. Did Susan and the rest of the staff know about my misdemeanors? Perhaps, but in true South Carolinian style they were as polite and gentle as daisies in spring—never said a word. Lindy? She pretended like nothing had happened at all.

Another ironic twist: the only person I now felt comfortable hanging out with was my old enemy, Belle. All that stuff she told me about Lily? That Lily had taken her own life by sinking herself in the ocean? And that I should go and look it up in the library et cetera? Belle told me she was pulling my leg, didn't expect me to lap it all up and be so gullible. She found the whole thing hilarious. Ashton had sworn to keep Lily's anonymity a secret, she said, hence his cageyness. Yet Lily, AKA Alex Leader (supposedly), still remained a mystery. There were times I was so curious I was tempted to hop on a plane to the Bahamas and track her down.

At first, I was enraged with Belle for playing games with my head. But my fascination with the similarities between us drew me closer. We became friends. It turned out that she and Ashton had broken up when he told her he never wanted to start a family. Brandon was waiting in the wings and snapped her up. Smart guy. I confided in Belle about operation-get-even. I guess she and I both had the same twisted sense of humor. Some people mistook us for sisters.

I would have loved to discuss all this with Dr. Becker: my bizarre friendship with Belle, the kid in the candy store who had lied and stolen yet who still felt cheated. But Dr. Becker had moved to another state, so my therapy sessions sadly ended.

Mariama, Georgia-May's wonderful nurse, returned to Heritage Park to look after her devoted patient once more. My mother-in-law is quite her old self again. Not the murdering-husband self, but the charming lady in pearls-and-pink self. I still visit. Which is another reason I have been dragging my feet about leaving Ashton. Georgia-May and I have become closer than ever. Oh, and last time I went to see her, she told me in the perkiest of voices how Ashton didn't deserve me… and something else rather familiar that caught my attention:

"You know, my dear, that I love you more than anyone in my own family?" she said in a sweet voice. "You really should leave Ashton while the going's good."

# CHAPTER THIRTY-EIGHT

### Nine months later

Ashton has arranged a marine safari for us, farther up along the North Carolina coast, four hours away from Beaufort—a mini vacation. It's the first chunk of time off he's taken since our honeymoon, and he needs it. They say neurosurgeons have the highest rate of burnout than any other medical specialist: emotional exhaustion or depersonalization are common. Not surprising when dealing with chronic diseases of the brain and nervous system, fifty-five hours a week, every week, nearly all year long. It's important for him to wind down, empty his mind of gray matter, his own included.

I secured my PADI diving certificate years ago in Mexico and had in mind that we'd explore the crystal waters of the Bahamas, warm and tropical. I wanted to see "my house." Vacation there. Meet his infamous sister Lily, whom he swears exists. But Ashton wants us to go diving here, in the Carolinas, with his shark conservation friends. Not quite the break I'd had in mind, but if Ashton can dive with sharks, I can too.

I haven't seen Cady since our fight, nor heard a word. Now eighteen, she's an adult. I have no choice but to let things be. Perhaps she puts me into the same bag into which I mercilessly slung my parents? Perhaps she wants me out of her life for good? Karma has a way of coming around.

So tomorrow's the day that Ashton and I go scuba diving with sand tiger sharks. They can be found in great numbers living in various sunken ships in the "Graveyard of the Atlantic," home to thousands of shipwrecks dating back to the sixteenth century, which have turned into reefs over time—now home to these predators and myriad other sea creatures. Perhaps these sharks are ghosts of those who perished? An ominous thought. Ashton is as excited as I am scared of my initiation with this "gentle" species of shark. "They're generally docile," he has told me. The word "generally" sends shivers down my spine.

We are to meet the conservation group and set off on the boat journey, fifteen nautical miles from the coast, towards one of the wrecks, *The Proteus*, a luxury liner that sank in 1918. I now regret I agreed to this. I can't "get on board" with Ashton's gung-ho attitude that all will be fine. It's not even the sharks that worry me so much, but the terror of something going wrong with the oxygen bottles, the tubes.

In your teens and early twenties, fear doesn't seem to equate the way it does when you're older. I guess that's why they send young people off to war, because people's fear barometer must not yet be developed fully. Scuba diving with sharks suddenly seems like an insane idea, but I have this need to prove to myself that I can overcome my most primal fears. Perhaps it's my competitive spirit; I can match Ashton in the bravery department. Being brave is not about not being afraid, but conquering any particular fear you have.

*I can do this.*

"But what if these sharks smell my fear?" I say to Ashton at dinner that night. We're outside, the cool sliver of a moon hung low in the sky. Around it, a halo, and a splatter of shiny stars. The Carolina air tells us it's the end of summer, but heady warmth still lingers, and the scent of oleander is thick in the air, sweet and cloying, and somehow nostalgic, yet I can't place a memory, nor a time. Maybe it's a twisted sort of nostalgia for my very own marriage, which I know I must abandon? The surf slaps in the distance: nature's heartbeat.

Ashton lays his large surgeon's hand on my knee. *What would he do without these hands?* I think, and push the thought away. "Just stay calm," he says in a low voice. "You have to understand one important thing: these sharks do *not* think of humans as food. Maybe if the water's really turbid, and there's lots of bait in the water, or a lot of wave action, and they can't differentiate one prey from the other…" He trails off, realizing he's exacerbated my fears. "Sometimes people feed them. We won't be doing anything like that. You'll be fine, Vivien."

"What if I panic?"

"We'll double-check all the hand signals beforehand. If you feel scared down there, we can come up slowly. Slowly, remember, because of the changes in pressure. Just the way we practiced in the pool this morning."

I pull a face. "The pool's one thing, the merciless Atlantic another."

"I promise, once you're down you'll become so enchanted with the incredible marine life underwater, you'll have no qualms. The sand tigers are very docile, pretty timid around humans. Just make sure you don't wear anything shiny—take off your jewelry or they might mistake it for fish scales. There'll be some barracudas most likely, too. They're attracted by anything glittery."

*Barracudas?* Goosebumps prickle my arms. "Great whites and tiger sharks have been spotted along this coast, too," I say. "What if we come across Pearl White?"

He laughs. "If that happens it'll make my year."

I've seen a video of a diver stroking the head of a shark, like a dog. Rubbing its nose, giving it an underwater massage. But I also know that their teeth and jaws are designed to crush the hardest of objects, like turtle shells.

"Great whites do pass through sometimes," Ashton admits, "but where we're going is the home of the very docile sand tiger. These wrecks have become their habitat, their shelter. It's been discovered the females return to the same place year after year. They call that 'site fidelity.' You'll be fine, Vivien, honey, don't overthink it."

I grimace.

"Such misconstrued creatures," Ashton goes on. "The true nature of sharks is so different from how they're portrayed. They need us to help stop the brutal slaying of them. The shark fin trade's gotten out of control in the last ten years. Sharks clean our oceans. They're a vital part of our ecosystem. We can help by educating people."

All I can think about is *Jaws* while he speaks, despite the beautiful footage I've seen of that cute shark having a love fest with the diver, like a puppy begging for attention. Ashton is not afraid, not one iota. But I am. Animals can smell fear, especially apex predators. *The sharks will hear my thundering heart, detect my panic*. Or they might nibble me out of curiosity with their dagger teeth. One little innocent bite…

This conversation was last night at the hotel. Now I've had the night to think it over—turning and tossing and revolving in my bed—I'm wavering toward a "no." It's before dawn, and we're scheduled to leave at six a.m. I have half an hour to decide if I join the boat trip or not. I've done some Google research. At around eleven feet long with razor-sharp teeth built to dismember and tear, these sand tigers are still awesome, to say the least, despite their "docility."

Ashton's all for it, raring to go. But then he's braver than I am. I don't want him to know that.

*There's no bigger bogeyman than a shark*, I think.

Despite my reservations, I get in the car with Ashton and we drive off.

"I have a big surprise waiting for you," Ashton says, as we get out of the car and approach the waiting boat by the dock.

My stomach dips. "What?"

"If I told you it wouldn't be a surprise." There is quiet menace in his eyes, which also, but not quite, is hidden by the charm of his smile. I want to jump back inside the safety of the car, tell him it's all been a mistake, that I've changed my mind.

But I don't. Curiosity pulls me forward.

We take off our shoes and get onto the boat. An ominous feeling overwhelms me, and I wish I hadn't come. Too late. A woman approaches, and I do a double take. She smiles at me. "Alex Leader," she says.

It's his sister Lily.

She grins and tells me how wonderful it is to finally meet, embraces me in a hug. She's just like the girl in Belle's photos, but a grown-up version. Long blond hair, skinny long legs, with an unhurried, musical drawl to her voice, and I'm glad she immediately talks about sharks because I'm tongue-tied. I half expected her to be dead or a phantom of Ashton and Belle's imagination.

"I'm so excited to share with y'all the true nature of sharks! I feel so privileged to have gotten to know these beautiful predators and make friends with them. There's no need for fear, Vivien, just knowledge." Ashton, I realize, has spoken to her about my misgivings.

"And the conservation team?" I ask Ashton. "Where are they?"

"I thought it would be more fun just the three of us."

Lily touches my arm in a sisterly way. I still don't know how to receive her. "And we'll be hooking up with my assistant, Tyler, a divemaster. Tyler's running late, hence the separate boat. Hope that's okay. We'll be a nice tight group."

While Lily's busy organizing the equipment, Ashton whispers in my ear, "The less Lily knows the better." He gives me the lowdown: Lily has no idea about our history—Ashton's and mine—the stunt I played on him, the fact we made a baby together eighteen years ago, or nineteen if you count conception. It turns out that it wasn't only Georgia-May who was committed to a psychiatric ward, but Lily, too, way back when. I read between the lines and deduce that the key for Lily's survival is being away from her mother and a stress-free life in Harbour Island as a marine biologist, the way Georgia-May's survival—apart from continual medication—appears to be linked to being joined at the hip with Mariama. Lily keeps a low profile. Hence the lack of close-up photos of her online.

"Lily's sensitive," Ashton warns me. "Let's keep things nice. She needs things to be happy. No skeletons in closets jumping out at her, okay? No confessions, no sharing secrets."

"You'll fall in love with these cuties, I promise," Lily shouts over to us. "Ashton told me your size. The wetsuit I picked out for you should do great."

She chats on about Tyler and the sharks and the trip, and I try my best to take it all in. There's a childish quality to Lily, an innocence. She is here right before me. A real person in the flesh, after all this time, after all my fantasies about her being dead.

She goes on, "A few things to be aware of. Don't touch the sharks."

*Are you kidding me?*

"Resist the urge to chase them. Sand tigers are curious but also afraid of divers. If you remain still, they'll be more likely to come to you. You'll be blown away by the shipwreck, it's pretty cool. Remember to always leave an open exit when you go inside. Don't corner a shark or it could turn aggressive."

*Corner a shark? Um, no, I hadn't planned on it.*

From more conversation, I glean that Lily has no children and few friends, just lives for these sharks and her dives, which usually take place in the Bahamas, where she lives in "my house." This is the first time since she fled her family, all those years ago, that she's been back to the States.

The boat trip to the shipwreck is beautiful. We motor across the deep green waters, pewter-blue flying fish shimmering through the air. They look prehistoric, half fish, half birds: evolution before our eyes. As we power along, Lily at the helm, Ashton and I go over and over the various hand signals. Ashton will be my dive buddy, and I'm glad because he's done this several times before.

The other boat is in sight when we arrive, but we don't wait for it or tie up together. Tyler. But the boat's too far off to see him. I'm concerned with my paraphernalia, trying to keep everything I've learned about diving from my PADI course and Ashton's refresher course in my head.

I'm trussed up in my neoprene dive suit, which sticks to me like glue. Ashton somehow looks attractive in his. However ungainly I feel, I see mine as a barrier between these great sharks' teeth and my flesh, although I know that's illogical and somewhat paranoid. Even though the weather's warm, Lily assures us we need these suits as if they were our second skin. It's cold down there in the deep Atlantic where the unknowable awaits. Plus, there might be jellyfish. I waddle in my outfit toward the back of the boat, careful not to trip on my fins.

Lily jokes, "I love the smell of wetsuit in the morning," and I force a laugh, because the idea of offering myself up to a host of sharks terrifies me. I want to pull out, tell them I'll stay on the boat, but pride and curiosity won't let me. I have committed to this madness so now I must see it through.

"Humans go into the water on average over eight billion times a year," Lily tells us. "Out of this insane number there are only eighty-five people who are mistakenly bitten, and only around five who actually die. Yet people do much more death-defying things every day, like drive in cars, for instance. Seriously, don't sweat it. The odds of anything bad happening to y'all are negligible."

The word "odds" gets my heart racing. Odds means chances. *There's a chance I'll be one of those five!*

We jump into the water, clad in tanks, masks, and flippers. I hold my nose and ease myself in with a splash, sink under the lapping waves. Beneath the ocean, I follow the lead. Lily first, then me, and Ashton behind me. I watch all Lily's signals. I look up for a second and see bright slices of morning sunlight streaming above the water in a brilliant fan of white. The sun brandishes its fiery heat on the ocean's lid, lighting up my bubbles. I'm suspended in a moving piece of art, both above and below me. It's another universe down here.

The deeper we descend, the darker and colder it is. Slowly, methodically, following the boat's anchor line to give us our bearing, we stop to equalize every so often so our ears adjust to the pressure. A new world opens up before me. A school of fish flit by, silvery-blue and luminous, and Lily points toward something then puts the peace sign to her eyes, which means "look." A turtle. I give her the thumbs up but realize quickly that's the wrong diver signal as it means "going up," not "how fabulous." I quickly change it to the "OK" signal. The turtle goes deeper, and finally I lose sight of it as it ghosts into the darker distance. But there are more fish darting one way and then another, moving as if they have one brain between them. I turn a little to my side. Ashton's behind me. He grins through his mask—or at least it looks that way. The deep turquoise-green is intense. Today we're lucky as it isn't choppy or turbulent. Today, Lily has told us, it's clearer than usual. The blue-green goes as far as the eye can see, varying in shades of cobalt, forest-green, and aquamarine. The color is so immense, so unending I feel it burst inside me. Depending on the day, there are sand tigers, bull sharks, lemon sharks, too, apparently. But we haven't seen any sharks at all yet, and I'm secretly hoping we won't.

We follow the anchor to the end of the line and reach the wreck. It humbles me to think that lives were lost here. Will we come across skeletons? New life has taken hold. The cycle of the universe.

I gaze into the windows of the destroyed ship, the great hunks of rusty metal overtaken with coral, algae, and sea crustaceans.

I don't know what fish species I'm watching now: shoals of black and white stripy ones, parrotfish also, spots and stripes, oranges and pinks, yellow edged with luminous blue—an angel-fish? Fish that look like the rocks they inhabit, too, eyes bulging and transparent. Colors so varied and shapes so prehistoric, it puts me into a trance. Thousands and thousands of smaller fish like suspended, glittery confetti. I'm just one little human amidst all this glory. And then a stingray zips by underneath, clouds of sand in its wake. Or maybe it's a manta ray. I'm too much of a novice to know the difference. I tilt my head up and spot a group of barracudas above, staring at me with interest. I left all my jewelry on the boat—like magpies, they're attracted by glitter. Then I see a beautiful striped lionfish with its venomous, spiky fin rays, and I instinctively paddle backwards. But I can't tear my eyes away, mesmerized as I am. It'll be on someone's dinner table before long, because it isn't an indigenous species and has been wreaking havoc in these waters. Ashton and I exchange glances. I can see how delighted he is.

I'm aware of how tiny I am in this vast space of bluey-green. I had forgotten that I'm only alive because of my tank and diving paraphernalia, and the second I remember this I catch my breath and an overwhelming sensation of both claustrophobia and agoraphobia engulfs me.

*Don't panic. Stay calm. Breathe.*

I still my mind, let my pulse steady, then focus on Lily ahead and regain my nerves, back being like a fish myself, a creature of the ocean. I have no idea how many meters down we are, or how many feet. But we all do the OK signal at each other—the thumb and index finger in a loop, other three fingers up. And then Lily does the thumb down… going down further. We follow. And I do feel like some strange fish now that I'm getting used to my surroundings and the impossibility that I can breathe underwater. As long as I don't make any sudden movements, the fish are fine with me, too, with all of us. We are just another marine species.

*Stay relaxed. Everything's cool.*

I hear a bunch of rumbling splashes. Another panic as I imagine our anchor coming loose and our boat drifting away, leaving us abandoned in the great ocean, but I turn and see the hull of our boat behind us. Then, in the distance, a cloud muddies the waters. Ahead, Tyler must have joined our group. I can't make out much detail, just arms and legs, bubbles floating upwards, Lily greeting Tyler, although it's very hazy and they are pretty far-off.

We all move forward, Ashton holding my hand, the other two ahead. The hull of the sunken ship looms beyond, yellow coral clinging on its edges like small trees. Weaving in and out of the wreck, I see sharks.

Lots of sharks. Sleek. Ghostly. Haunting. But very fricking real.

I stop swimming, my mind and body suspending in a numb bubble of fear.

One shark notices me. Its mouth hanging open, its snaggly teeth on full display set in a fixed, menacing grin. Does it smell my fear? Its round white eyes with the beady black centers are staring straight at my face, fastening on me like prey, making a beeline for my body. I can make out old scars slashed this way and that on its brownish-gray body, and two rows of pointy, serrated teeth in a machine of a mouth set below a sleek pointed snout. My body goes into a frozen shock. My heart—I swear—stops pounding. All I can do is wait to be eaten. I don't think to knock it on the nose or push it away from me like I've seen in videos.

*Maintain eye contact, maintain your ground, don't act like bait, let them know you cannot be ambushed.*

I do this… not from bravery, but with both awe and terror. I cannot move. I'm a stone waiting to be swallowed and chewed by this predator. Masticated by those great teeth.

At the last second, it swerves, nudging me with its passing fin. The shark is curious, nothing more.

As it moves away and I get ready to join the others, I freeze again.

I'm surrounded. There are more now; it seems as if they have appeared from nowhere, circling… their great bodies lithe, one second here, the next out of focus. Their agility is easy for them. I am a lump in the water. A blobby creature who blows bubbles against these awesome sharks that are a fine feat of God's creation. I'm counting now… one, two, three, four, five, six, seven, eight, nine… four is over there, three is… behind me. I can't keep up. I turn around, and it dawns on me that Ashton is no longer holding my hand. I can't see him anywhere. Lily and Tyler have floated away with the current. They're a haze. *Where's Ashton?* Cold blood runs through my veins, but only just, because I feel I might combust. The sharks can hear my heart thundering anew. A new fear has arisen inside me:

*Revenge is a dish best served cold.*

Is this Ashton's punishment, nine months after the fact? Has he brought me out here on purpose to abandon me? Lock me in the proverbial basement? Is Lily in on it too? They can simply drive away in the boat, leave me here to be eaten by predators in the cold Atlantic. This icy truth is more petrifying than even the sharks themselves.

These creatures smell my terror. In the distance, I see the others making signals. They're going up. *Wait! What about me?* I know now my fears are founded. They're leaving! I want to swim toward them but am too afraid my movements will excite the sharks. The current is pulling me further and further away from the group. Sea grasses shimmer in the cool underwater stream. Purple coral sways. More parrot fish. I'm floating backwards. The round sharky eyes are back, sizing me up, their streamlined bodies moving in for the kill… how many now? I can't count. My end is inevitable.

I think of my marriage vows: *Till death do us part.*

My time is up.

*Breathe! Breathe, Vivien, breathe.*

I've been holding my breath. I gasp, pull in air. My gloved hands are cold, closed into tense little fists. Tears fill my gaze, locked behind the mask. It's fogging up. I can't see. I'm too scared to take it off and put it back on. I can't remember what I was told to do. The human figures seem miles away now. *Why is nobody helping me?* That big shark is coming back for a second inspection. He/she is enormous but weightless, cruising the endless blue-green. The shark's home. I am an intruder. My muscles contract into spasms of panic.

*Stay calm. Stay calm. Eye contact. Eye contact. I am not prey. I am not prey.*

The oxygen burns cold as I sip in another breath. Again, that inconceivable reality that I am down here and I should be up there. Up. On land. Where humans are designed to live.

*Why? Why did I get myself into this?*

I exhale. Bubbles obscure my vision. I look up. That sun again, glaring down on the water, making prisms of blue and green. I remember:

*I. Am. All. Alone.*

A sudden thrashing flurry. Massive fish bodies swerving and propelling themselves through the deep, the sharks' tails steering left and right, up and down. The current has pulled me into the center of the wreck. Nobody can see me except these creatures. *I have been abandoned!*

Moving with their great fins, these voracious hunters sweep into a circular shoal of fish, mouths open, jaws snapping. Relieved it's not me they're after, I take the opportunity to swim toward my dive group, angling my body around the commotion. I could get mixed up with the prey! Then I feel a nudge on my arm. That shark is back! But no, it's a human in a wetsuit, coming up behind me, *out of the blue*. My mask's all foggy, thick with panicked tears from thinking I was all alone. It's a woman. I can't make her out. Limbs, arms… she's pulling me to safety with her gloved hands, away from the sharks. She turns me around to face her, grips my shoulders. Gives me a sign. Not the peace sign to "look" but two fingers like the number two. Is it Lily? I can't even see straight. What is the sign? It seems like an F-you. This bears no correlation to the diving signs we learned. As I'm trying to understand what the hell she wants me to do, she rips at my gear, her dark neoprene hands tearing at my regulator, which is the only thing connecting me to my tank. My air. I kick her away to reinsert it, putting the mouthpiece back on my lips as I draw in a lungful of my only life force. She's miming the number two again, coming upon me again in a flash, and I wriggle and oscillate my body—struggle to get away. *What does she want? Why is she trying to kill me?* I give her a momentous kick, harder this time, forcing enough distance between us. A shark cruises between us. Another body… I'm confused. The water has turned murky, currents are causing swells. It's not clear like before. Is it the same person? I swim into a corner of the wreck to balance myself. Hulking rusty metal acts as a barrier behind me. More sharks. Impaired vision. The figure comes into focus. The same? A woman… by the shape of her slim body. I see—I think I see, through the fog of my mask—who it is:

Cady.

No. Impossible! I'm imagining things.

I look again. I can't be a hundred percent sure.

As I squint at her, she swims toward me. Another shark. Heart thundering, I make to swim through the sunken ship's port window. Hands creep behind me… tear off my mask. I can't see. The current's stirring up the ocean floor; sand and particles fly into my vision. A jellyfish swims within inches of my face. I grab my mask and press it back to my face, but my vision's even worse than before without any mask at all. Everything comes at me at once: my desperation to survive, the realization that my daughter's alive and well but she's trying to murder me. I can't see. She lunges for me again, the lack of gravity making her movements slow enough for me to react. But am I seeing two bodies? Orange fins. Yellow fins. I'm kicking and gyrating my body in my effort to escape those gloved hands again. As I twizzle myself upside down, my gaze catches the top of the ocean: a rippling ceiling, far, far above. Impossibly far away. And even if I could get there, a rapid ascent could kill me, rupture my lungs or cause an air embolism—we've been warned not to go up too quickly. Then I feel another pair of hands—the same, different?—lunge at me with an object, but I sway my body from side to side, dodging. My torso moves too slowly; the density of the water feels like syrup. She—it's definitely a woman—has one hand hooked around my weight belt, pulling me toward her, stabbing at me with the other gloved hand. A knife. She has a knife. She rips at my regulator again. Slashes the knife back and forth, just missing my stomach. Cady trying to stab me anew? Open up my scar?

I hear myself scream, but the scream is a gurgle… the regulator's hanging down. My hand shoots to my face, I shove the apparatus into my mouth, and I seize another lungful of air. But she wrenches my hand away, yanks the regulator off again, grabs both my arms. Great shadows pass in my peripheral vision: the sharks in a feeding frenzy. Lashing through the water, gobbling and guzzling every fish in their path. I see red. I see blood.

*Think. Stay calm.*

I double my knees to my chest. No mask, no regulator, the figure pinioning me. Her vice-like grip on my arms impossible to escape. My legs ram at her chest with all my might, catching her chin and her regulator with the tip of my fins. Her head rolls back. She's off me, finally. My arms flail for my regulator again, practically blinded as I am, and this time I start to swim.

Anywhere. Just away from her. I don't aim up, but sideways, powering my legs with every scrap of strength left in my body. She catches me by my left fin, pulling at it, hooking me toward her like a fish on a line.

I can't see. I can't see her face.

A body, gray, hulking—a shark flits by, knocking me hard—a great punch in my ribs. I can't see. Orange flippers, my black flippers, sharks, yellow fins, flashes of gray, a knife spinning in the great space of the ocean, falling. I try to catch it, try to catch the knife on the descent, but it floats out of my reach.

Everything happening is both in slow motion and fast-forward. A mass of bubbles surrounds me, and out of the tail of my eye, I see two female bodies in an underwater dance. Then Ashton. I recognize his form. Three bodies in wetsuits. Someone has grabbed the knife. There's a swirl of the trio upside down upside down, under, over, as they tackle with one another. Round and round they spin. I can't see who's attacking who. Who's saving who. A slash of the knife. Blood… like watercolor paint, disperses. Red against turquoise. Turquoise against red.

Blood.

Bubbles.

Blood.

Is it me bleeding?

My ankle is slashed.

The sharks are moving in.

# EPILOGUE

## THE AFTERMATH

Swimming back up to the boat happened in a dream. I survived. But only just. I lived to tell my tale. But only just.

Someone died that day.

"Tyler" was Cady. The divemaster who had been helping Lily.

Somewhere along the line I had given Tyler a male persona—the name Tyler, I guess. The word dive*master*. Cady had started working as "Alex Leader's" assistant, at first not having a clue whom Lily was. Of course not. How would Cady have known beforehand that Alex Leader was her aunt? It wasn't long before she found out. The physical likeness to Ashton was too hard to miss. Cady, though, didn't let on who *she* was. She wanted time out alone to sort things out—didn't want me, or Ashton, or anyone tracking her down. She'd created a new identity for herself: Lana Tyler.

It wasn't Cady coming back for revenge. It wasn't Cady who ripped my mask off my face. But Lily.

Lily wanted me dead.

Did she plan it ahead of time? Or was it something she did on the spur of the moment? Cady—when she had started working for "Alex Leader" in the Bahamas—was suspicious that something might happen; the look of hatred when Lily talked about her brother's "bitchy new wife" had Cady on alert. I'd foolishly posted something on my Facebook page about our upcoming shark trip, a few weeks before. Lily told Ashton how fun it would be for her to join us. And persuaded him that we shouldn't go on the marine safari we had organized with his group of conservation friends, but with her, Alex Leader, the shark expert, the professional, his beloved sister. Ashton agreed and wanted to surprise me. I'd been hounding him so much about his sister, hadn't I? What better way for us to finally meet!

Lily surprised me all right. In fact, later I discovered that the intruder Cady and I had heard that night in the house was Lily. The noose? Made by Lily especially for me. She'd been creeping around Distant Sands. She missed killing me then so hatched a new plan.

After Cady rescued me from Lily's underwater attack and slowly brought me to the surface, Ashton and Lily remained under for another ten minutes. Cady and I were exhausted, slumped on the deck of the boat. We didn't even have the energy to peel off our wetsuits. We were alone together, praying for Ashton to emerge. I was mesmerized by shock at having been attacked. Cady, too, although she had handled it better than I did, because, being a divemaster, she knew what she was doing—she had been diving several times with sharks before. When Ashton realized that Lily was trying to kill me, he intervened.

We waited for him on deck. Staring at the water. *Waiting, waiting.*

As I fixed my gaze on the ocean in horror thinking I had lost my husband to the sharks, and Cady sat shaking in the boat, fearing she'd never see her father again, he surfaced.

Alone.

The three of us remained on the boat for hours, stunned into silence. Ashton could not speak. No sign of Lily. Our eyes focused on the water as shark fins circled then finally disappeared. No body emerged. No lone yellow fin. No regulator or oxygen tank.

Had Lily drowned? Ashton wouldn't tell me what had happened down there, in the depths, between the two of them.

Had the sharks swallowed her? "No, they're docile creatures," Cady insisted. "Impossible."

Cady finally called the marine patrol.

The police realized Ashton was in shock. It was an accident, they said, a horrible accident.

"It was Lily or you, Vivien, I had to make a split-second choice," Ashton whispered to me in confidence, later that night.

I had wished, for so many years, for Ashton Buchanan to feel that same bone-crushing degradation that I had suffered after getting pregnant with Cady. When something happens in your life that you are responsible for, yet you didn't plan. My wish came true that day. But not in the way I had envisioned. Lily's death broke him, stole a part of his soul, however wicked Lily's intentions. I thought of what I'd told Cady the year before: that Ashton, as a surgeon, did not get to pick and choose who lived or died. But as a man, that is exactly what had happened.

He had chosen me. He had chosen my life over his own sister's.

*How can I leave my husband now, knowing this?*

He had proven his love. He had sacrificed his very own flesh and blood. For *me*.

*I will not divorce him. I will stay. Our marriage is true. He really loves me.*

But then he whispered in my ear again… another confession. "You know, it wasn't Mama who killed Pa?"

The hairs on my neck rose. "What do you mean?"

I recalled what Ashton had told me about Georgia-May going out on the FlatsMaster with his dad, that when Buck was trying to scramble back onto the boat after he'd "fallen" in the water, woozy and happy from booze, she had smashed him over and over and over again on the head with a butt end of the oar till his skull cracked open, and how she had started the engine and motored away, leaving him bleeding out in the water. She was "cool as icebox pie," Ashton had told me. And I also remember, when Ashton recounted that story to me, how I couldn't imagine Georgia-May doing such a thing.

"It was Lily," he said in a low voice, with a small, creepy smile lingering on his lips. "It was Lily who murdered Pa."

"You *knew* this all along?"

*You should never have gotten involved with my family*, Georgia-May had told me. She had been trying to protect me. The note, the warnings. I looked up at Ashton to see if he was joking. He wasn't. His eyes flickered in a sort of gleeful dance.

His mocking laugh cut like a cleaver. "It was easy to get Mama committed. The two of us siblings—the 'duet,' Mama used to call us—against one of her, especially considering I'm such a respected physician. Oh, people always believe doctors' opinions, don't they? We hold such power in the medical field. People always think physicians know best. Mama did have a mild case of schizophrenia, true, but she wasn't *dangerous*. Strange how almost normal people can turn really crazy when they're all cooped up. And Mama… well, she wouldn't stop talking. To you, especially. Couldn't just let things be. Made me uneasy. The medication didn't quite cut it, so last week I treated her with ECT. You know, electroconvulsive therapy? Oh, I know, I know. The side effects can be quite debilitating sometimes. The exacerbation of cognitive impairment—memory loss—can be pretty drastic with certain patients. But with Mama that suits me just fine. You'll notice the difference when you next see her, honey. She's so much more… compliant. It's better this way."

I stared at him, my eyes, my mouth, my thoughts fixed in a silent scream.

"I'd hate to see anything like that happen to my lovely wife. Our marriage is everything to me, Vivien. Please don't slip up again. Please be a good girl and keep your pretty little mouth shut."

# A LETTER FROM ARIANNE

Thanks so much for reading *The Newlyweds* and I hope you had as much fun reading it as I did writing it.

A few years ago, I went to visit Beaufort in South Carolina and fell in love with the place. My mind, as usual, started ticking away with ideas. I always love to set my books in magical locations and take my readers on an emotional, visceral journey. I really hope you'll be sharing more literary escapades with me in the near future. Where next? Somewhere remote and eerie, definitely… so if you are curious, please join this mailing list for alerts on my upcoming novels. You can unsubscribe at any time, and your email address will never be shared with third parties.

*www.bookouture.com/arianne-richmonde*

If you enjoyed *The Newlyweds*, I'd be thrilled if you'd recommend it to your friends and family and, if you have a moment, leave a short review. I read all my reviews as it's so useful to get feedback and I'd love to hear your thoughts. Also, it's great for likeminded souls to find books that are right for them. People are reading more than ever and sharing favorite books… how wonderful is that? Thank you so much for spreading the word.

I'd love to chat with you, so please feel free to reach out. You can join me on Instagram or Facebook or Twitter. I also have a website. Thanks again for adding *The Newlyweds* to your library—I feel honored.

Until next time!
Arianne

@arianne_richmonde

AuthorArianneRichmonde

@a_richmonde

ariannerichmonde.com

# ACKNOWLEDGMENTS

Firstly, I would like to thank my publisher and editor, Helen Jenner, who has worked with me from the beginning on *The Newlyweds*. Thank you, Helen, for your ideas, input, and the picking and pulling of my characters and story, knowing where to cut, develop, and rein in my overactive imagination. And another huge thank you to the Bookouture team for always having my back and for the tireless work you do for your authors. In particular, Noelle, you are incredible.

I did a lot of research for this book about schizophrenia and care homes. Huge thanks to fellow Bookouture author and forensic psychologist, Ellery Kane, for your invaluable information about mental institutions and schizophrenia, and also to certified nursing assistant, Tiffany Anderson, whose insight and information about dementia and schizophrenic patients living in care homes and assisted living homes helped so much. My sister, Ness, thank you for your professional advice about psychotherapists; your feedback was invaluable. Any embellishments are my own. DISCLAIMER: As with all fiction, I have taken liberties and employed a certain amount of artistic license to provide an entertaining story. Although I take full responsibility for creating my characters, in no way do I condone their behavior or feel that their actions are typical of people suffering from these conditions or in these situations. Mental health and domestic violence are very real concerns, which I take extremely seriously.

There are themes about ecology running through *The New-lyweds*. Never have we, as humans, been challenged so much to protect our planet and our future. Thank you, Jim Abernethy, for your incredible shark videos—it has to be seen to be believed; you have educated me about the importance of sharks and their vital place in the ecosystem. The *Breaking Their Silence* team, who are doing so much to help elephants, rhinos, and all wildlife. To our beloved treasure, David Attenborough; you are my hero, I am your forever student. Also huge thanks to all of you fighting tirelessly for the environment and our animals. It makes me so grateful to be living on our unique rock that we call Earth.

And last, but never least, to you, dear reader, for sharing this journey. Thank you for encouraging me to delve deep into the human psyche and make up stories, and for the time and care so many of you take to review and share my books. I am forever grateful.